I0602401

# DEADLY RIPPLES

Other Titles by

PENNY GOETJEN

*The Woman Underwater*

**Olivia Benning Mystery Series**

*The Empty Chair ~ Murder in the Caribbean*

*Over the Edge ~ Murder Returns to the Caribbean*

**Elizabeth Pennington Mystery Series**

*Murder on the Precipice*

*Murder Beyond the Precipice*

*Murder Returns to the Precipice*

# DEADLY RIPPLES

PENNY GOETJEN

SECRET HARBOR PRESS

Copyright © 2024 Penny Goetjen | pennygoetjen.com

All Rights Reserved. No part of this publication may be reproduced, stored in a retrieval system or transmitted, in any form or by any means – electronic, mechanical, photocopying, recording or otherwise – without prior written permission from the publisher, except for the inclusion of brief quotations in a review.

This is a work of fiction. All characters, places, and names are a product of the author's imagination. Any resemblance to a real person, either living or dead, is purely coincidental.

For information about this title or to order other books
and/or electronic media, contact the publisher:

Secret Harbor Press, LLC
www.SecretHarborPress.com
secretharborpress@gmail.com

Cover and interior design by The Book Cover Whisperer:
OpenBookDesign.biz

Publisher's Cataloging-In-Publication Data
(Provided by Cassidy Cataloguing Services, Inc.)

Names: Goetjen, Penny, author. Title: Deadly ripples / Penny Goetjen. Description: First edition. | [Charleston, South Carolina] : Secret Harbor Press, [2024] Identifiers: ISBN: 978-0-9976235-2-9 (paperback) | 978-0-9976235-5-0 (ebook) Subjects: LCSH: Authors--Fiction. | Uncles--Death--Fiction. | Murder--Investigation--Fiction. | Inheritance and succession--Fiction. | Mothers and daughters--Fiction. | Missing persons-- Fiction. | Charleston (S.C.)--Fiction. | LCGFT: Detective and mystery fiction. | BISAC: FICTION / Mystery & Detective / General. | FICTION / Crime. | FICTION / Sagas. Classification: LCC: PS3607.O3356 D43 2024 | DDC: 813/.6--dc23

Library of Congress Control Number: 2024910896

978-0-9976235-2-9 Paperback
978-0-9976235-5-0 eBook
978-0-9976235-8-1 Audiobook

Printed in the United States of America


FIRST EDITION

*For my brother Kevin, whose generous heart, infectious smile,
and comforting hugs will never be forgotten.*

# PROLOGUE

With the convertible top folded neatly and tucked away in its slot over the trunk, the night air tossed his hair about and buffeted his face. The engine purred smoothly, shifting seamlessly on command.

Headlights had been bobbing in the rearview mirror for the last mile or so. At a distance. Not changing lanes. Not turning off. Just far enough back to avoid scrutiny. At that hour they were the only two vehicles on the road—save for the occasional flash of white light in the oncoming lane—the road that led to the bridge. Once on it, there would be no exits, no way off the two-and-a-half-mile expanse.

A second set of headlights appeared in the mirror, next to the first. Four white lights suddenly bearing down, growing larger. Getting closer. He could hear the souped-up engines. The car in the left lane zipped past with a roar he could feel in his chest. Just as the headlights of the other car splashed onto the rearview mirror, it sped around, nearly clipping his bumper, chasing the first car. Right behind were two more who screamed by, and the four crisscrossed up the road, disappearing over the crest.

His palms, tingly from the close encounter, made the steering wheel slippery. The street racers, now well out of sight, had startled him more than they should have. But two new headlights bobbed in the mirror. They were a good distance behind but seemed to be closing.

What had he been thinking, taking the car out so late? He needed to get back without wrapping the classic Austin Healey and himself around a light pole.

As the cable-laden towers came into sight, he pressed the accelerator, and the front tires crossed onto the Ravenel Bridge. There was no turning back. The peppy engine responded easily as if content to be challenged beyond the usual stop-and-go city driving.

His pursuer sped forward and closed the gap between them until the bumpers were so close, the headlights were no longer in the rearview mirror.

As he tightened his fingers on the wheel to switch lanes, away from the edge of the bridge, he felt the impact and his body lurched. It was suddenly eerily quiet—until a second impact and then darkness filled in around him.

# CHAPTER ONE

THE GRAND ELM TREE IN THE far corner of the backyard had always been my refuge from the family, particularly my mother, at least for a short while. But somewhere along the way she'd figured it out after I'd been gone for an extended period and would suddenly be standing at the base of the sturdy trunk, yelling up at me.

It was usually something like, "For God's sake, Kathryn, what are you doing up there?" or, "Get down out of that *damn* tree." And once, "Ladies don't climb trees. Certainly not at your age. And certainly not in skirts."

But this time it was, "Kathryn, your uncle has died." My mother didn't even bother to call me down from my perch on the branch that seemed to be trying to escape the compound like I was, reaching out across the wrought iron fence separating our property from the sprawling Beacon Hill estate next door. There was no looking into her daughter's eyes, taking me by the hand, and certainly no warm embrace to ease the pain. My mother hadn't even attempted to deliver the news gently. No, Rose Moore didn't sugarcoat anything. It wasn't her nature.

I'll never forget the jolt in my chest. As the air rushed from my lungs, my foot slipped, and I had to grab onto a secondary branch to keep from falling, although the thought of throwing myself off the broad arm I was balanced on sashayed through my mind, I'd have to admit. Tempting though that was, I wasn't going to give my mother the satisfaction.

Tucking the notepad and pencil I was clutching into the wide pocket of my gingham tiered midi skirt, I scooted up into the branches, not out of sight of my mother—even the tiniest of green leaf buds hadn't begun to burst from the branches—but farther away. Always the messenger of bad news and seemingly with a twisted sort of pleasure in the delivery.

My uncle... my kindred spirit. Gone? How could it be? The universe was beyond cruel.

"I'm sure you're upset. You may want to up your med dosage." That was my mother's attempt at compassion. The silence that followed allowed the recently arrived wrens to chirp their lyrical song that suddenly seemed out of place. "It was a shock to us too."

I knew my mother had felt nothing at hearing the news—nothing but a sense of relief her husband's younger brother, who she considered to be the family failure and an annoying influence on her impressionable middle child, was finally out of the picture and less able to influence.

"All right... well, I'll leave you to it." That was it. She'd come to deliver the news, and she'd done it. She could return to whatever it was Rose Cogswell Moore—or Posh, as she preferred to be called—spent her days doing.

# CHAPTER TWO

As LUGGAGE BOBBED ALONG THE CONVEYOR belt, my eyes slipped out of focus. It had barely been a two-hour flight from Boston, so it wasn't the travel that had zapped my energy. The mental whiplash from the past few weeks had me struggling to wrap my head around the news my beloved uncle was gone. And he'd left his Charleston home to me. But why? Why not my father—his brother?

Don't get me wrong. I was beyond flattered—more like flummoxed—but it didn't seem to make sense.

As I tried to refocus on the bags chugging by on the belt—had mine gone by already?—a familiar pain stabbed between my eyes until my vision blurred, and it felt as though the edges of my mind were sizzling.

"Oh no," I whispered to no one, grabbing for something to hang on to. I hated when it happened in public.

"Are you okay?" A short but stout, salt-and-pepper-haired gentleman offered his concern. I looked in horror at my hand clutching the rough tweed fabric on his upper arm.

"Sorry," was all I could manage, releasing my grasp and pushing past him.

Scanning baggage claim for a place to sit, I dashed for a row of small white bistro tables along the front windows, aiming to plop into the nearest available chair, stumbling as I went, catching my toe on someone's suitcase. I didn't make it. I went down hard, landing on my side with my shoulder taking the brunt of the impact, followed by my head. At that point, all I could do was close my eyes, willing the episode to pass without a lengthy vision. I heard a shriek and then could feel people gathering around me.

"What happened?"

"Is she all right?"

"Someone call 911."

I couldn't spit out the words, *Please don't. I'll be okay.*

"She's having a seizure. She's as white as a ghost."

*I'm pale because I'm from New England, and we're coming out of nine months of winter.*

*Give me a minute* wouldn't form on my tongue. Instead I uttered unintelligible sputterings and grunts while I fought with the images in my head. Per usual, they won.

This time I sensed I was in a vehicle. It was moving, but I couldn't tell if I was the driver or a passenger. It was dark, but uplights illuminated cables from a tall tower ahead. It wasn't clear what the structure was. Where it was located and the time frame I was viewing it in weren't coming to either. They rarely did.

My head felt detached from my body, yet I pushed through the vision, trying to discern what I was seeing. At this point I was all in. I could sense the crowd around me, but it felt as though they were watching the images along with me. But what was I *supposed* to be seeing? Did I need to keep moving through to the towers, or was there something there I needed to notice? It was quiet like the middle of the night, and I had the feeling of being alone. There didn't seem to be any other cars nearby. Suddenly things shifted and I was falling. My stomach lurched upward. It was difficult to breathe. Just when I thought I would run out of air, a voice penetrated the dark and I snatched a breath.

"Girl, you all right?" Her voice boomed, and the crowd seemed to take a step back to make room. Something wrapped around my forearm, constricting the blood flow. As my splotchy vision began to clear, I could make out bulging eyes and hair sticking out of her head like she'd overdone it with gel that morning. I didn't notice the blue tips until her face came into focus. Shiny from the heat outside. Dark, beyond what a month in the sun would look like. She yanked my arm like a tight end righting a quarterback after a humiliating sack. "You best be getting up. The floor of a public place is nowhere for you to be lying on. It's filthy. People walking all over it and all. Dragging luggage and whatnot across it. That same luggage gets dragged through public bathrooms. Yuck."

I was on my feet but teetering. Two bear claws steadied my shoulders. "You're Miss Moore, right?" she said in a hushed tone, but the words blared in my ear, and then she turned her attention to the gawkers, waving them away. "Go on now. There's nothing to see here. Go on."

*How did she know who I was?* Before I could ask, she tried again. "Right? Kathryn Moore?"

I struggled to gather myself. "How... how did you know... and who are you?"

"Well now. Forgive my atrocious manners. My mother would be plum embarrassed at me. I'm with Levinson & Levinson. I'm here to pick you up."

"Great... that's great. Thank you. I thought I'd have to grab a rental and figure out how to get downtown."

"No. I got you, girl. That's my job today." It sounded like she mumbled a few words after that, but I let it go. I was grateful for the ride and a connection in Charleston.

Offering me a water bottle, she said, "Here, looks like you might need this."

Deciding it was preferable for her to think I was simply dehydrated than for her to know what had actually transpired, I accepted the water and unscrewed the top, sensing the crowd I'd inadvertently gathered was finally dispersing. Nothing more to watch. Spectacle over. The wacko tourist had come around.

"How did you know it was me?" I tried again. My city girl instincts kicked in. Was she really who she said she was? One couldn't be too cautious when she first got to town. Even though my driver was female, she was no slouch. In fact, she could be described as sturdy, solid, or even a bit masculine. And tall. Most guys would think twice before messing with her.

"Your mother described you to a tee."

The nearby baggage carousel lurched to life again, prompting us to wander over to where my flight's bags were riding the belt. I hadn't noticed it had halted for a moment. I was too busy causing a scene.

"Really. What did she say?" I could hear my mother describing me as *rather plain, kind of frumpy, with dark rimmed thick glasses, which were simply easier to wear than fussing with contacts, unremarkable brown hair—finger combed and pulled back into a pony, flats that had been scuffed into submission, and a long dark print skirt that didn't quite cover them. And a notebook sticking part way out of the pocket with a pencil or pen attached somewhere on it. Lord knows what she keeps in it.* Nope, my mother wouldn't have held anything back.

She opened her mouth to answer, then thought better of it.

"Yeah, that's what I figured," I said.

She flashed the resigned look of someone who'd been caught between two sparring partners, both of whom happened to be women. A dangerous place to tread, for sure.

It was then I noticed how uncomfortable she looked in a white button-down shirt with a decidedly masculine feel to it, and khakis, the latter barely covering her ankles. Even though her cuffs were rolled up a couple of times, I sensed the sleeves were too short too.

"Oh, this one's mine." I lunged for the handle of a small black roller bag that had nearly snuck past and tried to yank it off, but she pushed me aside and said, "Yo, I got this."

Again, I found my world spinning and breathed in deeply to recover.

"Wow, it's tiny. You must not plan on staying long. How can you tell it's yours?" Her eyes scanned the length of the conveyor belt, a line of black rectangles. "They're *all* black," she declared, holding it chest high by the top handle with both hands.

Reaching over, I swatted like a kitten with a roll of toilet paper at a diminutive narrow turquoise ribbon tied to the side handle. "With that. And no, I won't be here long. I'm just here to put the house on the market."

"Uh… shouldn't we check the I.D. tag?"

"Nope. Not necessary. So how do we get out of here?" I turned toward the wall of windows, palms trees fluttering in the breeze just beyond. Certainly didn't see those in Boston.

She let it go and said, "This way."

"Wait, what did you say your name was?" I couldn't remember if she'd already told me while I was in my fog, but I needed to know.

"I didn't." Her eyes pored into mine. Was she trying to intimidate? After living with my mother for decades, it was going to take more than that for me. "It's… Stella."

Why the hesitation?

"Okay. Good to meet you, Stella. I'm—"

"Yeah, I know. You're Miss Kathryn Moore. Your uncle was William Gray Moore. Now we've got your bag. Let's go."

I cringed at her use of past tense with respect to Gray.

Trying to keep pace with her long legs, I fast walked to stay alongside my escort but stopped short at a display case that held intricately woven baskets. "Whoa. What are these?" I poked my nose close enough to the plexiglass to fog up an impressive circle.

Pulling up, Stella turned back. "Those are sweetgrass baskets. The handiwork of Mary Jackson. She's a local star."

"Absolutely gorgeous." I sidestepped along the case to get a look at all of them, a half a dozen spectacular hand creations.

"The Gullah people have been making sweetgrass baskets for hundreds of years. They're actually sewn, not woven. You'll find them in all shapes and sizes. *They* used them for practical purposes, but now they're considered works of art and a coveted souvenir for visitors," she said and was off again.

Taking one last look before I scurried to catch up, I said, "I may have to find room for one in my suitcase before I head back." I could have sworn she was mumbling again... something about tourists.

Stepping outside, I was struck by the expanse of crayon green grass between the concrete passenger pick-up area and the parking garage beyond. The late afternoon heat warmed my New England soul, chilled by months of frigid temps and not used to thawing out so early.

"It's so lush here. My glasses are steaming up." I removed them to wipe away the annoying buildup.

"It *is* the end of March. Spring in the Lowcountry. Has been for a while."

"Geez. We're still dealing with disgusting black snow piles in Boston."

Stella shot a puzzled glance my way. "I thought snow was white."

"It is when it first falls. It's beautiful. But then the snowplows get out on the roads and push it to the sides so the crap on the roads gets plowed up with it. Some of the piles get huge by the end of winter and take forever to melt. So on particularly gray winter days, it's depressing to have nothing pretty to look at—just dirty snow."

Having lost interest in my description of New England winters, Stella led the way to the trunk of a modest sedan, some sort of faded blue foreign job. The trunk protested when she opened the lid and tossed in my bag. I jumped as she slammed the lid shut.

"Yo, give the door a good yank." She pointed in my direction as I reached for the handle, which was good advice. The passenger side door acted as though it hadn't been used—or oiled—in a decade and groaned when it finally budged. I prayed I'd be able to open it again from the inside.

Sliding in, a pungent odor accosted my nasal passages—greasy fries?—and I wished I'd thought to brush off the seat first. The springs were shot, so I felt as though my rear end was resting on the undercarriage, my knees protruding unnaturally higher than my waist.

Chick-fil-A wrappers cluttered the dash, a battered briefcase took up half of my floor space, and Mardi Gras beads numbering in the dozens hung from the rearview mirror. I stole a side glance to watch her fold herself awkwardly into the compact.

As if aware of where my eyes had landed during my onceover, she snatched up the fast-food wrappers and shoved them into the pocket in the door, jamming them as far down as they would go. She coaxed the engine to life with a couple of raps on the dash and said, "You best put on your seatbelt. Drivers around here are maniacs. They're—" She stopped short of her full warning once she saw I was one step ahead of her.

After jamming the car into reverse, she floored it, leaving a puff of black smoke behind us, which she didn't seem to notice. We were on our way, windows down even after we got up to cruising speed on the highway. Apparently the A/C wasn't working. I doubted it was a recent issue.

Slipping my notepad from my pocket, I began to jot down my last vision before I forgot the details. They were a lot like dreams that way. The more time that slipped by, the murkier my memory of them.

"The *hell* are you doing?" Stella couldn't mind her business.

"Oh, uh… I'm just writing down a couple of to-dos. You know how it is, if I don't write them down as soon as they pop in my head, I forget them." It was a harmless fib. She didn't need to know.

Frowning, she said, "No, I don't, actually. I don't forget nothing… anything," she corrected. "I have an amazing memory."

Not willing to get into it, I let it go.

"So my assignment is to get you to your uncle's house," she said with a glance in my direction. "And I'm sorry for your loss." It sounded more like an obligation she needed to check off her list than a sincere gesture. No matter. She didn't know me and I didn't know her. Time would tell if it would stay that way.

"Thanks." I waited for her to continue, but she didn't. "So that's it? You're just supposed to drop me off."

"Hope you weren't counting on a tour guide, 'cause that's not what I'm here for."

"Is this what you do? Pick people up from the airport? Run errands? Seems a waste of your intelligence." I hoped she wouldn't see through my veiled attempt to hack through her crusty exterior.

"No, it's not. But you're right." She gathered her thoughts. "I probably shouldn't say nothin'—*anything*," she corrected. "But at times I feel like they forget I passed the bar too. I'm as qualified as the other associates in the firm, but I'm the one who gets the crap assignments." She fell silent. "God, I shouldn't have said that. I didn't mean it." She shook her head but wouldn't look at me.

"Hey, don't worry about it. I get it. It must be so frustrating."

Her shoulders dropped with an exhale I read as relief.

"Could I get your professional opinion on something?" I tried again with the flattery angle.

"Sure." She seemed to brighten at the thought.

"What do you make of my uncle leaving me his house here."

"What do I *make* of it?" Keeping her eyes mostly on the road, she managed a side eye.

I must have seemed odd to her, or at least my situation. But I pushed for more. "You know … doesn't it seem odd that he left it to me and not his brother? Is it even legal for him to do that?"

"Legal? Well, yeah. As long as it was spelled out clearly in a will, he could do whatever the hell he wanted to do." She paused to bite the edge of her lower lip. "Whatever *he wanted* to do," she corrected.

"I would have thought he would have given it to my father. Seems like it skipped a generation in a rebellious, nonconforming way."

"Girl, I have *never* been able to figure out rich people and why they do what they do," she spat while her head wiggled wildly back and forth as if her neck suddenly had trouble supporting it. It may have only occurred to her then I might fall into the category of rich people, but she didn't let on. She continued.

"As my mama would say, 'Don't look a gift horse in the mouth.'"

"A what?" I'd never heard that expression before. "That's a new one on me. Is it a Southern *thang* to say?"

She shot a glare my way and said, "Now don't you start poking fun. You best watch yourself. My mamma would also say, 'Don't bite the hand that feeds you.' I'm the one giving you the ride you need."

"I'm sorry. I didn't mean to poke fun. Just…" I let it go. Figured it would be best if she was going to be so touchy and didn't seem to have much of a sense of humor.

As we rode in silence, strands of hair that had escaped my ponytail flapped in the breeze, smacking my face until we took the exit that dropped us into what looked like downtown Charleston. Clearly on my own to figure out what I was looking at, my head was on a swivel. Modest—some might say dilapidated—houses sprinkled in among mom-and-pop retail at first. Commercial docks on the harbor side. A gloriously restored factory that now housed some sort of an event venue, and a coffee shop, but I didn't catch the other businesses on our way by.

Without a prompt, she got chatty again.

"So when was the last time you were here?"

"In Charleston?"

"Uh, yeah." Her words were dripping with impatient sarcasm.

"I've never been." Taking her eyes from the road, she shot me a look.

"What? Are you kidding me? You've never visited before."

"No. Guess it was never on my radar," I said with a pang of guilt, trying to make it sound as casual as I needed it to. Uncle Gray had lived there for years, but it had never been a priority to come down? It was more like I knew my mother never would have let me come.

"So you have no idea what your uncle has left you. You've never been to his home."

"No, I don't. But my mother says it's probably a dump."

Her foot slipped from the gas. "I can assure you it's not a dump. Nothin' south of Broad is a dump."

"South of Broad?"

"Broad Street. It's the line of demarcation—" She broke up the word into four distinct syllables as if she were practicing to get it right. "—for real estate on the peninsula. There are all kinds of beautiful Charleston homes that would fetch a stupid price but your uncle's property—" She whistled through pursed lips and left it at that.

I suddenly wanted her to get out of my business. For someone in her position in life—a struggling legal associate driving a car that should have hit the scrap metal pile years ago—I would imagine there were very few dwellings she considered dumps. The Moores had standards, and my mother would never allow me to keep a modest home, even if it was in picturesque Charleston.

"As I said before, I'm just here to put it on the market and get back to Boston."

"Back to civilization."

I started to laugh, then I realized that was a barbed stab. "Something like that." Was the tension I was sensing part of a North/South struggle going back to the days of Lincoln?

We slowed as the road narrowed to two lanes, approaching a line of cars at a light that gave me more time to look. Some sort of an open-air market on the right. The U.S. Customs House on the left. A candy store with its front door wide open, allowing the sweet aroma to entice passersby. My mouth watered. The sign offered free samples of pralines. My hand crept toward the door handle. I didn't know what pralines were, but my taste buds were dying to find out.

"What are pralines like? Are they worth the calories?" I welcomed the frivolous topic to lighten the mood.

Stella pulled in a breath between her teeth as we crawled through the intersection. "Girl, they are to *die* for. A yummy heap of Southern pecans, covered in a sweet mixture of caramelized sugar, butter, and cream. Addictive. But see for yourself. You saw that candy store back there—Savannah's Candy Kitchen?" she asked, pointing her thumb backward as if she were hitchhiking. "Lord knows why it's called that and not Charleston. Well you go on in there and they'll give you a sample and you can make up your own mind."

"I think I may have to. That smell was incredible."

"And they've got candy apples, caramel apples, fudge, all kinds of handmade candy, and a bunch of old-fashioned stuff you don't see anywhere else."

"Yum."

"You won't be able to leave without buying something. Might be illegal if you do."

We shared a chuckle.

"And there's a vendor in the market back there—pretty much an outdoor market with a roof, across from the candy store—where you can get candied nuts. Not just pecans but almonds and cashews too. Those are also addictive. She'll give you a sample if you ask."

"I'll have to try those as well."

Stella was turning into a quasi-tour guide after all—at least for snacks. Free ones. I could picture her swapping out hats, jackets, and sunglasses in order to make return stops for samples.

"And both are walking distance from your uncle's place—that is, if you're a walker. If not, you could hail a bike taxi."

I forced a laugh to keep from reacting to the insult. "What's a bike taxi?"

Her guffaw came as a surprise. I thought it was a legitimate question.

"You'll figure it out. They're all over downtown."

Restaurants lined both sides of the next few blocks. I wanted to try them all. I'd heard the food in the Holy City was fabulous. A couple of cobblestone streets came into view on the left, presumably heading to the waterfront. When we stopped at a second light, Stella nodded toward the wide street perpendicular to the one we were on.

"That's Broad Street."

I allowed my eyes to meander down it. "Looks aptly named."

"Yeah, well, everything south of here on the peninsula jumps in value, rarely goes on the market, and costs seven figures and up when it does."

Could that be where my uncle's house was? Could my mother have been so wrong? Surely there were more modest homes mixed in.

Her expression turned sour. "And it was all built on the backs of slaves. People ripped from their homes. Families broken up. Shipped here like cargo in nasty living conditions to do backbreaking work so the wealthy white plantation owners could get richer."

The air in the car turned frigid. A line was drawn between us. Was I to blame for the actions of a few generations ago, just because I had the same skin color? I had no control over my ancestors any more than Stella did. It was horrible what they went through. Hard to imagine slavery being an accepted practice. It turned my stomach to think about it. I understood why it upset Stella, but I decided not to engage in the dicey topic, and thankfully she dropped it.

From that point, the street took on a quaint neighborhood feel. Rows of pastel-colored homes with window boxes overflowing with blooms, trees lining both sides of the street.

"This is so picturesque," I said as a horse drawn carriage *clip-clopped* by. "Like something out of a Hallmark movie."

"Ha! Wait until you see your uncle's place. Well… yours now."

Before long our view opened up in front of us to the expansive harbor to the left and in front of us. I drew in a quick breath. "Wow, that's beautiful. I could look out at that all day."

"Girl, that's a distinct possibility." As she turned onto a brick driveway on the right, something under the car rattled. Her muffler? She ignored it as though it happened all the time and tapped the squeaky brakes in the shade of a towering tree with stout branches that reached across the property and over the wall to the next. It reminded me of my tree in our yard in Boston, but this one was thick with a cover of deep green narrow leaves, what with spring arriving much earlier in the South.

A light pink structure with expansive side porches and a view out to the harbor towered next to us. A much smaller building lay just beyond where the driveway ended—smaller but large enough to live in. A cottage? I supposed it was called a carriage house.

"This is it?" I nodded toward the more modest building. Surely the monstrosity couldn't be my uncle's property.

Stella chuckled. I was grateful her sense of humor had returned.

"Take a gander out your window." She gestured to the passenger side.

Shifting in my seat I had to crane my neck to take in the grand three-story structure that looked more like a museum than a home.

"What? This is… my uncle's house."

"The word *house* is an insult. Are you kidding? Just look at it. For God's sake, who lives like this…. Well, I guess you do now. That is, if you keep it." Clenching her jaw with a slight wag of her head, she couldn't stand it.

It wasn't my fault the property had been dumped in my lap. I'd have given it back in the blink of an eye if the gesture would have brought back my uncle.

Seemingly eager to complete her assignment, she was already at the trunk, yanking out my suitcase and slamming it shut. I was barely out of the front seat when she was back in. I leaned into the open window.

"All right, girl. You're all set. The key is on your suitcase. I'm outta here," she said.

"Thanks… and thanks for the ride."

"Yeah, no problem. Enjoy your new… *house.* Hope you can deal with the guilt." With that she hit the gas and pulled out with a screech onto the street. She couldn't resist having the last word and yelled out her window with a wave, "Just don't go in the basement."

*Don't go in the basement.* I stood there in the driveway with the key to my uncle's house clutched tightly in my fist. No doubt there was a distinct outline forming in the folds of my skin.

Her five words transported me back to the basement of our family home on Beacon Hill. I was nine. My brother was twelve, and he had locked me in the cold, dark, creepy basement while he was watching my younger sister and me one evening when my parents were out. It was supposed to be funny. Payton was the only one who thought so. I'd like to think he'd forgotten about me, but he even went so far as to stuff my bedcovers with blankets so it would look like I was sound asleep when our parents got home and peeked in on me. He left me to sob on the steps until I eventually fell asleep. My mother finally found me the next morning once she noticed I was missing. I was a mess. My mother, in all her twisted parenting, thought it was humorous, which only screwed me up even further.

I felt excruciatingly alone even though Stella sat in her car idling in the street. From her expression I couldn't tell if she was pitying me or laughing at me. Either way it was unsettling. *Just go already. Get out of here. You've had your fun. Now go. Get the hell out of my life.* I choked up and swallowed away a sob. I didn't need her. *Go!*

As I started to turn my back, the loud metallic crash shook me before it could register Stella had been rear-ended by a massive truck.

# CHAPTER THREE

"No!" I shrieked and ran down the driveway. "Holy shit… this didn't just happen. Let her be okay," I pleaded for what seemed like an impossible ask, which felt absurdly insincere. I'd just been hating on her and wishing her out of my life.

Sirens in the distance. How could they have gotten word so quickly? The truck driver was out of his cab. He seemed okay. Not even staggering. What condition was Stella in? There would be blood everywhere. Had she had time to fasten her seatbelt before the impact?

Then a car passed alongside the accident, heading in the other direction, obliterating my field of vision momentarily. I pulled up and hesitated. Why wouldn't they stop for a nasty collision they must have seen as they were approaching?

As that car cleared out of the way I saw the truck. Dark green. One you would see at a construction site. But Stella's car was not in sight. *Oh God, it's under the truck. Her tiny car got crushed.* I started running again only to reach the end of the driveway and halt to avoid being hit by another passing car. Why was no one stopping to help?

Then I saw it. In front of the truck was a dumpster. Blue. Very similar to the color of Stella's car. Sitting in the middle of the road. Just ahead of it was the flatbed it had fallen off and its driver walking back to assess the situation. The two men began to chat. Stella's car was nowhere in sight. Neither was Stella.

What had happened? Why did my brain twist what I was seeing and hearing into a terrible crash involving someone I'd just met. Yes, she'd hurt my feelings. And unearthed a traumatic childhood event that could very well have initiated my bouts of anxiety. But did I really want her to be hit by a truck?

"Jesus, Kathryn. Pull it together."

Starting back up the driveway I tried to shake it off. Maybe my mother was right, and I needed to up the dosage on my meds. Taking hold of my rollaway handle, I headed toward the porch. Under more ordinary circumstances the rocking chairs would have seemed downright inviting. Now they beckoned in an eerie sort of way.

I peeled the key off my sweaty palm. To hell with the basement. I would simply steer clear of it. What secrets was this beautiful structure hiding? It was an incredible home.

"She's a magnificent lady, isn't she?" Her voice had a Southern lilt to it, friendly and not in a hurry.

I turned to watch a tall, older woman making her way up the driveway, perhaps my uncle's age but well preserved, her ankle-length open caftan in warm peach, muted yellows, and cool white fluttering in the breeze off the water. Her ash blonde wavy tresses fell to just below her shoulders, pulled back on one side with an encrusted hair comb that sparkled in the sunlight.

There was a seductiveness to her stride I thought should have been saved for her male counterparts, but perhaps that was always how she walked. Her eyes were fixated on Uncle Gray's house as she sauntered.

"Indeed." I loved how she referred to the impressive home as a lady.

It certainly seemed to fit with its pink exterior. I'm sure Uncle Gray wouldn't have minded.

I offered a smile and nodded as the woman came within a few feet and halted, dropping her glance to my shoes and back up again, assessing the newcomer. Suddenly feeling on display, I jammed my hands into my skirt pockets.

"You must be Gray's kin." Her last word was two syllables.

"Yes… Kathryn Moore. His niece."

"I can see the resemblance, sweet thing." She pronounced thing like *thang*.

Again, I nodded, but my throat tightened and words wouldn't come.

"Shame he never married. Such a fine-looking man. Even though he wasn't born in the South, he sure turned into a right fine Southern gentleman. You know, if I'd been a little more assertive while we were on earth at the same time…" She left the thought for the breeze to whisk away.

I wondered if she'd hoped he would be a proper suitor but remained silent to see if my visitor would continue, and she did.

"Anyway, enough of all that wishful thinking. I'm Annalee." She flicked a graceful, diamond-ring-adorned hand toward the house and, presumably, whatever lay on the other side of it where she'd walked from. Annalee took in the grounds around us. "It's been tough to watch the gardens go to shambles since—since he's been gone. But now you're here, so I'm sure they're in good hands."

"Oh, I'm not much of a gardener," I confessed. "I wouldn't know a dandelion from a daffodil. Besides, I won't be here long enough to—"

"Well bless your heart, darlin'," she said with a teeth-bearing grin in a tone so sugary, it could put a pitcher of sweet tea to shame. "It's not hard, sweet pea. And I can give you some pointers." The woman wandered over toward a mass of greenery with light purple flowers.

"A little weeding and these plumbago will be thriving again." Her last word sounded more like uh-gee-un. She bent at the waist and cradled a cluster of blossoms to her nose. Straightening up, she said, "Just be careful of the oleander."

I couldn't tell which plants she was referring to.

"They're pretty blossoms but the leaves can be deadly." With a chortle, she headed back down the drive. "Well, I just wanted to stop by and welcome you to the neighborhood. You know, Southern hospitality and all," she said over her shoulder and then disappeared around the edge of the brick wall, the bottom hem of her breezy caftan the last to flutter out of sight.

It wasn't until then I realized I was back to clutching the house key so tightly the edges were cutting into my palm, so I stretched out my fingers to unlock my vice grip. Was I suddenly protective of my uncle's house? Afraid it could be thrust from my grasp as quickly as it was plopped on to my lap?

The time had come to see what he had left to me. An uncomfortable pinch in my stomach reminded me I'd never visited him there. Regrets.

Three grand porches stacked one on top of the other lined the side of the house. Hand railings framing the steps up to the first-floor porch splayed outward, giving them a welcoming flair.

"All right, Uncle Gray. Thank you for entrusting me with this incredible home. Let's take a look." Leaving my suitcase on the driveway, I approached the front door with its ornate woodwork, and my eyes landed on the tarnished brass knob.

Folded up, unread newspapers—some stacked on the welcome mat, others scattered across the porch—didn't seem to be enough to be one for each day since his accident. Someone had to have stopped their delivery. It wasn't surprising he still received the print version of the *Post and Courier.* I could imagine him sitting on one of the porches, looking out to the harbor, having his morning coffee, and reading the paper. Downright romantic. He *was* a writer, after all.

Pulling out a paper from the bottom of the stack, the headline caught my eye. Local Man in Ravenel Bridge Accident. I tossed it back on the pile. Sidestepping the papers, I inserted the key into the antique slot. It slid in easily but didn't budge on the first try to turn it.

"You have to give the knob a good tug toward you while you're turning the key."

Jumping at the sound of a voice, I spun around, my back thudding against the door as the key hit the wooden floorboards.

"I beg your pardon, angel. I didn't mean to frighten you." Annalee had reappeared. I hoped this wasn't going to be a regular occurrence.

Gathering up the key by its chain, I did my best to wave off the awkwardness, willing the burning in my cheeks to subside. "It's fine. I'm fine. Really. I didn't realize you'd come back." I sucked in a bit of the invigorating sea air and followed Annalee's advice. After a couple tries with a firm tug, I heard a muffled click and the knob turned easily. With my shoulder leaning into it, I was able to push the massive wooden door open.

"Hey, it worked. Thanks for—" I scanned the yard and spotted Annalee bent over, busy in the garden, apparently not able to stand the condition of it any longer.

The air inside the home was tinged with mustiness, but it wasn't as bad as I'd expected. The foyer was grand with a room on either side. It looked like a small dining room on the left with the living room across from it, which I decided to call a sitting room. Seemed to fit the house. Except for the dust coverings that looked like old sheets on the furniture and the foyer chandelier, it must have been the way my uncle had left it the last time he'd walked out the door.

Where had he been heading? What had gone wrong? A car accident.

They happen all the time. But to other people. Not someone you looked up to and adored and wanted to be like. He was supposed to always be there. Now he was gone. He'd taken a part of me with him and left a gnawing emptiness in my gut I imagined would always be there.

"Uncle Gray, your home is absolutely stunning. Looks like you did all right for yourself." As soon as I uttered the words, they sounded trite with a tinge of insincerity. *Find the right words, Kathryn. Remember, you're a writer. Or are you an imposter?* "What I mean is I'm proud of you and what you've accomplished. I can only hope to follow in your footsteps." I thought of how slim my chances were of actually doing that now. "I don't know that I can. You were so encouraging. And I appreciated that." My words still sounded hollow.

Just beyond the foyer's curved archway, a graceful, winding staircase beckoned me upstairs. Light filtered through the branches of a magnificent magnolia tree splashed onto the stairwell through a two-story pane glass window.

Passing under the chandelier, I couldn't resist a playful swipe at the covering and instantly regretted it. Swatting dust from my hair as I reached the first step, I glanced down a hallway toward the front of the house and the door I imagined visitors would have been welcomed through. A curved transom with artfully arranged circles and stylized stars sat atop, letting in a dusty ray of waning daylight. I had expected it to look more like a spiderweb but it would undoubtedly not be the first surprise in a house of this size and age.

With what felt like an afterthought, I caught the toe of my shoe on the lip of the second step, clearly at an odd height. Grasping for the railing too late to keep from face-planting into the balusters, I heard a snap and felt a sting across the bridge of my nose. Gravity took over and sent my glasses—now in two pieces—toppling down the stairs like a couple of slinkies let loose by a child. Whirling around, I plopped my backside onto the closest stair.

"Damn it!" On the floor at the foot of the steps lay what was left of my thick-lensed spectacles. All because I was clumsy. My mother—always quick to distance herself from her middle child—would have said I took after my father's side of the family. I was okay with that. My uncle was on that side of the family. And I adored him.

Retrieving the plastic rimmed remnants, I realized I'd have to start wearing my contacts—something my mother had been urging me to do for years. I'd been limping along with what was comfortable even though my glasses prescription was outdated. I'd never wanted to invest the time in learning to wear plastic discs on my eyeballs. How uncomfortable did that sound? At least I'd thought to bring them on the trip. Ever the planner, I sometimes took preparing for the unexpected to a new level—the single trait I regrettably shared with my mother. *Shudder.* Although my mother's planning was for parties, mine was for the worst.

Fitting the two pieces of my glasses back together, I balanced them on my nose in the hopes of checking out the rest of the house and resumed shuffling up the stairs, ever careful of where I placed my feet.

At the top, the open space mirrored the grand foyer below with another massive chandelier peeking through its sheer wrappings. What would one call this space? It was more than a landing. The upstairs foyer? Pre-event room sounded closer. Recalling an intro to architecture class I'd taken as an elective, I plucked the word entresol from my distant memory. A grand place to entertain, for sure. Like a ballroom. Three rooms opened off it.

The first room toward the front of the house was smaller than the other two and appeared to be a library or a study of sorts, lined with floor-to-ceiling-stuffed bookshelves that ran the length of the three walls I could see, interrupted only by an ornate writing desk to the left and a floor to ceiling window that looked out to the harbor. The desk sat open to reveal an impressive array of slots and small compartments. A Windsor chair sat tucked under the open flap as if inviting me to sit and write, inspired by the view. A tarnished brass telescope on a stand pointed out the window as if someone had just stepped away from surveying the harbor and beyond.

A narrow opening connected the study with the room next door where a harpsichord and harp were on display, along with an ornate metal music stand and more seating under protective wraps. Toward the back of the house and occupying space nearly the size of the two front rooms was a formal dining room with a long table with more chairs surrounding it than I'd seen in a dining area before. "Who lives like this?" I asked the essence of Uncle Gray that lingered there. I could hear Stella's voice with the same words. "Geez, this is over the top." I wondered if he had ever used the rooms as they were originally intended.

French doors leading out to the second-floor porch opened easily, and a breath caught in my throat by the view out to the harbor off to the left. I imagined the view from the third floor was even more spectacular. Could you also see rooftops and church steeples?

Cars that seemed to be intruding into the wrong era, given the homes in the neighborhood, passed by on the street down below. I imagined horse-drawn carriages in their places.

It was a magnificent home, nothing like I could have imagined. It had a museum feel to it—a museum that hadn't been visited in a while, so the funding had dried up and its future was uncertain. And that future was in my hands.

If my mother had had an inkling of what it was like, she would have figured out a way to wrestle it from my grasp—hire the best estate attorney in the state of Massachusetts to find the best attorney in the state of South Carolina to get her hands on this property.

The sheer size made me feel uncomfortable—like I was not just an outsider but an interloper. Not worthy of having something so grand placed in my care, much less in my name.

Reentering what I'd named the entresol, I noticed a closed door to the left of the stairs. Compared to the rest of the floor, it was quite plain. Its location suggested it was connected to the wing that extended into the backyard.

The tarnished brass knob only turned so far and didn't open when I yanked on it. A skinny black skeleton key sat cockeyed in its slot but slid easily and the door opened to a darkened narrow hallway. A modern light switch looked out of place, but when I flicked it, nothing happened. With the daylight streaming into the rest of the house, I hadn't needed additional light up to that point. It hadn't occurred to me the utilities would have been shut off.

Slipping out my cell, I tapped the flashlight icon to illuminate a long hallway lined with closed doors, but it didn't seem as bright as usual. Undeterred, I pressed farther into the dimness. The bedrooms were likely down this hall, and I would need to select one to use. Before I got to the first door, the light went out.

"Come on. Really? Shit." The movie I'd watched on the flight down had zapped the battery. Had it been worth watching *The Thomas Crown Affair* for the fiftieth time? The familiarity of the movie had helped distract me enough to manage my flying anxiety.

Who didn't love a movie with everything in it? A clever art heist at the world-famous Metropolitan Museum of Art, a forbidden romantic encounter interwoven with an intellectual game of cat and mouse, and a full emersion into the world of the elite—all in the city that never sleeps—with a fling to the Caribbean thrown in for good measure. The storyline never got old as I imagined myself in Rene Russo's shoes as Katherine Banning. Stunning, confident, successful, and able to run in the same circles as the exceedingly wealthy. Each time, when the credits started to roll, I'd ask myself the same question: Would I have gotten on that plane?

So yes, it had been worth it. Until now.

From behind came the unmistakable sound of the door slamming shut, thrusting me into complete darkness. Then came the sound of a click. Or had I imagined it?

Had someone followed me? Was I locked in? Was Annalee back? Had Stella returned? Was this her idea of a hilarious joke? I wasn't amused. It wasn't a basement, but I was trapped in the dark.

# CHAPTER FOUR

"Annalee, is that you?" Running a hand along the wall with the other out in front, I shuffled back to where I'd come in until my palm smacked the door. The knob turned, but the door wouldn't budge. Turning the knob in the other direction, I yanked hard but it didn't move. Grabbing ahold of it with both hands I tried again, panic welling up inside. My breaths became rapid and shallow as my imagination kicked in, conjuring up what was lurking in the dark behind me: elongated hands poised to grab my waist, a furry critter with sharp teeth looking to gnaw on an ankle, or pursed lips to blow cold air on my neck.

"Annalee, the door seems to be stuck. Can you push from that side?" I knew I wasn't talking to anyone, but the charade helped me believe the stuck door had a simple explanation and I'd figure it out. The mind games I had to play with my own head. I also figured if anyone had followed me in, they'd think there was someone else in the house and might be scared off.

"Why can't I open this door?" I whispered to myself. "Think, Kathryn. Think." Releasing the knob, I thrust both fists at the door, pounding and pounding. "Help," I shrieked, hoping against hope someone would hear me. "Please, someone help," I pleaded. I couldn't get stuck in an old house that no one had any reason to enter. That would be my last stupid mistake. When they finally found me, my body barely recognizable from the extensive decomposition, what would my mother say? I didn't want to think it through any further than I already had.

No phone to call for help. No neighbors within shouting distance. I kept pounding. "Help! Please, someone."

"Miss Moore?" His voice was muffled, but it sounded like he was close. "Are you in there?" The knob rattled in place.

"Yes, I'm stuck. Can you open it from that side?" Who was there? I wondered.

Then came the sound of the key sliding in the lock on the other side. The door popped open, flooding the hallway with light.

"Miss Moore?" His robust tone sounded like it had been smoothed over by the burn of a steady diet of Southern bourbon.

I looked up into a deeply tanned face with warm azure eyes that seemed to say, *Welcome to the Lowcountry.* He would have been a much sweeter Southern welcome at the airport than the one I'd experienced. But I wasn't going to complain. He was here now.

His broad shoulders and bulging biceps threatened to burst the seams of his button-down oxford, rolled up to his elbows.

I pushed my glasses up on the bridge of my nose, trying to keep them from falling apart, to get a better look at the specimen of a Southern gentleman. "Yes?"

"Ma'am, I'm Mason Levinson from Levinson & Levinson," he said, offering a warm hand.

I took it, considering him for a moment, suddenly painfully aware of my sweaty palms. He was the professional attorney material I would have expected. In spite of his sizable frame, his mop of wavy dark blond hair and peeling, sunburned nose read harmless. But he also didn't strike me as the kind of guy who would get chewed up and spit out in a courtroom.

He glanced at the knob with his head cocked. "How the hell did that happen?"

"I… I'm not sure," I said, pushing past him, desperate to get out of the dark hall, glancing to the French doors to the porch to confirm I'd shut them and hadn't created a draft. "I'd left the door ajar, but it slammed shut behind me."

"Maybe there's a window open down the hall. It might have been opened so the place wouldn't get too stuffy." He fiddled with the key in the lock. "This *is* pretty loose. Turns easily. Must have fallen into the right spot when the door slammed. Funny."

"My phone died so I had no way of calling anyone."

"Good thing I came along when I did. And this is why I'm here." He held out his hand, a key resting in the center of his palm, a Levinson & Levinson logo on the keychain. "This is for the carriage house. You won't want to use any of the bedrooms in this wing." He tilted his head toward where he'd just rescued me from. "The main house doesn't have any electricity at the moment. Hasn't had for a while. Just the carriage house. Your uncle had contracted with a management company to handle renting it as a B&B. From what I understand, it was quite popular. Tourists love the idea of staying in such an old place. Even if they can't get into the main house, they can peek in the windows and feel like they're stepping back in time—or something silly like that. Anyway, the utilities for the rental property were set up as a separate account and got left on."

As Mason rambled on about the old house and the tourists that flocked to it, I felt one half of my glasses fall askew on my nose.

"Oh, ma'am, your glasses are broken." He broke off his narrative.

"Yeah." As I took the two pieces off my face, his lit up. He regarded me thoughtfully. My face was probably pale from my spine-tingling, paralyzing scare.

"Why don't you head out and get some fresh air. I think you could use it. I'll do a quick check of the wing to make sure everything is the way it should be. There must be an open window...." His voice trailed off as he headed down the hall.

Feeling a bit silly for putting myself in such a vulnerable situation but grateful for being rescued, I took his suggestion and headed for the stairs. I'd seen enough, and the scare in the hallway had me rattled. Even if the house had had electricity I wasn't about to sleep anywhere down that hall. The sprawling old house was suddenly too creepy. The rest could wait to be explored. When I had proper lighting. And maybe some company.

As I made my way back to the lower level, careful where I placed my clumsy feet, I noticed an old black typewriter—an Underwood—that took up most of the top of a small desk just inside the sitting room. It was doubtful that was where my uncle had written his novels. He simply appreciated antiques. *Just look at the house and its contents.* A blank sheet of white paper was cued up on the roller as if someone were going to start typing the next *New York Times* bestseller.

Stepping out onto the first-floor porch, the briny sea breeze brushing my face helped to settle the nerves. That was until I realized my suitcase wasn't where I'd left it.

# CHAPTER FIVE

DID SOMEONE HAPPEN ALONG WHILE I was busy getting locked in a dark hallway and decide to snag my suitcase? There wasn't much in it besides a few days' clothes, some toiletries, and a couple paperbacks I'd hoped to devour. Perfect. A dead phone, a creepy old house, and no change of clothes or toothbrush. I looked to the carriage house in the hopes it could offer a more welcoming place to stay.

Mason reappeared, pulling the massive door shut behind him.

"Sorry about that in there. Hell of a way to start off. And please accept my condolences for your uncle. Terrible tragedy. Senseless."

I nodded my acceptance, and we stood gazing out to the harbor.

"This whole thing is my uncle's?" I asked, drawing a circle in the air above my head with an extended index finger like a cowboy with a miniature lasso.

"It *was*. Now it's yours, Kathryn."

Why did everyone have to keep reminding me?

A shiver ran through me. Nothing was *ever* how I anticipated it—I should have been used to the idea—but this was so far out of my ability to imagine, I struggled to take in the impressive home.

"This lady is one of the oldest properties south of Broad, so she's seen a lot of action. Built in the early 1800s… she's withstood the ravages of the Civil War, the earthquake of 1886. And we can't forget about the Great Fire of 1861, although it didn't get this far down on the peninsula so fortunately she survived unscathed. Many others weren't so lucky. And there have been many hurricanes over the years, but she stands proud in spite of her history."

He fell silent, as if in reverence to a grand historical figure. But he wasn't finished gushing.

"Check out that view."

I glanced back out to the harbor.

"It doesn't get much better than this."

Yet my attention was drawn back to the main house. Such an impressive structure. I hadn't pictured anything close to the size of it. Southern belles in colorful ballgowns must have sipped sweet tea and fanned themselves on the porches.

"Is it haunted?" I couldn't resist asking.

"Could be. I don't have any firsthand knowledge about that, but with the history of this area, I would say just about every structure on the peninsula has at least one spirit still hanging around. Some don't know when they've outstayed their welcome."

He made his way over to one of the rockers.

"So except for that scary hiccup, how does it feel to be back in Charleston? I wish it were under better circumstances. You must be reeling from everything that's transpired." Mason's question was innocent enough, a conversation starter, but it made me squirm.

"Back to Charleston? I've never been before," I hated to admit.

He wagged his head once as if it would help him make sense of that. "Didn't your uncle live here the last couple decades?"

"Yeah. As long as I can remember, he's always been here."

"And you never came," he said with an expression that came close to a scowl. I felt the weight of his judgement on my entire body.

I let out the air in my lungs. "Here's the thing. You don't know my mother. Okay? And she would never have let me come down here to visit him."

"What? Why not? How old are you? No—don't answer that. My point is you're obviously old enough to make your own decisions. Why would you let—" Thankfully he let it go. I really didn't want to have to explain my life back in Boston. "Well, listen. Since this is your first visit, I think I need to take you on a little tour of the peninsula.

"That's very nice of you to offer, but I'm sure you're busy." Of course I would love to be escorted by a handsome Southern gentleman, but I had to push back a little bit. After all, wasn't that what a Southern belle would do?

"I insist. It wouldn't be right if you didn't have a proper introduction to the Holy City."

"Well, if you're sure you have the time. Wait… I don't see my suitcase. I left it—"

"Oh, I took the liberty of bringing it over by the carriage house. I figured that's where you'd be staying."

Relieved there was a logical explanation for its disappearance, I thanked him for his gesture.

Eyeing a dark sports car he'd clearly arrived in, I couldn't wait to climb in and be seen with him. I don't claim to know one fancy car from another, but this one sat so low to the ground, looking like something a British spy would drive in the movies.

He held the door as I climbed into the passenger seat as gracefully as I could manage, flustered by his chivalry—no doubt, flushing. He'd slipped behind the steering wheel before I'd noticed he'd opened the driver's side door. His head didn't touch the ceiling, but he filled up his half of the front seat. It was then I caught sight of the unmistakable Jaguar ornament threatening to leap off the hood.

As he backed down the driveway, with a bit more touch than Stella had, I thought I'd throw in my own conversation starter, the continuation of a poll of sorts.

"So, Mason, let me ask you this. Don't you think it odd that I was left with my uncle's house?" Maybe I'd get further with him.

He didn't respond right away, perhaps focusing on pulling out into traffic.

I waited. Dead air had a way of getting people to talk. About anything, just so it wasn't silent. And I had no problem keeping my mouth shut so he would open his.

"Ma'am, nothing in this business surprises me anymore." A politically correct and noncommittal answer all wrapped in one.

"Really." He couldn't have been in *this business* much more than a few years.

"Yes, ma'am. But it's also not my place to pass judgment."

"You know, you can dispense with the *ma'ams*. I'm sure it's a Southern thing and you're trying to be polite, but it just… I don't know. It sounds so old." But it was certainly a refreshing way to be spoken to after Stella—the way I would have expected, being in the South.

He nodded his acknowledgment. I couldn't tell if he was agreeing it was polite or it sounded old. Maybe both.

Allowing the silence to hang for a moment longer as we headed up East Bay, I ran my hand along the buttery soft mocha leather on the seat that covered the rest of the interior. Not a bad ride. I guessed he was also an associate. "Company car?" I tested.

He stole a glance my way before refocusing on the road ahead. "Uh, no. It's mine."

*A gift from Daddy?* I refrained from asking.

"Sorry. I didn't mean to pry."

The side of his mouth turn up slightly. Was I providing amusement of some sort?

"I'm not the office errand boy, if that's what you're thinking."

"I didn't mean to imply that." Offending him would not be in my best interests. But surely an attorney—was that what he was?—would have more of a backbone than that.

He laughed. "No, I give people that impression a lot. I look younger than I am. 'Course, I skipped a couple of grades in school and graduated from law school early, so by default I *am* younger than most associates at my level."

Impressed by his resume so far, I asked, "And I suppose you passed the bar on the first try?"

The corner of his mouth turned up again. "Yeah." Which I interpreted as, "Of course."

My mother would have been proud of him. A real go-getter. A high achiever. Unlike myself who hadn't followed in the footsteps of my parents in a successful business like my brother and sister had.

"So who do you think your uncle *should* have left his home to?"

I was pleased he was returning to my original question.

"He wasn't married. Had no children."

"How about my father, his brother? That would seem to make more sense."

"He must have had his reason not to. What was their relationship?"

"I mean… I don't know. I guess they weren't that tight. But they're brothers."

"And you're his niece. Did you two have a close relationship?"

"We did." The thought gave me a strangely warm chill, coaxing a smile, but the raw ache from losing him reawakened in my gut. We'd had a special connection. A real bond from when I was quite young. He was the successful writer I looked up to and wanted to emulate.

"Well, then. That explains it." Clearly Mason was satisfied we'd figured it out and was done with the topic.

Not to be cut off, I kept the questions coming. "So what made you want to be a lawyer?"

He glanced over and said, "Guess it runs in the family."

"So you work with your father?"

"Actually both parents initially."

*Seriously Kathryn?* I mentally kicked myself for assuming the attorney in his family was his father. The more we talked, the more his situation smacked of familiarity with my own family. Not a comfortable talking point, but I pressed on.

"What's *that* like?" Nothing like an open-ended question to see what spilled out.

Cocking his head while he fashioned an appropriate answer, he said, "It has its ups and downs. My father passed away several years ago, which changed things." He grew silent, suddenly intent on adjusting his rearview mirror.

"Did your mother ever remarry?" I knew the question was borderline nosy, but the more I knew about him, the better.

"Boy you Northern ladies don't mince words, do you? Get right to asking what you want to know."

"Why, would Southern ladies have considered that an invasive question?"

Mason smiled and glanced my way, a glint of amusement in his eye.

"No, they would have asked. Just not in the first fifteen minutes of meeting someone."

We shared a laugh.

Mason took a moment and then finally added, "Yeah, she got

remarried a few years ago. Also an attorney." He went back to fiddling with the mirror as if trying to catch a glimpse of his past.

At that point, I let it drop. He wasn't going to be any more forthcoming than he had been already. I could tell I'd pushed too far. But I knew firsthand it could be hellacious working in a family business. If he still lived at home, dinner conversations must be riveting.

"Did Stella bring you down East Bay along the harbor when she dropped you off?"

"Yeah, that sounds right."

"If I had picked you up from the airport I would have brought you in along the Ashley River and done a loop along The Battery. There's so much to take in there, and you really get a feel for Charleston's history, which you now own a part of. We'll cut over to that side of the peninsula by way of Broad."

He took a left at the light and negotiated his way through traffic. Broad, which I had gotten a glance of earlier, was laid out like its name implied. Two lanes wide and straight as far as you could see ahead.

"Some great restaurants along here on both sides." He pulled a large, tanned hand off the steering wheel to gesture. "Up ahead is what we call the Four Corners of Law. There's the post office, the county courthouse, city hall, and St. Michael's Church. So you've got federal, county, city, and ecclesiastical law on the four corners." A horse-drawn carriage passed us from the opposite direction just after the intersection.

My attractive chauffeur was also a capable tour guide, giving me a very different ride than that from the airport. More welcoming, exuding warmth. The same Southern hospitality as Annalee had shown me. The congestion at the start of Broad dispersed as the road narrowed, and the area turned more residential.

"That's Colonial Lake over there on the right, but I'm going to take Rutledge to get back down to the waterfront."

He made a left onto a narrow street with lovingly maintained quaint houses lining it. Gas lanterns flickered on either side of front doors. Wrought iron gates forged in intricate designs, nestled between the openings of brick walls, invited passersby to peek into the meticulously manicured gardens, down the brick walks to babbling fountains tucked in among the greenery. It seemed we had slipped through a wrinkle in time and were now somewhere in the past—1700s? 1800s? There was something very familiar about Charleston—like I'd been here before, perhaps in a previous life? It was so romantic to imagine.

"You are now south of Broad again. This is where you'll see some of the most beautiful examples of Charleston Singles. Absolute specimens."

"Charleston Singles?"

"That's what they call a good number of the homes downtown. The part of the house that faces the street is the narrow side—it's a single room wide—then the rest of the house runs deep into the lot, usually with a piazza or stacked piazzas on the side."

"Piazzas?"

"You probably call them porches. But here, they're piazzas."

I made a mental note not to call them porches anymore.

"They were built that way to take advantage of the breezes to stay cool in the warm months. Your uncle's place though, is in a different category altogether."

Mason slowed the car to a crawl, and I pressed the button to open the window to feel closer to the surreal scene. I imagined the *clip-clop* of a horse pulling our carriage. Layers of heavy fabric pooled at my ankles. A pleated paper fan clutched in my gloved hand.

"I see you have a few of our Charleston rice bead bracelets." His gaze had landed on my wrist. Reflexively I ran my fingertips across the three strands of small, elongated silver beads nestled between a variety of sterling cuffs.

"My uncle gave them to me for my last birthday."

"Nice. They represent a piece of Charleston history."

Suddenly I felt trapped inside the slow-moving car. I wanted to hit the sidewalks and explore. As my fingers connected with the sun-warmed door handle, I realized Mason was speaking again.

"This is Tradd Street." He indicated the crossroad. "It's the only street that runs all the way across the peninsula from river to river."

An expanse of water opened up in front of us. "We're back to the Ashley River. It's on the southwest side of the peninsula. The Cooper River is on the northeast. The two rivers meet to form Charleston Harbor." He took his hands off the wheel long enough to touch his fingertips together.

Turning to put the water on our right, he pointed up ahead. "White Point Garden. Nice green space to hang out. The cannons are left over from the wars. We're up on a seawall that's supposed to keep the sea out, but it doesn't always work. Downtown floods during a hard rain, let alone a big storm. Sometimes during high tides you'll see water coming up through the sewer drains. It can be quite a show but detrimental and a real headache to homeowners here."

Grand homes from a bygone era similar to Gray's flanked the road behind the park. I imagined the wealthy families who occupied them. Or were they museums now? My mother could have moved in and felt right at home. But she'd have hated the hot summers.

"Way out in the harbor is Fort Sumter." He pointed. "That's where the Civil War started. Beyond that is the open ocean."

"Stop. Can we get out?" I wanted to take it all in, not zip by in a blur because he'd seen it all so many times before.

Mason slid the car into an open spot along the sidewalk where it curved around the tip of the peninsula. I scrambled out before he could kill the engine and headed to the metal rails that ran the length of the waterfront. The cool briny breeze gently brushed my face and tickled my nasal passages while dark water lapped at the base of the seawall well below my feet.

"Kathryn, meet Charleston Harbor." He'd joined me along the rail.

Peering in the direction he'd indicated the fort was situated, I didn't see much but a grayish structure that was barely discernable. Closer in, the harbor was alive. A cargo ship stacked high with rectangular tractor trailer containers silently steamed in among sailboats bobbing lazily on the sun-speckled water. A red and white Coast Guard helicopter buzzed overhead.

The sidewalk curved around to follow the palm-tree-lined road. More grand homes looked out to the harbor, separated from it by the road and sidewalk where it was now raised. The waning afternoon sun reflected off a structure in the distance. Some sort of tower with cables extending out from both sides.

"What's that?" I asked.

"Behind the buildings?"

"Yeah."

"That's the Ravenel Bridge." He let out a soft chuckle. "I never realized you couldn't see it from this vantage point on the peninsula. I thought you could see it from everywhere. But from here, you can only see the top of one of the towers."

Considering his observations, I stayed silent.

"It's iconic. You'll have ample chance to get a better look at it. Anyway, I need to get back to the office. Let's get you back to your uncle's house. I'm sure you'd like to settle in."

"Oh, no," I whispered. Then more loudly, "The bridge. That's not where..." I looked to him for a reaction, but he'd returned to staring at the fort out in the harbor. "Tell me, Mason. Is that the bridge my uncle had his car accident on?"

He didn't answer.

"I need to know. I have a *right* to know."

Mason pulled away from the water, refocusing on me. "You're right. Yes, that's the bridge."

"I need to see it."

He squared his jaw.

"You know exactly where it happened. I want you to take me there."

"There's nothing to see. It was an accident. Nothing much left behind but I'm sure if there was any residual, it's all cleaned up by now."

"I need to see it."

His body stiffened. "I need to get back to the office." He brushed past me and headed for the car.

"What? No." I held my ground. "Mason, how long could it take? I don't have a car. I can't get there. Besides, you know exactly where it happened," I repeated, pressing to see how far I would get.

"No, I don't know *exactly*. Even if I did, there would be nothing to see," he called back.

"Just show me where. I need to know." I ran to catch up.

He aimed his key fob toward the hood. I hadn't remembered him locking it.

"I gotta go," he repeated.

Reluctantly I climbed back in, and we zipped out of the space before I could buckle the seatbelt. Up the road, he steered the Jag through the open wrought iron gate in the red brick wall onto the matching brick drive.

Reluctantly I got out and thanked him for the tour.

"You'll get your chance to see more of the bridge. I'm sure of it."

I stepped to the side and watched him back out.

It was just me and the grand Pink Lady.

# CHAPTER SIX

THE CARRIAGE HOUSE SAT IN THE shadows of a grand oak. A couple of French doors and square windows punctuated the side visible from the street. Its construction looked more recent but not less than a hundred years or so. I was counting on it to be a suitable place to stay while in town to conduct my business.

The key Mason had brought opened the door with ease. Inside was a small living area with a fireplace as the focal point. The entryway hall led to the doorway of what looked like a small kitchen. I took the stairs on the left of the entry, suitcase in tow, running my free hand along the smooth dark wood banister. I could feel indentations under my fingertips, evidence of many years of use.

At the top was a cozy bedroom—my suitcase and I took up most of the jockeying space—with a mahogany four-poster, queen-sized bed, matching armoire, and bedside tables. Roughly hewed beams ran the length of the ceiling, lending it authenticity. The room had an inviting, comfortable feel to it.

"You might want to change the sheets."

I jumped at the sound of his voice. "Jesus, Mason. Could you not sneak up on me like that? My nerves are rattled enough as it is." Was it a Southern thing? First Annalee, now Mason.

"Who's sneaking, Kathryn? I walked in like I normally do."

I flashed a glare his way while wondering if I'd remembered to take my morning med.

"Like I said, you might want to change the sheets. Who knows if the rental manager took care of it once she learned she was canned."

"Duly noted. Thanks," I said, rifling through an armoire stacked with sheets, towels, and extra toilet paper. "So what brings you back? I thought there was some urgency to you getting back to the office."

He ran his fingers though his golden mop, fluffing it out more than it already was. "Yeah, well, I didn't feel good about the way I left things. I'm sorry. You had every right to ask about the bridge. I just wasn't prepared for you to ask."

Suddenly feeling trapped by him standing inside the doorway, I said, "Why don't we head back downstairs." The living area was a much more appropriate place to receive a guest.

Spying an armoire next to the fireplace, similar to the one upstairs, I strode across the room and started opening doors. The top section held a flat screen, and the lower part held a nice assortment of liquor bottles and a supply of glasses. "Ooooh, guests had everything they could desire in a B&B. Care for a beverage?" I held up a bottle of Tito's, my favorite.

"Kind of you to ask." He checked his watch. "Guess I could be officially off the clock. It's Friday afternoon. Sure. But my druthers would be a belt of bourbon."

"Bourbon."

He leaned in and pulled out a bottle with an auburn liquid sloshing inside.

"Okay, I'll try that." Wouldn't want to insult a new Southern friend.

"Yeah? Allow me to pour." He relieved me of the vodka bottle and reshelved it. Grabbing two stout glasses, he headed for the kitchen. I could hear him scooping ice from the freezer. Returning to the sitting area, he poured a generous splash into each glass and offered me one, then settled into one of two light-colored wing chairs framing a low coffee table set in front of a matching sofa. "Not bourbon ice cubes, but they'll do. Thank God for the electricity in this building." We clinked. "Cheers. Welcome to Charleston."

"Cheers." I stifled a cough as the bourbon burned on its way down. To my ears it sounded more like clearing my throat, but I may not have fooled him. It wasn't anything I couldn't get used to, I decided.

He held up his glass. "First time?"

"What?" I'd already drifted off, imagining what it must be like to stay in the carriage house as a paying guest instead of a mess of a woman who was mourning her uncle.

"Have you ever had bourbon before?" He tried again.

"No, I don't think so." My head was already buzzing, reminding me I hadn't eaten for a while. The granola bar on the plane hadn't carried me very far.

"Well, you're handling it very well."

I appreciated his words of encouragement.

"Of course, there are other drinks and food you'll need to try while you're here. You know, to be fully indoctrinated into life in the Lowcountry."

"Like what?"

"She crab soup… fried green tomatoes… sweet tea and shrimp and grits… beignets . . . oysters. There are some great local beers too, if you're into beer."

"I'm not going to be here *that* long." I wasn't going to mention it to him, but just the smell of beer made my stomach turn, having to smell it every day at our family's brewery.

"Then you'd better get started." We shared a laugh.

"What's she crab soup?" I'd never heard of it. "Is that some kind of a Southern crab?"

"No, it's just that they use the roe from female crabs to give the soup a lot of flavor."

"*She* crabs."

He laughed. "Yeah."

"Odd name."

"The taste more than makes up for the name."

"Got it." I was in. Hopefully I'd track some down before I headed out of town.

"So what are your plans for the property? Donate it to the city? Keep it and continue to run a B&B out of the carriage house?" He scanned the ceiling from corner to corner as if to assess its worthiness.

"Oh, I'm just here to put it on the market." I felt disloyal as soon as my words spilled out.

"Well, you'll certainly get top dollar in this market. As I mentioned earlier, properties like this don't go on the market very often."

"They don't?"

"No, they often stay in the family and get handed down from generation to generation."

To which I felt a twinge in the gut.

Would Gray want me to keep it? Had he expected me to? How would I manage that? My mother would be pissed if I did. The thought made me grin. Maybe that was a reason *to* keep it.

"But lately it seems our generation doesn't want the hassle and are open to a buyout." He nodded in the direction of the grand home across the yard. "They do require an immense amount of upkeep, so you'd have to have deep pockets to keep that up. And anything on the outside of the house you want to do, you'd have to go through the proper channels to get approvals and then once you do, you have to use someone from the list of approved contractors. You don't have a lot of say in it all, but that's why the peninsula has maintained its charm."

"Assuming I *am* going to sell it, would you have any recommendations for a Realtor?"

"Of course. We could get you connected with the right people. Any of them would kill for a listing like this. But I would make sure you entrusted the sale to the right firm."

When one bourbon turned into two, we moved to the chairs outside. The conversation turned to Gray.

"Did you know him?" I asked as a conversation restarter.

"Your Uncle William? No, not well."

"He went by Gray. William *Gray* Moore." I enjoyed the cadence of the four syllables across my tongue. "I always thought that was the coolest name, especially for a writer."

"Seemed like a great guy. Well-liked in our office. I only met him once when I dropped off some paperwork to him."

"I miss him terribly. Even though I didn't get to see him often, we were close. Technology made that possible."

Mason remained silent but nodded his understanding.

"Can't believe he died in a car accident. Just the meaning of the term means it could have been prevented. It didn't have to happen."

"Life's unfair at times."

"You think?" I snapped. His flippant remark smacked of disingenuousness. It felt like a dismissal. But not everyone was able to find the right words when they needed them, so I let it go. "Is there some sort of an accident report I could look at?"

"I would imagine there is. The officer on scene would have filed one. But why would you want to put yourself through that?"

"I need to know."

"To what end? It's not going to bring your uncle back."

"I *know* that." I grew annoyed at his steering me from my objective, the second time in the short while since I'd met him. "I have a right to know what happened." I rubbed at the tension building at the base of my neck.

Scooting to the edge of his chair and condensing the space between us, he softened his voice and said, "Kathryn, let it go. You're not going to accomplish anything but giving yourself more heartache. I know you're hurting. I can see it in your eyes, and I don't really know you. It was an accident. Plain and simple."

One thing I'd learned from my mother, when someone tells you it's *plain and simple*, it never is. Dig deeper.

She arrived today. I noticed her
From the window in my hiding space.
At first, I thought her a neighbor
Then spied hesitation in her face.

She's a fine young woman.
Attractive in her own sort of way.
Not to tread long in my world.
She'd never want to stay.

A precarious situation is at hand.
A need to intervene, no doubt.
It's hard to predict what lies ahead
And how it should turn out.

# CHAPTER SEVEN

I WOKE EARLY. THOUGH THE MATTRESS was comfortable, I'd tossed the covers about all night, agonizing over my next move. I needed to know more about how my dear uncle had been snatched from my life. If Mason wasn't going to help I'd find my own way.

During my fitful sleep, the dreams had come in fragments that made no sense, except that I seemed to be revisiting memories. Trying to put the pieces together in some sort of logical order, I recalled riding on my uncle's shoulders. I was a child and my brother and sister were fighting over who would be next. I had the sense they wouldn't get a turn.

Another clip that surfaced looked like a birthday party. Mine. Gray had lifted my chair off the ground—he was always so strong—and he was pretending to have transformed it into a helicopter. He was giving me a ride around the dining room—complete with his improvised whirring sound—before plunking me at the head of the table, to the cheers of those already assembled. It was pure delight being the center of his attention. Nowhere in the dream segments did my mother or father appear. Was it just wishful thinking or an accurate depiction of what would have happened in my younger years once Uncle Gray had arrived at the house?

With my glasses in pieces, I started the day struggling with my contacts—it had been a while since I'd first tried to wear them, a half-hearted effort at that—but finally triumphed and got one attached to each eye. Who had come up with the concept? I would have hated to have been one of the test subjects. Barbaric, if you asked me.

Yet with this recent attempt, I was astonished at how comfortable the contacts were and how clear my vision was. I'd fought the idea of wearing them because it had been my mother's—not mine. But at times obstinance didn't pay off. This was clearly one of those times. *Damn, I hated when my mother was right.*

Half a bottle of eye drops and a lot of blinking later, I'd been liberated from my coke bottle glasses. I was sure I'd hear an *I told you so* from my mother. I didn't care. It was worth it.

A brisk walk to gather my thoughts took me by a quaint cobblestone street, one of only a few remaining from the early 1700s when Charleston was first built, past the brightly painted houses on Rainbow Row, to a cute café farther up the street, past where East Battery turned into East Bay. I grabbed a chai latte and a chocolate croissant. Parked at a bistro table on the sidewalk, I was soon serenaded by the *clip-clop* of horses pulling carriages filled with tourists gawking at their surroundings and listening intently to their guides.

If only I could have been as carefree as them, here to explore charming, historic Charleston, leaving my worries behind. Instead, I needed to dig deeper into the car accident that caused my uncle's death. Ask the unasked questions. Perhaps the unpopular ones. Figure out why Mason was not only reluctant to fill in some blanks but actively discouraging me from pursuing my quest for answers.

What was he hiding? Or perhaps closer to the point, what was he preventing me from learning?

Returning to the Pink Lady, as I'd begun calling it, I peeked into the windows of the free-standing garage. Two bays. My eyes went to the one that was empty but for a bike that leaned against the side wall, and I tried to picture the car back where it should have been, next to the Aston Martin. Uncle Gray had had a passion for classic British cars. I imagined he would have owned more if he'd had room to store them. The one he'd been driving when the accident occurred was an Austin Healey. He'd sent photos to me when he'd first bought it. He was so proud and knew I'd appreciate it too. It was a deep navy with a luscious dark tan interior. A convertible.

The creaky doors of the garage opened out like a barn's. The metal spokes of the spare mounted on the rear of the car glistened in the wedge of sunlight I'd introduced to the dim space. Running my fingers along the side of the metallic green body, I knew I wouldn't be going anywhere unless I could find the key to start it.

Slipping behind the wheel onto the soft, supple leather, I ran my hand around the top of the stick shift. It brought back memories of when my uncle had taught me to drive a stick during his visits to Boston. His frequency bordered on seldom but when he did show up for family events, he did it in style—renting a different classic car each time. I'm sure he didn't go through Hertz. As a young girl, I thought he was the coolest. Still do.

Where would he keep the key? Somewhere in the house? It would take forever to locate it there. Scanning the interior, my eyes landed on the console between the two seats, and I popped it open. A pair of leather driving gloves that matched the interior was tucked inside. Slipping them out to pull them on—longing to feel close to Gray—something dropped into my lap. A key on a chain with an Aston Martin logo. Rather obvious in his key chain choice. And trusting as well, leaving it in the console. But I was in business. As long as it started, I had a way to get around. Come and go as I pleased.

"Thanks, Uncle Gray." Yanking in the folds of my skirt, I closed the door gently and jammed the key into the ignition, one foot on the clutch, the other on the brake. It stalled as I pulled out of the garage, but by the time I was up to speed on East Bay, driving with a clutch was coming back to me.

The ride to the Charleston Police Station took me along the Ashley River, past the marina with a slew of white boats ranging from the modest fishing vessel to the outrageous *my boat is bigger than yours.* Must be nice to live so close to water. It had such a calming effect. I could use that. Maybe I could get rid of the meds—or at least reduce the dosage. Perhaps I should stay at the Pink Lady with her views out to the harbor.

Once at the station, I followed the signs to the records department, produced my ID, and provided the pertinent information about my uncle and what little I knew about the accident. The female officer behind the counter couldn't have been more pleasant—not what I'd been expecting—and spoke in a delightful Southern drawl, drawing out the last two syllables in each sentence.

"I'm so sorry for your loss, Miss Kathryn. Where exactly did it happen?" she asked. Her fingers clicked along her keyboard, but in spite of her efforts laced with Southern hospitality, she was having difficulty locating a report in the system.

"On the bridge."

"The Ravenel?"

"Yes."

"Any chance you might know where on the bridge?"

Not understanding why that would make a difference, I said, "No, I don't have any more information than the date and that it was an accident somewhere on the bridge." My patience was starting to wear thin. How difficult could it be?

The sound of typing stopped abruptly, and she pulled her hands from the keyboard. "Oh, *that* wreck. A local man. A reporter for the paper." Her voice trailed off.

A reporter? No, that wasn't right. But she was on a roll so I waited to correct her.

"I'm not finding it in our records. I'll call over to Mt. Pleasant PD. If it happened closer to them, they might have taken the call."

I plunked an elbow on the counter with most of my upper body weight under it as the officer went to a desk along the wall and got on the phone. Before long she hung up but didn't return. She held up an index finger and went off to talk to another officer. He accompanied her back to the counter. The records officer spoke first.

"Ma'am, this is Sergeant Michaels." She stepped to the side to let him handle it from there. I looked to him to explain the issue.

"Ma'am, I understand you're interested in a wreck that involved your uncle. William Moore. I'm afraid there isn't a report yet. It's in the hands of the state police. There's an investigation going on."

I pulled in a quick breath. Not what I was expecting him to say.

"Why would there be an investigation? I thought it was an accident."

"Ma'am, when a car is pulled from a river, it's not always a simple accident."

The sergeant might as well have delivered a punch to my gut with his fist. It took a moment to process. "From the river?" No one had said anything about his car going into the water. "Were there other cars involved?" The question spilled out before I knew it was coming.

The officer squared his jaw. "I can't really go into it."

"I know. The investigation and all. Are they doing an autopsy?" Again, where were my questions coming from? I was beginning to sound like my mother.

"If we had a body we would."

# CHAPTER EIGHT

The sergeant's revelation had hit me hard: *When a car is pulled from a river.* What had happened to my uncle? Had he fallen asleep at the wheel and gone over the side of the bridge? Was it distracted driving? What would the investigation uncover? And why wasn't there a body? Was he still in the harbor somewhere? Were they actively searching even though it had been a few weeks since the accident?

My cell rattling on the seat startled me back from the rabbit hole I'd started down. Downshifting as I approached a traffic light, I grabbed the phone and switched it to speaker, not able to catch the caller ID.

"Hello?"

"Kat, how's it going down there?"

I should have let it roll over to voicemail. She was the last person I wanted to tangle with right now. Didn't think I had the energy for it.

"Mom, could you *please* stop calling me that? I *hate* it." I regretted my admission as soon as I'd said it. It gave my mother reason to continue to do it, not that she needed one.

"I think it's a cute nickname for you." My mother came up with a nickname for everyone, whether they wanted one or not. She'd changed her own name to Posh—legally—saying it better reflected who she was as a successful, accomplished woman. I'd always thought it sounded silly, especially for someone her age. But all her silly friends went along with it. My father did too, which was disappointing. Then again, he seemed to go along with all her ideas, silly or not. It was probably just easier that way.

My mother's signature color was jet black—for her hair and her clothes—with a splash of hot pink added for good measure. I thought she looked hideous at times, but I kept my opinions on her appearance to myself. It was easier that way. Like father, like daughter.

I remained silent, not engaging in any further discussion about the nickname.

"So how is Gray's house? Have you gotten a good look at it? You're not staying there, are you?" From her tone, I could picture her expression of disdain with a wrinkled nose and turned down mouth. "It's a dump, isn't it? That's the way it is with bachelors. They're perfectly happy living in a pigsty until a woman enters their life to get them straightened out. It's disgusting. But he never was able to hang on to a woman long enough for that to happen."

"Geez, Mom. *Enough.*" Never missing an opportunity to disparage her brother-in-law's image, my mother finally paused long enough to take a breath.

"All right. All right. But you know I'm right. So what's the house like?"

With no intention of cluing her in, I said, "It's old." True, but she would get the wrong idea.

"Old? So not new construction. Huh. Old houses are *money* pits." Leave it to my mother to veer down a thorn-laden, negative path.

"And he has a lot of old stuff in the house too." I wasn't going to divulge they were stunning, not to mention valuable, antiques.

"Probably a hoarder. I never knew him to be much of a housekeeper. What a mess you must have on your hands. Well, don't *you* worry about cleaning out the house. There are companies that handle that kind of thing. Hire someone to do it and then have a Realtor list it. Get what you can for it and get your sorry self back to civilization."

My mother's barbs stung, but I loved she had no idea about Uncle Gray's impressive property. And I intended to keep it that way.

"Oh and some mail came for you, Kat."

My body bristled at the despicable nickname. I would never get used to it, no matter how many times she insisted on using it.

"Mail?"

"Yeah, from Simon & Schuster. You know, one of those form letters you've been getting ever since you've been whoring your rough draft around to every Tom, Dick, and Harry in the publishing industry."

"You opened my mail?" I slammed on the brakes, nearly ramming the car in front of me that had stopped for a pedestrian.

"Figured I'd save you the trouble. I knew it wasn't going to be good news. It's just another rejection. Shall I read it to you or toss it in the trash?"

"How could you? That's *my* mail." I brushed a tear from my cheek. My own mother not only couldn't encourage me to go after my dreams, she tore them down and ridiculed me for having them. She couldn't stand they were the same as Gray's.

"For God's sake, Kat. Wake up. It's not going to happen. Stop chasing after this ridiculous daydream. You're not going to be a published author like your crazy uncle was. You've wasted all this time trying, so give it up before you piss off the rest of your life."

If only Gray were still around to be my cheerleader like he'd been doing since I could remember. I'd have to go it alone now while enduring Posh Moore's constant verbal tearing down—her way of trying to change her daughter's mind, take a more practical path that included taking over the family business.

Then I realized my mother was still ranting.

"—I mean just look at what your brother and sister have accomplished in the time you've been fooling around with this. On their way to becoming wealthy beyond anyone's wildest dreams with their entrepreneurial skills. They've followed in your father's footsteps. They used their trust funds wisely. You could take a clue card from them."

My mother didn't need to remind me how successful Delaney and Peyton had become with their startup business that had something to do with bitcoins—an industry I couldn't begin to comprehend and had no desire to try. As expected by our parents and seemingly society at large, my brother and sister had majored in business in college. I had gleefully gone the arts and literature route in spite of my parents' coaxing to consider a more marketable major, but I wouldn't be deterred. Unlike the rest of the family, I'd always loved to paint with oils and acrylics, at times with pastels and colored pencils, read anything I could get my hands on until the wee hours of the morning, and wrote tucked away from the rest of the world, preferably on a limb of my favorite tree at the far end of the yard.

My brother and sister had paid their dues and did their requisite five years working for our father's beer brewing company before they were eligible to draw from their trust fund and start off on their own. At thirty-one, I was *still* working there, even though my five years had come and gone, and only as a middle manager in his shadow, even though I awkwardly wore vice president as a title. I'd never had to ask but knew our father saw me as his last hope to pass along the hugely successful company he'd worked so hard to build from the ground up.

But I had other plans. While I dragged myself into the brewery Monday through Friday, saddled with the responsibility of product quality control, and returned home each night reeking of beer, I'd been biding my time until my acceptance letter arrived from one of the Big

Four publishers. Simon & Schuster had been the fourth. It was time to send out a new batch of query letters to the smaller firms, but it would have to wait until I'd taken care of business in Charleston.

My mother was still droning. "—amazing if you think about it. We're so proud of them."

She didn't have to put into so many words that she and my father weren't proud of me. I lived with it every day. The embarrassment hung out in their sprawling Beacon Hill home like a sixth member of the family. But I wouldn't be swayed from my dream.

"All right, well carry on. Keep me posted." A click on the other end signaled my abrupt dismissal.

I wasn't done with the conversation so I called her back. It rang a few times as if she was trying to decide if she would pick up. Finally I heard a click.

"What. We just talked."

"Yes, Mom, I know. I was part of the conversation too."

She could be so condescending. "Then what's up?"

"I had a chat with the Charleston police." I paused to listen for a reaction but couldn't detect one. "Why didn't you tell me they never found Uncle Gray's body?"

Crickets on the other end. Got her.

"Well?" I asked.

"What difference does it make?"

"What difference? Are you kidding me? It makes a huge difference. You told me there wasn't going to be a service… that his friends here were going to do something small… that that's what they thought he would have wanted. When I kept asking you about it you said it had already happened and to let it go. Do you have any idea how much that hurt? Or was that the point?"

"Kat—"

My body stiffened.

"—there was no point in schlepping all the way down there."

"Mom, there was never a service. I searched the obituaries. There hasn't been any closure. There's a police investigation going on. What were you thinking? That I'd forget about it? Clearly *you* have."

"Sweetheart, he's gone. He's not coming back. Whether there's a funeral service or a memorial service or whatever, it's not going to bring him back. You need to figure out how to get over it and move on with your life."

She was a cold, crass woman. I hadn't felt anything remotely resembling fondness for her in a very long time. How did my father live with her? Perhaps their marriage had reached the stage of merely coexisting. But how did you share a bed with someone who despised your brother? Who knew, maybe they didn't share a bed.

"It's not that simple. I'm sorry you feel it is." This time I hung up on her.

I knew I wasn't supposed to hate my mother. But it felt like I did.

After pulling the Aston Martin back into the garage, shutting it down, and tucking the keys back into Gray's gloves in the console, I slipped my notebook out of the pocket in my skirt and flipped it open. Besides my visions, it was also where I kept my story ideas for potential books. There seemed to be a lot of overlap in that little book.

I kept flipping the pages until I got to the one I was pretty sure was there:

Car goes off bridge. Car retrieved. Driver never found.

# CHAPTER NINE

From the foyer, I could see the paper in the typewriter was a few inches higher out of the roller than it had been. My body stiffened when I realized there were words typed on it. Taking a few steps closer, I read:

IT WASN'T AN ACCIDENT

Stumbling back from the typewriter, the arm of a sofa caught me behind the knees, buckling them, and toppling me backward. I rolled off the upholstery, landing hard on a coffee table. I lay there for a moment, stunned by the unexpected tumbling sequence. Then came the sound of wood splintering before I dropped to the floor onto a pile of wood pieces. My lower back had had enough of the antics and sent a stabbing pain through my lower lumbar.

"What the hell." Dazed, I gathered myself and stood to survey the damage, rubbing the throbbing pain from my back. "Uncle Gray, I'm so sorry. You probably loved this… what used to be a beautiful antique table." Thank God my mother wasn't there to witness my spectacular stumble. When she had finished guffawing she would have told me to lay off the chocolate chip cookies.

No matter how much my mother wanted me to be tall and sinewy like her and my siblings, it wasn't going to happen. I had a different body type. That was all there was to it. Her middle child must have gotten the DNA grab bag, which was often nothing more than a consolation prize.

My eyes went to the typewriter again and the bold black letters on the white paper. Someone had been in the house. And that someone was trying to send me a message. Who had another key? For all I knew, half of Charleston had a copy.

Suddenly my priorities shifted. Finding a real estate agent was going to take a back seat; instead, I needed to find out what my uncle had been working on when he passed away. His genre was espionage suspense. But fiction. Not true crime. Had he dug up something during his research that steered him in a different direction? Had he uncovered information that was meant to stay buried? Could the perpetrator have learned of his delving and silenced Gray to keep his or her secret? Perhaps that was why the state police were involved. *It wasn't an accident.*

*Think, Kathryn. Where in the house would he have worked on his novels?* The stunning, imposing desk on the second floor.

Taking the stairs two at a time, careful to maintain a solid footing on each riser, I reached the landing and headed to the desk. The surface of the opened flap was uncluttered. Was his writing area the exception to his usual "lived-in" look my mother suggested he was known for?

"Come on, Uncle Gray. Help me out here. Show me where your zip drive is." One by one I opened the line of petite doors by pinching the tiny knobs between my thumb and index finger to reveal unused envelopes, stamps, fountain pens, notepads, and a yellowed newspaper clipping, but no zip drive. Folding up the writing surface, I focused on the larger drawers below where I found advance reader copies of his first few paperback novels, what looked like a rough draft the size of a reem of printer paper, and a threadbare quilt tucked neatly in the bottom drawer. No zip drive.

"What am I looking for, Gray?" Taking another look at the quilt, I yanked it out of the drawer. As I unfolded it to get a better look at the pattern, something hit the floor with a thud. A small black revolver.

"What the… Why would you need this?" I whispered.

Gingerly, I picked up the handle of the gun with two fingers and tucked it back into the folds of the quilt, praying it wasn't loaded. It was unsettling to think my uncle needed protection. Guns scared me. I didn't want anything to do with them.

Jamming the quilt back into the drawer—perhaps I got my sloppiness from my father's side of the family—I slid it shut and opened the desk flap again to leave it the way I'd found it. My eyes returned to the row of small doors, and I started to open them again, one at a time. There had to be something else to them. This time when I pulled out the contents, I left them scattered across the writing top and the doors agape. Each compartment looked identical to the one next to it. Until I got to the last one. It didn't seem as deep as the others.

Sliding my fingers into the slot, I ran them along the five walls. At one point my hand wouldn't budge. I snatched a quick breath. The last thing I needed was to get my hand stuck with no one around to come to the rescue. My mother would have said I had my father's pudgy hands. Always the encouraging one, she was.

Once I pulled my hand free and the panic had subsided, I elongated my fingers as best I could and reinserted them, keeping them extended so my hand wouldn't get stuck again. This time they caught on what felt like a latch at the back of the slot toward the top. I couldn't get it to move. Which direction did it go? Bending down to see what I was dealing with, I flipped on my cell's flashlight.

A couple more tries with my fingernail slipping off each time, I finally got it to slide a bit. Pulling my hand out I yanked off what was left of my fingernail hanging off the tip of my finger. Shoving my hand back in I tried another nail and got the latch to move again. This time it was just enough, and the back of the slot popped open.

In the light from my phone I could see the space wasn't very large—but it was just big enough to hide a zip drive. I grinned and slipped it out. "Nice, Gray." There was no label on it. No discernible markings. I shoved it into my pants pocket.

After tidying the desktop, I scampered down the stairs and returned to the carriage house in search of my laptop.

Easing the zip drive into the side, I closed out the word file I'd had open for weeks, trying to come up with a fresh idea for a manuscript, and scrolled through the names of the folders on it. Nothing jumped out. But I figured he wouldn't make it obvious in case it got into the wrong hands.

The knock made me jump. I snapped the computer shut, slipped out the zip drive, and padded to the door to peek through the side window. A man in a light khaki polo shirt and matching cargo pants, his cruiser parked halfway up the drive. I hadn't noticed him approach.

The knock came again and I pulled the door open, doing my best to keep my voice even. "Yes?"

"Kathryn Moore?"

"Yes, what can I do for you?"

"Ma'am, I'm Sergeant Jennings with SLED."

"SLED?"

"State Law Enforcement Division."

"Oh. Never heard of that." I had nothing to add so I kept quiet so he could go on.

"I understand you're William Moore's niece."

Bad news and the fact I was staying in the carriage house of my missing uncle traveled fast.

"Yes, but he went by Gray," I corrected.

"Yes, ma'am. Could I talk to you for a moment?"

"Of course. Would you like to come in?" Not knowing what the protocol was for being questioned by a state police officer, I opened the door wider and he stepped inside, pulling his baseball style cap off.

Unsure if I should invite him in farther, I stood awkwardly in the entryway. "So you're investigating my uncle's death?"

"Yes, ma'am." He ran his thumb and forefinger along the rim of his hat.

"You don't think it was an accident, do you? What have you found out? The Charleston police said the car ended up in the water. How did that happen?"

His face said he hadn't been expecting an interrogation. "I'm afraid I can't answer your questions. The investigation is ongoing."

"But you have plenty of questions for me, I'll bet."

Tucking his hat securely to his side and trapping it with an elbow, he retrieved a notepad and pen from his shirt pocket.

"Can I at least ask if you found his body?" I tried another angle.

The trooper pressed his lips together and curled them in until they'd turned white and were barely visible.

"I'm afraid I can't go into that yet."

"If you haven't found a body, how can my uncle be declared dead?" In order for his will to have been executed, I would have thought there would have to be a death certificate. And here I was in Charleston because the will had been executed—much to my mother's dismay.

"I didn't say we haven't found a body. I just can't get into it with you."

I leaned back against an antique sideboard and folded my arms. He wasn't going to be very helpful so I needed to decide how helpful I was going to be. Fair was fair.

"So what do you need from me?" I asked. The sooner I addressed his needs, the sooner he would leave, and I could get back to the zip drive.

"Do you know if your uncle was friendly with any of his neighbors?"

"I would imagine he was." How much more ambiguous could I be? "His next-door neighbor has stopped by a couple times. Very friendly. Helpful."

"Were you aware of your uncle befriending or helping out any of the homeless population?"

"I didn't know Charleston had any homeless."

"Every city has homeless." He regarded me with a look of irritation.

The sound of a shotgun getting cocked ricocheted in my head, and I wanted to shove him back through the door I had so politely let him in through. I was losing my patience with the way he was playing it close to the chest.

"Well, I don't know of his involvement in that. He did have a huge heart. Maybe he did volunteer."

"How about alcohol, drug use, dealing drugs—"

"What? Now you're going too far. My uncle wouldn't have been into drugs." I felt my voice getting louder but had no intention of lowering it. "Don't you dare turn this into a drug-deal-gone-bad."

"How often did you see him?" He wasn't deterred by my pushing back.

I hesitated. He had me. I had no idea what my uncle was into. I only saw him when he ventured to Boston for a family event, but as the years progressed, the less frequently he seemed to pop in. My mother undoubtedly had a hand in that. And he could have only shown us the side of him that would be acceptable to the family. I often wondered why my father allowed her to keep him away. It could have been another case of it just being easier that way. Or perhaps he had his own reason. I'd never asked.

"Not as often as I would have liked," I hated to admit.

"Where are you from?"

"Boston."

He considered my answer and said, "And when was the last time you visited your uncle here."

I hesitated. He had me again. "This is my first time here." Why that was so important to everyone was beyond me.

"First time." He nodded a couple times in thoughtful succession.

"Yes. But I know my uncle, and he would never get into anything bad."

"Okay, well I think I'm good for now. Thanks for your time. I just need to get into the main house."

"What for?"

"To look around."

"I don't know that I can let you do that."

Slipping a paper from his chest pocket, he said, "I'm afraid you don't have a choice, ma'am."

Again with the *ma'am*. What was it with these Southern gentlemen? I wasn't used to it, but I thought I might be starting to like it. My mother would hate that I was softening.

The paper he unfolded and held up was emblazoned at the top with *Search Warrant*. There was to be no discussion or negotiation to be had.

"And we'll be conducting our search without any outside assistance."

I understood that to mean me.

"Did you remove anything from the house?"

"It's exactly the way I found it."

"So you've been inside … all throughout the house?

"Not all. Just some of it." I recalled the ordeal in the second-floor wing.

"I'll ask again. Did you remove anything from the house?"

I fingered the zip drive in my pocket. There was no way they would have found it. I replied, "As I said, I left it exactly the way I found it." Was that non-specific enough to satisfy my conscience? I maintained a sober face until he'd turned away. What had I just committed? Obstruction of something. The investigation? Justice? Hopefully what was on the zip drive was worth the length of incarceration associated with my infraction, if it got that far.

Returning his hat to his head, he slipped out and strode past his cruiser as another vehicle pulled in the drive with a man and woman in street clothes but looking no less official. Trailing behind the trooper on the way to unlock the door, I suddenly felt outnumbered. Then I remembered the paper in the typewriter.

Waiting on the piazza until all three officers had slipped inside, I crept back to the door they'd left ajar. It sounded like they were in the front entryway so I pushed through and headed for the drawing room. I'd only made it as far as the threshold when the trooper appeared in the foyer behind me.

"Ms. Moore, apparently I wasn't clear with my instructions. You need to wait outside until we're finished. Is that clear?"

"Of course. I'm sorry. I just wanted to see if you guys needed anything."

"I think we're good."

"Water? Soda?" I was beginning to sound like a flight attendant, but I needed to get him away from the typewriter.

"We're all set. Thanks." He stood resolute.

I had no choice but to walk away, shooting a glance to the small table near the door. The paper that had been in the typewriter carriage was no longer there.

# CHAPTER TEN

SETTLING INTO A BISTRO CHAIR OUTSIDE the carriage house, I had an unobstructed view of the side door to the main house—the one I'd let the police in through. A paperback I'd been meaning to get to lay splayed open on my lap, but I knew I wouldn't be able to concentrate on it while my uncle's house was getting ransacked. It was more of a prop to feign disinterest.

"Who are you?" A young boy—maybe ten or twelve—appeared in my peripheral and spoke in a sweet voice, higher than what I would have expected for his age. He practically blended into the towering hedge behind him. "Are you a friend of Gray's?"

"Oh, hey. I'm Gray's niece."

The boy considered my answer.

"Who are you?" I asked. If he was going to barge into the yard and start asking questions, I could too. It was my yard now.

"I'm Andy. Gray was very nice to me. I miss him. I want him to come back."

"We all miss him. I want him to come back too. But unfortunately that's not going to happen." I jolted at the sting from my words.

The boy jutted out his lower lip, but that was the extent of his demonstration, which was a relief. I didn't have a lot of experience entertaining, much less cajoling, children.

"Maybe he'll come back when the bad guys go away." He took a couple tentative steps toward me and then rocked on his heels, his thumbs hooked on this belt loops.

It was a shame some kids thought police officers were scary, but I didn't have an appropriate comeback. I glanced toward the main house as the face of the female investigator came into view in a side window. Given the size of the property, I imagined they'd be a while.

"I'm sorry about his car."

"Yeah… me too." The car at the bottom of Charleston Harbor was collateral damage. A mechanical problem? Swerving to miss something in the road? Or was it something more sinister than that? If I could have shoved his other classic car off the bridge to bring him back, I'd have done it. I'd throw in the bike too if that would help.

"I went for rides with him."

"Did you?" Wishing I'd gotten to ride in Gray's cars with him, I felt a pang in my gut that a neighborhood kid got to—on more than one occasion, apparently—and I'd never been. "I bet that was fun." I was doing my best to keep it light.

He nodded, regarding me for a moment. "I've never seen you around here before." If it weren't for the guilt I was trying to shake off, I would have laughed at how much it sounded like an overused bar pickup line.

Everyone there seemed to be fixated on my absence from my uncle's life. I wasn't going to explain to a kid why I hadn't been to visit him. Even I didn't understand how I'd let that happen. My mother was very good at orchestrating so everyone around her did what she wanted them to do and accepted it willingly.

That was where our little chat would end.

"I gotta go. Got a phone call to make." I pulled out my cell.

His expression darkened. "Okay." He turned on his heel and headed back to the hedge.

Occupied with my phone, I didn't notice the opening he'd used to slip through.

"Mom, the police are investigating Uncle Gray's crash. It might not have been an accident." It took a couple turns before I realized I was pacing the patio in front of the carriage house.

"What? Not an accident.... What the hell did the fool get himself wrapped up in? See, Kathryn? You've been idolizing him all these years, and he wasn't the person you thought he was."

"We don't know that. It's too early to jump to conclusions. But you've always wanted to crucify him."

"You don't know him like I do. I mean, if whoever hadn't finished him off, I probably would have before long."

"My God," I said, shocked at her admission. "You can't be serious."

"You haven't seen him in years. You don't know him," she repeated.

Why had I called to bring my miserable mother up to date? I should have known she would have reacted this way. The answer was I had no one else to cry to. But my mother's shoulder was not one that welcomed a tear-stained cheek. There was never any compassion on her part so there was no point expecting it.

"Oh, I got his number early on. He was a quick one to figure out."

"I think there should be a service," I tossed out to revisit the topic and see what would come back. It was worth a try to shut down her rant before it really got going.

"You mean a funeral service?" She scoffed on the other end. "I'm certainly not going to arrange that. But for who? If he has any friends, they can do something. We're the only family he's got, and we don't need a service. You *do* realize funerals are for the loved ones left behind, don't you? Not the deceased."

Unwilling to engage my mother any longer, I let it go. I enjoyed the lack of her talking on the other end and fantasized she had hung up. But the dial tone wouldn't come.

"Any word on a body yet?" my mother asked.

"What? I don't know anything about that." Figured she would jump to that grotesque thought.

"Just curious. You might want to find out. Actually, yeah. Find out. I want to know."

# CHAPTER ELEVEN

WHEN THE POLICE APPEARED ON THE main piazza with a small clear plastic bag in hand, I hustled over to meet them at the bottom of the stairs.

"All finished?"

"For now." The sergeant paused on the expansive piazza while the other two headed to their car. "We could be back."

"What did you find?" I knew he wasn't going to tell me, but it was worth a shot. No telling what else he might actually reveal.

His jaw tightened. "You know I can't say." He started for his cruiser.

"All right, well hopefully you didn't leave a mess for me to have to clean up." I didn't want to be in the house any longer than necessary; I found it rather unsettling.

"It's not too bad," he called back. "We've done worse." I caught a glimpse of a smirk—seemingly uncharacteristic of him, at least in uniform. "Oh, and what's the story with the coffee table on the first floor? Looks like there may have been a struggle." Braced by a fist on the door frame, he leaned across the roof of his car, waiting for an answer.

It crossed my mind to shrug it off as something I wasn't aware of, but if it sent their investigation in the wrong direction, I would have regretted it. "No. Nothing like that. I had a… a clumsy moment."

Creases appeared across his forehead as if he was trying to picture it. Did his eyes flick down the length of my body? How dare he. After a beat, he let it go.

I was grateful.

Stepping through the doorway they'd left wide open, I caught sight of their handiwork. The furniture dust coverings were strewn about, lying where they'd been tossed. Seat cushions in the sitting room looked as though a couple of children had just finished a pillow fight, lying cockeyed on the couches and leaning up against the harp and harpsichord. I shuddered to think what the library with its hundreds of books looked like.

I set to work returning upholstered cushions to the furniture they belonged to and wadding up the dust covers, starting a pile in the expansive doorway. There was no point in re-covering everything. The house would show better if it didn't look like it had sat empty for a while.

After making my way through the downstairs, getting everything back in place where my uncle had had it, I trudged to the second floor—my thighs burning climbing the stairs—and started the process there.

The worse-case scenario I'd pictured proved to be all too accurate in the study. By the time I'd reshelved all the loose books, my cavernous stomach had grown impatient, and the carriage house refrigerator was calling, so I abandoned the clean-up task for the time being.

On my way by the sitting room, my eyes darted to the Underwood. Was I hoping or dreading there would be a note left there?

Sitting on the roller was a fresh sheet of white paper. On it was typed: THEY DIDNT FIND ANYTHING USEFUL. YOU DID.

I could only stare at the words. Why hadn't I heard the typing?

"Uncle Gray?" My words seemed to echo, so I brought it down a notch and asked, "Is that you?" I waited for a sign—more typing?—but nothing came. The monstrous house grew quiet again. Only quickened breathing in my ears. I hoped it was mine.

Leaving the note in the typewriter, I started back to the carriage house. My stomach would have to wait. I needed to take another look at the zip drive.

As I let myself into the carriage house, my cell vibrated. Jennings from the state police.

"A body was just pulled from the harbor."

I heard a click somewhere in my head but couldn't make my mouth form a response. His words hung in the silence.

"Ma'am?"

I managed to clear my throat, hoping to kick start my speech faculty. Only a muffled grunt came out.

"Miss Moore?"

Finally I could force out an intelligible sound. "Yeah."

"Did you hear me?"

"Yeah … you just pulled a body from the harbor." The words sounded distant, like someone else was speaking them.

"Actually it was over on James Island. The current took it and it washed up there."

"Do you think it's my uncle?" I was starting to come around.

"We don't know. It's on its way to the coroner."

*It.* How quickly my uncle went from being a person with a soul and a life to a thing that had been yanked from the muddy waters of Charleston Harbor. I pushed aside a grotesque image of pale skin, soaked clothes clinging to his body, and a brown mop of hair plastered to his head.

"How long will that take?"

I willed him to say *a couple days* or *it shouldn't take long at all.* Instead, he said, "It's hard to say." About as noncommittal as it gets.

"Well, you're bursting with info."

"I'm sorry. That's all I have. But I thought you would want to know. Just got the call."

Regretting my sarcasm, I added, "You're right. I'm the one who should be sorry." As an afterthought, I said, "Do you need me to donate some blood or scrapings from the inside of my cheek or anything like that? You know, to compare the body's DNA to?" I hoped he would go for the less painful option.

"No, we're good. When we searched your uncle's house we collected some samples."

"Samples?"

"His hairbrush, toothbrush, and other items with possible DNA on them."

"Okay." I pictured Gray's personal effects rattling around in an evidence bag and then dumped onto a lab table where they would be pulled apart, piece by piece, and undergo thorough testing—all while his body was spread out on display on a cold metal examining table, blinding lights from above, as he was cut open and dissected like a lab rat until they could determine with one hundred percent certainty it was him and how he'd died. Was it blunt force trauma from hitting the water? Or drowning from being knocked out by the impact and trapped in the car?

"But thank you for offering. We'll let you know as soon as we hear from the coroner."

I heard myself thanking him but didn't really want to hear the results I knew he'd have. It was then I noticed one of my rice bead bracelets was missing. One of the three Gray had given me. Yanking up my sleeve, I searched in vain but couldn't locate it under any of the silver cuffs. It was gone. Just like my uncle.

# CHAPTER TWELVE

MASON WAS AN AMUSING SOUL, AND he seemed to be exerting an inordinate effort to keep me amused. Or was it distracted? Lord knew I could use that. To a certain extent it felt as though I was letting myself get sucked in but I didn't know into what. Did he have an agenda?

This morning we were on bustling King Street, known as the shopping mecca of downtown Charleston, perusing the array of boutiques and national brand shops—for what, it wasn't clear yet. Mason held up the most colorful print Lilly Pulitzer capris at Palm Avenue, stunning floral dresses at Gretchen Scott, and smart sportswear at Vineyard Vines. From there, the names of the shops escaped me seconds after I took in the logo on the way in the door and the assortment of offerings became a blur.

Mason encouraged me to try on everything from white eyelet, ruffled skirts to cowboy boots—none of it really my style, but what was? My look hadn't evolved since I'd graduated from Brown where I'd developed a distinctive retro granola boho vibe with my wardrobe. I mean, who did I need to impress? I worked for my father. I went for comfort. And I was comfortable wearing long skirts in understated— read boring?—prints and solids. My flats were also comfortable. A girl needed to take care of her feet. Those high heels the other girls wore had to be so painful. And long term, what was it doing to their backs? Not for me. No thank you.

A couple stores in, Mason halted his pawing through the racks and asked about my wherewithal to be shopping—a rather personal inquiry, but a practical one as well. He needed to determine if we were wasting our time. He did it in a teasing sort of way but it stung nonetheless. After assuring him of my secure financial situation, the search resumed.

Never having enjoyed clothes shopping in the past—was it because it was usually with my mother and she'd always compared me to my perfectly shaped sister?—I was tickled with how much fun it was with Mason. I clutched colorful shopping bags, each brimming with new-found treasures.

Back out on the street, sparkling gems in a small jewelry store window caught my eye, and we paused to admire the display.

"Look, they have the rice bead bracelets like yours." He pointed to one side of the window.

I held up my wrist and offered a turned down lower lip, much like the young boy had in my uncle's yard. "I lost one."

"Sorry to hear. What happened?"

"I don't know. I just discovered it was gone."

"Bummer. Do you want to pop in here, and I'll treat you to a replacement?"

"That's very sweet of you." Perhaps too sweet. "But it wouldn't be the same. Thank you though."

"I get it. Can't fault a gentleman for trying." He chuckled and moved on to the next window. "Hey, let's stop in here. This is a fun shop. They even have a men's section I can look through. It's frustratingly small, but at least they make an attempt."

Was Mason enjoying our shopping excursion a little too much?

Weren't gay guys really into fashion? I'd never known a gay guy before, not intimately anyway. If Mason was, could I be falling for a guy who never would have an interest? Yet, he seemed to be. We were making a connection. Or was it simply for business purposes? Keep the client happy, no matter how miserable it might be.

Off on a self-deprecating thought, I allowed Mason's voice to bring me back to the bustle of the charming shop we were poking through.

"—and why are you still living at home? Sounds like you're doing okay and could have your own place. Or is it a requirement of working for your father?" He shifted the bags he'd been holding to one hand so he could rake his fingers through a rack of men's jackets with the other.

I was relieved my reaction was to laugh. "Don't be silly." I knew there was more than a shred of truth to the notion, but I did my best to conceal it. "Of course I could live on my own. But honestly, the house is so big, I don't really see my family members that often." That sounded ridiculous as soon as it spilled out. Grateful he didn't challenge me on it, I thought the safest thing was to change the subject.

Before I could, I sidestepped to avoid an oncoming young mother with a double-wide stroller and my foot slipped off the curb. As I flailed to remain upright, Mason grabbed my arm, catching me before I landed in the open storm drain that was essentially a cutout in the curb. The shopping bags sailed off my windmilling arms, but Mason quickly scooped them up, settling their contents back into place.

Once composed, I took a good look at the drain and was aghast at the size. "My God, that is *gargantuan*. You could lose a…" I shuttered to think of what would fit down it. "Why is there no grate on it? Are they all this way?"

"Yeah, as far as I know." Mason didn't sound too concerned.

"You've got to be kidding me. That's dangerous. Water is powerful. Can carry heavy objects like cars along with it."

Mason sized up the opening to the drain. "I don't think a car's going to fit through there."

A nervous giggle slipped out. "Of course not, but a child… or a dog. That would be horrible if that happened." The images my brain conjured up at an alarming rate, at times like that, were frightening. Was it just my overactive imagination or were they real? And if they were real, had they already happened or were they a glimpse into the future? I was sure I didn't want to learn the truth.

He scrunched his brows and said, "I've never heard of anything like that happening, but I guess it's possible. But God, Kathryn, don't start getting dark on me."

I shook it off and got back up on the curb, embarrassed I'd slipped off and created a spectacle. After all, I'd finally ditched the coke bottle glasses, which seemed to have been the source of my clumsiness in the past, throwing off my depth perception. Sadly, for years I guess I'd accepted it as a way of life, and my mother had reinforced the belief I was simply uncoordinated—just one on a long list of traits that made me different from my siblings. The woes of a middle child.

"All right, let's get out of here." Glancing back, I added, "That's just wrong. Really wrong. Are they really all like this?" Without waiting for a response, I said, "That shouldn't be."

As we walked along, glancing into storefronts as we passed, I felt my energy waning. "Hey, all this shopping has made me hungry."

"What? You're not throwing in the towel yet, are you?"

Pausing a moment allowed him time to check his phone.

"No, you're right. We've been at this a while. And you've done great." He nodded to the bags we were both holding, brimming with tissue-wrapped tops, capris, shoes, and wraps.

"Let's go grab a bite. He glanced up and down King Street as if getting his bearings. "167 Raw isn't too far from here. You okay with seafood?"

"Raw?"

"Not just raw, they've got both."

"Okay, then sure." Even though I hailed from Boston, a huge seafood destination in its own right, I preferred mine cooked.

Then it hit me—and I was uncomfortable it had taken so long—our morning shopping outing had had a purpose. He'd been doing his best to give me a mini makeover. A glance in a nearby glass door allowed a moment to self-assess. It was hard to take in. I was a mess. I could have been a model for the local Goodwill Store. He'd done me a huge favor by taking me on a shopping spree. The contents of the bags I clutched with sweaty palms and the loss of my geeky glasses the staircase had claimed would have me on the way to looking more like a fine young woman, an independent woman—perhaps a Charleston woman. How grand that sounded. I decided I loved Mason whether he was gay or not. I had a new dear friend.

# CHAPTER THIRTEEN

PRESSING THE PHONE AGAINST THE SIDE of my face, I wasn't sure I'd heard correctly.

"I'm sorry, Sergeant, you said the body they found isn't my uncle's?" Mouthing an *excuse me* to Mason, I headed out to the sidewalk to take the call.

"That's correct, ma'am."

"But if it's not my uncle's, then whose body is it?" *And where the hell is my uncle?*

"They're still working on an exact ID. They know it's a male. They're working on a few theories, but nothing I'm at liberty to speculate about."

I admired his professionalism, but I needed more than he was willing to give. The empty pause grew awkward.

"I mean, the possibilities are endless," he added. "He could have been giving someone a ride somewhere. A friend could have borrowed it. If it was stolen, that blows the field wide open."

"So, if he *was* giving someone a ride, they were both in the car when the accident occurred." I was still going to call it an accident when speaking about it but inwardly didn't trust I had all the facts yet. "But only the passenger's body has been found."

It pained me to ask the question, but I blurted it out anyway, "Do you think they'll ever find my uncle's body?" More dead air. *Just answer the damn question.*

"I can't say for sure. We've had divers scouring the area around where this body was found. I know they're trying. But currents are funny. It's hard to know where to look. They could end up in very different places… or get caught up on something underwater."

My brain conjured images of divers in full scuba gear making their way slowly through the murky water, not being able to see much in front of their faces until they were right up on top of it, the monstrous cargo ships chugging along over the top of them, stirring up the water, churning up debris in their wake.

"All right, Sergeant. I appreciate your call."

I took a minute to consider what Jennings had said—and what he hadn't—before stepping back inside to rejoin Mason and bring him up to speed.

"What if they don't ever find him?" I tossed his way after I'd finished, not fully expecting an answer.

"What do you mean?" Mason perked up.

"I don't know.… Maybe I'm really just asking myself that question. What will I do?"

He left the question for me to tussle with, seemingly disinterested, but I had every intention of pulling him in.

"Actually a better question is how they were able to declare him dead when they haven't found his body." I *hated* referring to my uncle as an inanimate object. "My uncle," I corrected.

"If you have enough evidence to establish someone is no longer living, they can be declared deceased by a court of law," said Mason, sounding annoyingly scholarly in an obviously delicate situation.

What had been the rush to do so? How long was it after he'd gone missing that it happened? A month? A couple of weeks?

Mason took my silence as a nod for him to continue. "With the eyewitness report they were able to pinpoint where his car ended up."

"But no one was inside."

"No. Apparently neither set of seat belts had been in use.... Not only that, the convertible top was down. There was nothing to hold them inside the vehicle. Not that wearing seat belts would have saved either man during a plunge into the water from a bridge the height of the Ravenel, but it certainly would have helped to retrieve their bodies for the loved ones they'd left behind."

I hated how he didn't hesitate to blurt out the grim reality of the situation. Just let it splat on the table and drip off onto the floor. It was irksome he knew so much about it.

"Not many people own an Austin Healey, and they were able to easily run the plates to determine it was his."

"What if someone switched the plates?" I held out hope it wasn't Gray's car.

"The VIN would also have been matched up. The vehicle hadn't been submerged long enough to rust out yet. His wallet and license weren't there—probably in his pocket—but the registration was still securely stowed in the center console."

"So you saw the accident report?"

He nodded.

A breath caught in my throat. "I thought there wasn't one yet?" How could he have seen it?

Our eyes met, but I couldn't discern if he was scrambling to come up with a cover.

"Before it was pulled."

"Pulled?"

"Yeah. The officer on scene filed a report, but it was quickly pulled when SLED got involved."

"But you were able to see it before it was pulled?"

His half-grin was unsettling, like someone hiding something and enjoying keeping it from everyone else.

"I was quick about it."

I studied his expression. All evidence of twisted humor had dissipated.

"That still doesn't seem like enough to prove he's no longer living."

"Well… all that and the time that passed since anyone had seen him. Not his agent, his neighbors, The Navigation Center, the newspaper—"

"The Navigation Center?"

"It's a place where the homeless can go. From what I understand, he volunteered there."

"And the newspaper?"

"*Post and Courier.* The Charleston daily."

I considered that for a moment. He read my expression.

"You didn't know he worked at the paper?"

"Guess not. I knew he wrote spy novels."

"Yeah, but those don't always pay the bills. He was also a staff writer. Did a lot of investigative pieces. Must have come naturally to him. He had to have done a lot of research for his novels too."

"So back to the idea that enough people hadn't seen him and assumed he was dead… and a judge bought all the evidence?"

"Bought? If you mean *believed*—then, yes. I don't think it was that much of a stretch."

I wasn't sold but suspected I was suffering from a serious case of denial. My body ached with the thought Gray had perished in a car accident. If I could ease the pain with a flicker of hope, so be it. At some point I'd have to come to terms with it, but not yet.

The interrogation wasn't over. "So who pushed for having him declared dead. Who would want or need that to happen?"

Mason cocked his head, as if turning the question over in his head. "I don't know that anyone *pushed* for it. I don't know the specifics—it's not my area of expertise. I'm in real estate law. But I think it's a fairly common procedure. It could be initiated by the family of the—"

"Well that didn't happen. We didn't even know he was missing." *At least I didn't. What else was my mother keeping from me?*

"It could also be initiated by creditors who are looking to make sure they're included in the dissolution of the estate."

"Do you think he had creditors on his back?"

Mason's palms went up as if to disassociate himself with the notion. "I honestly don't know the answer to that question."

I hoped Gray hadn't left me with a messy financial situation to have to untangle and resolve.

"I'll admit it does seem to have happened more quickly than usual. Did he have any other family locally?"

"No, we're all in Boston."

"A significant other?"

I felt my jaw clench. Had I been so selfish not to imagine Gray having someone special in his life? Would he have told me?

"A girlfriend?" Mason asked.

Disappointed I might have been sharing my uncle with someone else, I didn't dare speak for fear my tone would betray me. In my head I was sounding rather narcissistic. *For God's sake, Kathryn.*

"Boyfriend?" he tried again.

*Could* he have been involved with a guy? How well *did* I know him?

"I… don't know. I'm not aware of a significant other, but that doesn't mean there wasn't one." There was no point in speculating. It was becoming painfully clear I didn't really know Gray.

"No one that I know of has stepped forward," said Mason.

"But if there was one, she… or he could have initiated the legal proceedings to have him declared dead?" I needed to know if that was a possibility.

"In theory, yes. Especially if they could establish they'd been in a serious relationship with the missing person. Like… living under the same roof for an extended period of time."

"Wouldn't that also make them a suspect?"

"I really don't think that would automatically make them a suspect."

"The police might think otherwise."

As I reached for the glass of pinot grigio that had magically appeared at my place setting while I was outside, my cell rang again. "Hello?" I answered, expecting it to be the SLED sergeant again with something quick to mention and then hang up.

"Kathryn, it's Teddy Spinzali."

Instead, it was my doctor—our family doctor.

I swallowed hard, making a click in my throat. If there was nothing to discuss he would have had one of the nurses make the call.

"Is everything okay?"

"I wanted to let you know that your bloodwork came back."

"My bloodwork?"

"Yes, and everything looks great. You're a specimen of good health. Keep doing what you're doing."

"So everything is okay?

"Absolutely. Couldn't be better…. I mean, your bad cholesterol is slightly elevated so just be aware of that and make better food choices. You should be fine."

"Well, you scared me there for a moment, Teddy. My appointment with you was a while ago. A few months, in fact. You're just getting back to me now with this?"

"No, no need for alarm. Sometimes bloodwork takes longer than expected. In this case though, I'm afraid my staff dropped the ball. There was a notation in your file that a call was made, but I knew I hadn't spoken to you. So I apologize for their blunder. Fortunately it's good news."

"Yeah, thank goodness I wasn't dying of some sort of horrible disease and only had weeks to live." I was ticked at him but we still shared a laugh.

"Hopefully I won't see you again for another year. Everything looks good."

I hung up and frowned at the cell before tucking it back in my pocket.

"What's up?" Mason had only heard one side of the conversation. I'd almost forgotten he'd been within earshot.

"Nothing. Really. My doctor called to say all my bloodwork from my checkup looked great."

"Your doctor? That's a little strange. What doctor takes the time to do that? And you're on a first name basis?" As he slung an arm across the back of the booth, leaning back with a nonchalant magazine-ad pose, his jacket splayed open and a pistol secured in a side holster came into view.

Averting my eyes, I couldn't imagine why an attorney would need a gun but kept to the conversation. "He's a dear family friend. I think he made an exception for me."

"Your doctor is a family friend?" He screwed up his face like he'd tasted key lime pie for the first time. "That's even stranger than the phone call."

He had a point.

# CHAPTER FOURTEEN

Settling into a corner of the couch in the carriage house living room, I finally had a quiet moment to get back to my uncle's zip drive. Per usual though, as soon as I flipped open my laptop I was distracted by all the tabs I'd left lined up across the screen and pulled an Alice in Wonderland, scurrying down one rabbit hole after the other.

Googling my uncle's name. Checking out missing persons websites. Scouring his newspaper's online presence. Not to resurface until my stomach demanded nourishment. I ignored the abhorrent grumblings but when the lightheadedness advanced to a sensation of whirling, I headed for the kitchen, running my hand along furniture, the walls, and anything else that would steady me.

No wonder I was famished. It was the middle of the afternoon, and I hadn't tackled what I'd set out to do midmorning. Wiping the raspberry vinaigrette from my lips, I left my salad bowl in the sink and returned to the cozy couch. I slipped my uncle's zip drive from my pants pocket and inserted it into the side of the laptop.

The collection of files read like a bestseller's list with all the titles of his novels: *The Man in Moscow, Red Horizon Burning, Wounded Eagle, The Spy and the Woman in Red, The Traitor Wore White,* and one called

Current MS. I was curious how far along he had gotten on it. There was also a file named recipes that made me smile, not aware my uncle was into cooking to the extent he would collect his recipes on a zip drive. *What else don't you know about him, Kathryn?*

At the bottom of the list was a folder named XXX. I scrunched up my nose, hoping that didn't suggest the contents were porn but knew it wouldn't be outside the realm of possibilities. He was a guy with, I imagined, desires like most other guys. I vowed a quick peek and then an exit just as quickly if that were the case.

Clicking on it produced a smaller window on my screen with blanks to fill in. The folder was password protected. Would he feel the need to keep others from seeing his porn? Or was it something more significant than that?

Perhaps he was researching an article for the newspaper and the files in the folder were for his eyes only. But why would he put work files on a zip drive where he kept files for his novels? Wouldn't he keep those two areas of work separate? Or was it so secretive that even his coworkers couldn't have access to it? What was the risk he was taking?

A hard rap at the door broke the stillness in the cozy space. I startled and my hands skated across the keyboard. Clicking out of the list of folders, I ripped out the zip drive and shoved it securely back into my pocket.

Sneaking a peek through a front facing window, I could see Mason had returned. He fidgeted, waiting for me to answer the door. It was the first time he seemed uncomfortable in his own skin.

As soon as I gave the heavy wooden door a yank, he stood erect and plastered a grin on his face. The peeling on his nose wasn't as bad as the day I'd arrived.

"Hey, Kathryn. I was going to knock off a little early today so I thought I'd stop by and see if you wanted to get out and do something."

"Like what?"

"Let's go find out where the Holy City leads us."

Amused, I agreed to venturing out with him again. I was enjoying getting to know Charleston and him as well. As I pulled the door shut, I noticed an older man with graying dark shoulder length hair hurrying down the driveway toward the street, a bundle tucked under one arm. There was a wobble in his step as if he needed a cane but was too vain to use one yet. Perhaps it was the uneven brick surface of the driveway.

"Who's that?" I cocked my head in the direction of the trespasser Mason had paid no mind to.

"Him? Probably just a tourist. They can be annoying at times. Walk right up to people's windows and peek in. He probably wanted a closer look at this stunning property." He gestured toward my uncle's grand home. "At the airport they should hand out a guide to being a tourist in Charleston. Some of them think it's okay to open gates and walk right into people's gardens to take pictures. They don't seem to realize these are people's homes, not museums for them to gawk at. They get obnoxious at times."

I watched the man disappear around the brick wall and couldn't help but wonder if that was all he was. A tourist. I had felt like I was being watched since I'd arrived. Was it just the curious neighborhood boy? Spirits who were still hanging around? Or this guy? Was he stalking me? If so, why?

Mason had insisted we take a horse-drawn carriage ride. A charming idea. One that felt a tad romantic as well. That was until we entered the barn and I got a good whiff of hay and horse manure. The heat of the day no doubt accelerated its permeation. *Kathryn, you're not in the big city anymore.*

Our carriage was dark blue and sat up high with silky gold fringe along the flat roof that stirred at the slightest movement. As Mason took my hand to help me in, I realized I didn't have to gather the extra fabric of my skirt to climb in. I wore tapered ankle pants in a spring print, a coordinating solid gauze top tucked in the front, and strappy lace-up sandals. No doubt he'd noticed as well.

Once each of the four rows of the surrey was shoulder to shoulder tourists—Mason and I shared one with a couple from Cleveland—we were off with a lurch, pulled by a blond draft horse named Clarabelle. We passed through what our guide called the employee break room—my first indication the ride would be filled with tongue-in-cheek remarks that bordered on Dad jokes—where a row of horses had their noses in feed and water buckets. Oscillating fans and misters labored to keep them cool.

After each carriage row had had a chance to shout out where they were from, during which I flashed back to field trips in elementary school, our guide filled us in on Clarabelle and her much more rigorous previous life on an Amish farm until we pulled up to a small wooden booth on the corner of North Market and Church streets. This was where the city determined which of the five districts the guide could take us. Once selected from numbered balls much like a spinning metal bingo cage, we could go on any streets within the district. I didn't catch what the winning number was, but it didn't matter to me. I wouldn't have known which was which.

The guide's monologue drifted in and out of my consciousness as questions surrounding Gray's disappearance swirled in my head. But the *clip-clop* of the horse's lumbering soon felt soothing.

I half-tuned in as I gazed upon the impeccably maintained Charleston singles as we moseyed past, their window boxes bursting with colorful blossoms and trickling ivy. The narrow side of the houses faced the street with long piazzas on the side for entertaining and enjoying the breezes off the water. Wrought iron gates invited passersby into intimate gardens with worn brick paths, walls covered with fragrant confederate jasmine, and babbling water features. I learned the pineapples that adorned walls and gates symbolized hospitality. Apparently a larger-than-life example was on display at the waterfront in the form of a fountain. I made a mental note to check it out later.

Church steeples on what seemed like every corner explained Charleston's moniker: The Holy City. But given its history of the revolutionary war, the civil war, fires, and earthquakes, and the number of deaths on the peninsula associated with these events, Charleston was also called the most haunted city. Was the Pink Lady part of that eerie dimension?

Hailing from the 1600s, a handful of quaint cobblestone streets made from ballast from ships arriving in the New World reminded us of Charleston's humble beginnings. Gas lanterns whose flickering flames never went out gave a newcomer the feeling she'd stepped back in time.

When the guide got to the story of America's first female serial killer, I perked up. Along with her husband, John, Lavinia Fisher ran an inn called Six Mile House located, as its name implied, six miles outside of Charleston. It was frequented by merchants on their way to King Street, the center of commerce in the 1800s. After a string of disappearances authorities were struggling to solve, they got a break when a guest of Lavinia's inn happened to dislike tea.

As the story went, she'd been poisoning her guests, the ones with valuable goods to take to market, with tea made from oleander leaves. Once they were dead, she disposed of their bodies in the basement of her inn with a special contraption on their bed that dropped them through the floor.

The fortunate guest without a taste for tea didn't want to be rude when the beverage was offered, so he took it when his host offered it to him but tossed it out when she wasn't looking. Later he woke up when his bed suddenly fell into the basement. He was able to get away and alert police. One could only imagine the gruesome scene they discovered upon their arrival.

After our horse-drawn jaunt around charming downtown with tall tales mixed with a bit of paranormal and history, Mason helped me down from the carriage and whisked me off to dinner at Poogan's Porch, a longstanding Charleston institution on Queen Street known for its soulful Southern cooking. Its namesake was a dog who had lived in the building when it was a home and was buried in the front yard under a stone marker.

Mason asked for a table in the back, which turned out to be a small, brick patio, walled in and very private. It was a warm evening with a gentle breeze that kept any annoying bugs away. We certainly wouldn't have been having dinner outside if we were in Boston.

Spring in Charleston. No wonder it was a huge tourist destination. Absolutely beautiful. Almost magical.

At his insistence, I ordered shrimp and grits but shied away from the Mint Julep, not expecting to like the bourbon in it, having overdone it my first foray with the potent brown liquid. When Mason's drink was delivered, he offered to let me have the first taste, after which I flagged down the waiter and ordered a new one for him. I hung on to the chilled copper mug with the mint sprig poking out of the top. I'd found another Southern favorite to add to my growing list.

As we nibbled on pimento cheese and crackers, the conversation wove through the delightful carriage ride until the entrees arrived. Mason plowed into his plate of fried chicken and chuckled when he cautioned I might just be turning into a Southerner. I was okay with that. I'd been trying it on for size, and it was starting to feel right.

At the waiter's recommendation, we finished off the meal with a piece of key lime pie with two forks. I wasn't all that keen on the sour-tasting dessert, but our time together felt more like a date the later in the day it got. I hoped I wasn't blushing at the thought.

"Do you get to take off early from work often?" I asked.

A corner of his mouth turned up in amusement. "I suppose. But part of my job is entertaining clients. So I don't think my bosses will have a problem with it." He laughed. "Besides, I work hard. Once in a while I should be able to spend some time with a lovely lady."

Not having heard that from anyone except my father before, I ran a quick self-assessment. The image I'd seen in the mirror that morning reflected a considerable upgrade from what had arrived on the peninsula mere days earlier, thanks to the shopping spree with Mason and my glasses biting the dust on the stairs in the main house. I'd felt pretty when I walked out the door after Mason's unexpected arrival, and he'd noticed.

But this kind of attention wasn't something I was used to. And certainly not from a successful—not to mention attractive, okay *hot*—attorney. My inner voice was screaming, *He can't be serious. Check your authenticity meter. He's got an agenda. Think about it. In the same breath he used to describe you as pretty, he called you a client. You can't have it both ways. At a minimum, it's unprofessional. Don't fall for it. You know what someone like that is called.* I grew painfully aware how much time I'd let lapse.

Finally able to meet his eyes, I could see his cheeks were flushed—undoubtedly like mine—which surprised me. Maybe it was his second Mint Julep.

"Very sweet of you to say," I finally said.

Maybe he was sincere after all. But I'd keep my guard up. One thing seemed certain though. I was falling in love with Charleston.

# CHAPTER FIFTEEN

"WHAT DO YOU MEAN WE NEED to work together?" I asked as I shook off the surprise from finding Stella, my reluctant airport shuttle driver, at the door. I glanced behind her to ascertain her weathered-blue death trap was still intact and had not been flattened by a Mack truck—neither had she. The images still rattled around in my head. At times, I couldn't trust what went on up there.

"You have to realize not everything is making sense in your uncle's death. Because of my job I have access to certain things you do not. I can help you out. Otherwise you'll be at this for a very long time, and who knows what you'll be able to find."

There had to be more to it than she was letting on. "What do you get out of it?"

"Me?"

"Yeah, I seriously doubt you're willing to do this pro bono as they say in your profession. You must have some sort of an agenda."

Her eyes widened at the suggestion. "How about I'd like to see justice done? I'm a Libra. I can't stand it when things aren't fair. And things are *never* fair. My mama drilled into my head from early on that life isn't fair, and it's not. Far from it. But there are certain times where we can right wrongs, fight for justice. Even a small gesture can make things right again. I think this is one of those situations."

Impressive. Sounded well-rehearsed. "Is that why you became an attorney?"

Her eyes narrowed as if no one had ever asked that question before. "Yeah… I guess I would have thought that was obvious."

"One thing I learned from *my* mother is that most things—people, situations, events—are not obvious. And if they seem to be, it's only because you haven't delved deeply enough to find out what's really going on," I said, cringing that I was quoting Posh, who I despised. But Stella didn't need to know that.

"Sounds like your mama taught you some important life lessons like mine did."

"What happened to your mama?" Did I dare push further? I sensed she was no longer in Stella's life. "Is she still around?"

Stella fell silent and suddenly grew fascinated with the welcome mat, scuffing it with the toe of her shoe.

"You don't want to talk about it?" I pushed a little further.

Shaking her head without looking up, she said, "Not really." Her voice had turned ragged and barely audible. I'd touched a nerve, but that was okay. I needed to get to know her. What was her background? What was her motivation?

"I get that, but if I'm supposed to trust you, I really need to know more about you."

When she finally made eye contact, she brushed away a tear before it could escape.

"Why don't you come in." I stepped back and motioned down the tiny hallway.

Reluctantly she followed me into the kitchen and settled onto one of the chairs at the small table in the corner, one foot tucked under a thigh. I made tea and put out lemon cookies I'd picked up at the bakery down the street. She didn't touch the tea but snarfed down half the plate of cookies. When had her last meal been?

"I really don't want to talk about it. I understand that you feel the need to know me better in order to trust me, but it should mean something if I'm going to jeopardize my job in order to help you."

Although I saw her point, it didn't make me feel any better about it. I remained silent to encourage her to keep going, and after a while it worked.

"Let's just say… my mother had some *issues.* She was a single mom. I never knew my dad." She gazed out the window to the backyard as if looking for answers she'd never been able to find.

Stella took a sip of hot tea before returning the floral porcelain cup to the saucer. She needed her hands to talk with.

"I can't imagine how hard your childhood must have been," I said and instantly regretted it. It felt lame and she couldn't resist jumping on it.

"Of course you can't imagine. Jesus Christ, you have no idea. Born into money… in some snobbish Boston family."

I sat back in my chair and let her unload. Sounded like she needed it. I had nothing to add anyway. No defense. She was right. I had *no* idea what she'd been through. Without realizing it all these years, I'd lived quite comfortably in my surreal bubble, a miserable bubble.

With two siblings who were Type A personalities like our parents, going after what they wanted in life, embarking on a business venture that landed them in *Forbes'* Up and Coming Entrepreneurs list, somehow I got lumped in with them in her mind as highly successful and outrageously well-off.

Would I have given it all up to trade places with Stella? Was I actually contemplating the thought if it were possible? Give up egocentric and eccentric Rose Moore for a single mother? It would have sent Rose over the edge. It took everything I had not to grin at the thought.

"Let me spell it out for you." Perfect. My lame comment turned into the impetus to get her talking. "Got kicked out of our apartment." She swallowed hard. "Lived in our car for a while until social services caught up to us. That's when they took me away."

"Oh, Stella, I'm so sorry."

"Never saw my mother again." She was plowing forward as if the momentum kept her from stopping.

"Did that happen around here?" Did it really matter? Perhaps not. But I wanted to give the impression I was interested to keep her talking.

"Not too far. I came here out of college for a fresh start."

"If you don't mind me asking…" I ignored her scoff. "How did you get into college?"

"I was fortunate to have a couple people in my life who were my cheerleaders and coached me to finish high school, apply for college— my admissions essay had to have been an eyeopener. They recognized I had something going on upstairs in spite of my circumstances. I will be forever grateful to them.

"Then a friend from college convinced me to apply to law school after I'd scraped through undergrad with hardly sufficient financial aid, two backbreaking jobs, and a staggering pile of student loans. It was hard for me to see blurry-eyed past my damn debt and how I was going to repay it, but she talked me into a couple more years one night after dinner and too many glasses of wine at her place. She stroked my ego reviewing my academic awards, GPA, and telling me I was the smartest person she knew. *Don't you just love good friends?* There was also something in her logic about my earnings potential significantly increasing with a law degree and it made sense at the time. It still makes sense, but my student loans and the need to repay them hover over me like a nun at Catholic school during a math test. And I lost three years of earnings while in law school, only working enough to cover the immediate bills, needing every possible waking hour to study."

Fascinated with her story, I was impressed by how her speech had become more refined as she talked, as if she were doing an interview she'd prepared for over and over until it was perfect. I refilled our tea-cups and she kept going.

"But life is still not fair. I struggled to get a job at a decent law firm even though I graduated from USC School of Law and passed the boards in the first sitting. I didn't ask the dozens of firms who passed on me if it was the background check that did me in, but I have a good sense that was it. That and the color of my skin. I just needed a chance to shake loose from my past and that DUI that's clinging to my back with its sharp claws, refusing to be forgotten.

"Finally, I got a break. Levinson & Levinson let me in their door as an associate. Did they get sloppy? Did someone forget to do a back-ground check? Ha! I live with that possibility *every* day. That someone will wise up. Dig into my file, my background. Come after me and do a real follow up. When someone approaches my desk, my nerves tingle until they spit out their first sentence and it's obvious they're not stop-ping by to let me know I'd been found out and I'm canned. Mentally I got my dukes up and I'm ready to go at it with them. I can't make any mistakes. Bring the wrong kind of attention on myself, that would give them reason to dig deeper."

She scooped up the delicate cup and took a long sip, holding it in her mouth for a moment before gulping it down.

"Or maybe they *did* do the background check and the head of HR pulled in enough air to inflate a latex balloon on the first try at a child's birthday party when she read the report but decided to give me a chance anyway based on the rest of my credentials. And then word spread throughout the firm, and they're just waiting for me to screw up so they can kick my sorry Black ass out of there."

So much for the interview. We were back to the first-year associate with a huge chip on her shoulder.

"In the meantime, they're paying me barely enough to pay rent and eat—at least it's not fast food, unless I choose that and I rarely do. I'm still driving the same beat-up Toyota I had in law school, but it runs good so I'll keep driving it until it doesn't. On top of the ongoing anxiety of being found out, they're not trusting me to do actual associate work."

The kitchen fell silent except for the sound of the grandfather clock in the hall. *Tick. Tock. Tick. Tock.* It sounded too much like some sort of explosive device in the last seconds of its countdown sequence. Was the universe sending me a clear hint?

"So this is my shot. *You're* my shot to prove to them what I can do."

I didn't think I wanted to be anyone's *shot.* There was too much at stake. What was she dragging me into?

"You have to sense there's more to what they're telling you about your uncle's passing. I do too. Together we can dig deeper and figure out what's really going on."

"So you think you'll find something at Levinson & Levinson to explain what happened to my uncle?"

Her eyes became slits, peering intently at me. "The attorney who handled the case to have him declared dead works in our office."

She threw back the remainder in her cup. "But you have to keep this between us."

"Why? Would this be illegal?"

"What? No, I just mean I need to do this without anyone at the firm sticking their nose in before we come up with what we need. Otherwise we'll get shut down so fast, and I'll be out of a job quicker than—Well, you get the idea."

I loved her enthusiasm, but I didn't like how often she used the word "we."

# CHAPTER SIXTEEN

I'D GROWN CONDITIONED TO CATCHING MY breath when the phone rang and the ID was the South Carolina State Police. What did they have to report now? Had Gray survived the plunge into the river and just woke from a coma in a local hospital, unable to tell them who he was? I hoped beyond realistic hope that was the case.

"Hello?" It was more of a continuation of my exhale than an actual greeting.

"Miss Moore, this is Sergeant Jennings."

"Yes." I didn't bother to say I could see from the caller ID who he was.

"I just heard back from the state lab about your uncle's car."

"And?" In my head, I urged him to get to the point with stronger words.

"Upon examining the body of the car, they found the back left bumper and quarter panel bashed in. Initially it was thought it was from hitting the bottom of the harbor. Further inspection revealed silver paint had been transferred to the Austin Healey, consistent with getting bumped from the left side by another vehicle."

It took a moment to grasp what he was saying.

"Ma'am?"

"Yeah," I answered, my voice raspy.

"This shifts our investigation. We're now looking at vehicular homicide. Although premeditated murder isn't out of the question either."

Murder. The word hit me firmly in the gut. I'd been spending so much time in denial it hadn't entered the realm of possibilities. Regardless, I was going to cling to the idea Gray had survived the fall and was somewhere in a local hospital. For the time being, I would play along with his investigation.

"So the search is on for a silver vehicle with damage to the right front bumper and side."

"Yes, ma'am."

"Can I ask you something?"

"Of course." His words were nearly drowned out by the sound of traffic whizzing by on his end.

"What time of day did my uncle's car go off the bridge?"

"I believe it was around two a.m."

Not what I was expecting him to say. My father's voice suddenly thundered in my brain saying, *Nothing good ever happens after midnight.* "So no witnesses at that hour."

"Not on the bridge or the road leading up to it. I would imagine it was downright deserted at that hour."

"What about cameras?"

"Unfortunately, no. The closest one wasn't functioning. However, we got lucky and a cargo ship was heading out of port. The captain happened to catch sight of the car catapulting off the bridge and enter the water. He phoned it in."

Why would Gray have been out at that hour? *For any number of reasons, Kathryn. You don't know your uncle. Stop pretending you do.*

The officer continued. "It took a while for the captain to stop the ship—those monstrosities don't stop on a dime—but he was completely cooperative. Helped us pinpoint where the car had ended up. Delayed his voyage until we were satisfied we had all the details he could offer."

"What day of the week was it?" The more I knew, the better.

"It was a Tuesday."

It didn't seem likely Gray would have been out for a night of drinking on a weeknight and heading home at that hour. *So presumptuous of you. Again, you don't know your uncle. You don't have a clue.*

"Have you checked the hospitals in the area?" I wasn't going to let that go, and I wasn't going to let the state police let it go either. It was a very real possibility that my uncle, who could conquer anything, could survive a fall into the river if he was safely strapped into his car.

Dead air on the other end signaled I'd lost him for a moment.

"Checked the hospitals for your uncle?"

"Yeah."

"Uh, ma'am. I'm sorry to dash any degree of hope you might have, but a fall like that… from a bridge… from that height…" I detected a wisp of a breath out as he struggled to deliver the cruel reality.

"You don't think he would have survived."

"No, ma'am."

"Well the body you found may have been his passenger. And just because the other guy didn't survive, doesn't mean he didn't. You don't know my uncle. He's an amazing guy. Very determined. Resourceful. Tough. Resilient. Could accomplish anything." I sounded like a child defending her implausible theory against all odds.

"I don't doubt that. From everything I've heard about him, he sounds like he was quite a guy."

"And just because the seatbelts were both disengaged doesn't mean he didn't have his on. He could have simply taken it off after impact and swam to the surface."

More crickets on the other end.

"That's certainly an interesting theory."

"I think it's worth pursuing. Could you have someone check the hospitals? I would do it, but I'm sure they're not going to give information to a random caller asking about a patient in a coma. But they would have to talk to you."

This time, no hesitation. "All right. I'll get someone on it."

At least he was humoring me. Like a child gets humored so as not to hurt her feelings.

# CHAPTER SEVENTEEN

Hoping against all logical hope there was a reasonable explanation for Gray's disappearance, I replayed the phone call with the trooper over and over in my mind. Foul play. It was so much more difficult to wrap my head around to think someone meant Gray harm than if it had just been a matter of distracted driving or falling asleep at the wheel. I supposed it still could have been an accident even though they now knew another vehicle was involved. But if it wasn't an accident, but a deliberate act to kill Gray, who would have wanted him dead?

Recalling how much my mother despised Gray, my desperate thoughts jumped to her with alarming speed. A rush of heat from this despicable sin filled my core and crept slowly to my extremities. I could only wonder if that was what an old lady's hot flash was like.

What a terrible daughter I was to consider my own flesh and blood could be associated with killing someone—especially a family member. I was simply trying on the idea for size. Right? Would my mother's disdain for her brother-in-law compel her to harm him? Would she take it that far? Maybe she wasn't capable of doing the dirty deed, but she could have hired someone. It happened all the time—at least in the movies it did. She certainly had the wherewithal to pay someone. And having

Gray out of the picture would remove the unsavory influence he had over me—at least in her eyes. Problem solved. No more silly ambitions to become a writer. I would have been lost without his guidance.

Then I would have to get on with life and get serious about a career at J.W. Moore. Someone had to take over when Posh and Joseph retired. It wasn't going to be Delaney and Peyton. They'd gone off on their own venture, a very successful one, so they wouldn't be returning to the family business anytime soon, or at all. The last thing my mother wanted was to have the company fall out of their family holdings. Their empire.

But murder? Was she capable? Would she do it? I hated that I couldn't rule it out. I hated that my mother gave me reason to think that way of her. But my mother, a murderess? That was hard to swallow. But if it was her, I'd show her I could become a successful writer even if my idol—my inspiration—was out of the picture. I'd show her.

The only way to take the glare of the spotlight off my mother as a suspect was to come up with a viable alternative. Who else could want Gray out of the picture? It had to be related to his work. What was he working on? What had he delved into recently? Who had he pissed off? What was he getting too close to?

It was time to revisit his zip drive. Snatching it from my pants pocket, I slipped it into the drive on my laptop, scrolling through folder names again. The one labeled XXX caught my eye. It was password protected—all the more reason to take a shot at deciphering it.

Double clicking on the folder, the inset window popped up again. Well-versed in my uncle's email since I'd sent numerous writing samples to him for feedback, I typed that in for the username. Then the blank for the password loomed in front of me, the cursor line blinking in a steady beat as if tapping a finger on the desk and waiting impatiently for me to continue.

"I'm thinking," I said, as if my laptop was animate. "Give me a minute." Sometimes it could be rather pushy.

A logical password—may be too guessable—would be his birthdate. I typed in several versions—letters only, letters and numbers, numbers with dashes, numbers only, the year written as two digits and also as four, upper case, lower case. None of these attempts worked. I tried the Pink Lady's East Battery address in a variety of versions but without any luck.

Considering for a moment what was important to him, I typed in AustinHealey68 and 68AustinHealey. Then I tried Aston Martin the same way. Nothing. How many tries would I have before the system locked me out? I needed to think like my uncle would. What would he choose for a password that no one else would think of?

Then it came to me. I typed in April21993. My birthday. When I hit enter, the password input window cleared from the screen and the spinning buffering icon appeared. I was in.

The list of files popped up, and I was delighted to see they didn't have names that suggested anything inappropriate. Instead, it was a list of luxury British cars. Jaguar. Bentley. McLaren. A dozen or more high-end brands made up the list. Were they dream cars he hoped to own one day? Perhaps. I needed to dig deeper.

But when I clicked on the individual files, I was again prompted for a password. None I could think of worked. Gray had stumped me again.

# CHAPTER EIGHTEEN

My vision started to blur. The tiny dark spots almost twinkled in my peripheral. I knew what was coming, so I grabbed onto the nearest sturdy object.

Only her profile was visible, but her unmistakable stark features could belong to no one else. Her slender nose that turned up ever so slightly at the end. The high cheekbones that made her face appear concave. Even at night, by the light of the dashboard, I could see the Botox-enhanced lips were painted fuchsia. I swear she went to bed in full makeup with her signature color slathered on thick so it would last until dawn. Who did she think was going to see it? I suppose if the furnace malfunctioned and she died of carbon monoxide poisoning, at least she'd look her best for the police photos. Had my mother come to that realization? It wouldn't surprise me. Not much surprised me about Posh.

I had the sense it was late at night. My mother driving an unfamiliar car. It felt as though I was in the passenger seat, but she didn't know I was there. We were driving faster than I was comfortable with. I tried to speak but couldn't form words. I desperately wanted her to slow down. Her jaw was set, and her fists clamped around the steering wheel. We came up fast behind the car in front of us. The unmistakable rear end of an Austin Healey. Navy blue. Just like my uncle's. A vanity plate. Just like my uncle's. Right before she rammed it, I realized it was his. No! Stop. No! I screamed.

As we hit hard on my side of the car, I looked into Gray's car. He jolted from the collision, jamming the steering wheel to the right. He became airborne and was up and over the Jersey barrier for a fleeting moment before dropping out of sight.

My shouts, demanding my mother to stop pulled me out of the vision. It scared me. This time my subconscious was trying on the idea of my mother carrying out her idle threats and harming Gray. Could she have? Was this what really happened? It was replaying in my mind's eye? Or was my vulnerable brain taking my fears and running with them in a twisted, yet unlikely, scenario? I had no way of knowing. I didn't want to believe it. But she gave me no reason not to consider the likelihood.

CHAPTER NINETEEN

THE BLIND TIGER WAS A LIVELY place. But dark. And the bar seemed to take up most of the area we'd walked into off Broad Street. Mason led the way to the back and spoke to a twenty-something with unnaturally dark hair barely past her ears that looked mussed from taking a too-small sweatshirt off, balancing a small round tray teetering with drinks. Her three eyebrow studs looked painful. I wondered why she would go through with having it done. Had she lost a dare?

Turning to me, Mason nodded in the direction of a windowed door that opened to the outside patio area, grabbing a couple of menus from a nearby slot. He held the door as I walked into a lush, brick courtyard—an oasis of sorts in the midst of the city. Leading me to a small round table on the outskirts of the patio, Mason pulled out one of two wooden folding chairs and handed me a menu.

I took a moment to scan the space. It felt private, like you had to know it was there and who to know to get in. Perhaps he'd used a secret password, I mused.

"You *have* to try the beignets," he said as he settled his hulking torso into his seat that suddenly looked like a chair from a kindergarten classroom. "They're the best here. Mind if I order for us?"

The same girl with the drink tray in the bar delivered a tray of biscuits and gravy, a generous slice of quiche, a colorful salad, and avocado toast to the table next to us. Probably everything on the menu was amazing or he wouldn't have brought me there.

"Sure. No problem." There was no point in protesting. I would have ordered what he suggested anyway. When in Rome...

Tucking the tray under her arm, the girl turned her attention to her new arrivals.

"Hey, Mason. What's up?" Her voice was even and void of any cordiality.

Gathering himself up from the wobbly seat, he gave her a brief, but warm hug. It looked awkward on her end. "Great to see you, Scyler. This is Kathryn." He gestured across the table. Scyler offered a, *Hey*. "She's visiting but perhaps will fall in love and stay."

Did he mean with Charleston or him? Scyler nodded in acknowledgment but wasn't interested enough to engage. I sensed there might be a history between the two of them. Call it strangely placed jealousy, but I didn't want to know.

Settling himself back at the table, Mason put in an order for a mimosa carafe and beignets.

The waitress shot him a look I couldn't interpret.

"Come on, Scy. You can make it happen," Mason goaded.

Her eyes darted between Mason and me before she turned and headed back inside.

"What's going on?" I asked.

"Beignets aren't technically on the menu anymore, but if you know to ask for them, they usually make them. Depends on who's in the kitchen."

Grabbing the table with both hands, I took in a breath as my line of sight shimmered into flickering light along the edges and the immediate surroundings faded into a vision with our server speaking to a man with a chef's hat. The stabbing between my eyes returned. The man I was watching grew animated and they exchanged words. He picked up a carving knife, waving it at her. Scyler recoiled but pointed at him while she spoke.

Wriggling away from the altercation and settling back at the table, I said, "You've asked too much of her."

"What?"

"Scyler… she's getting into it with the chef over our order."

"No, she can handle it. She's worked here for a while. And we go way back."

"No, seriously. You've put her in an awkward situation. She's doing it for you but it could cost her."

"No need for dramatics, Kathryn. She's a doll and has pull in the kitchen."

"She may have been here for a while, but the chef is new. He doesn't like being pushed around in his own kitchen."

"What? How would you know—"

"It doesn't matter how I know. I just do."

"She'll be fine. You'll see." He added a single decisive nod, as if that would make it all right.

"May be. But she may have a price to pay." I glanced down at the table at my scrawling on the napkin. Usually I used my own pad of paper, but I'd only gotten as far as retrieving my pen from my pocket and started in on the nearest writing surface. The entire napkin from edge to edge was covered with inked lines in remarkable detail. It was the two individuals I'd seen in my vision in a commercial kitchen, one with a knife in his hand. The expression on the woman's face was one of terror.

"What the hell is *that?*" Mason's expression hardened.

The last thing I wanted to do was expose my quirky habit of whatever it was I could do. I didn't completely understand it and fought hard to keep it from happening but was not always successful. But I liked Mason and wanted to open up to him. Perhaps he would understand. Or perhaps he would run in the opposite direction.

"I'm not exactly sure what happens, but I have these visions.... They're more like a *peek* into someone else's world. Kind of a *snoop*. I call them snooks, combining the words together." I snickered, trying to keep it light. "Snook actually is a word—I looked it up—it means to move stealthily."

"Visions," he repeated, as if trying it on for size and looking for me to elaborate.

"Yeah, I can't really control when it happens. It seems to manifest when I'm particularly anxious or concerned about something."

"And you saw what was happening in the kitchen after Scyler left?"

"I don't know." I retreated from the idea what I saw was in the present. "I can't always discern what time frame I'm observing. It could have been in the past."

Mason fell silent. It was hard to tell if he was buying into it or writing me off as an irrational lunatic.

"Could it also be from the future?" he asked. Seeming more interested than I would have liked.

"I don't know. I suppose that's possible. Why not?"

His head was wagging. "I... I'm not sure what to make of it."

"Funny. Me neither. So let's move on.

Scyler returned in no time to plunk down a mimosa carafe and two wine glasses. I examined her face, but she showed no outward signs of recent tension. Had I merely seen a replay of an event in the past? I hoped that was the case.

Mason ordered our entrees as he filled the glasses and handed one across the table. We clicked rims and were on our way to the bottom of the carafe.

A couple glasses in, I decided to see what I could learn from him—extract might have been a better word for it.

"So, I'm trying to understand why someone would want to have my uncle. . ." I struggled to say it.

"Would want to have him killed?" Mason filled in the blank for me. "You think that's what happened?"

Flopping back against the flimsy rungs of the chair, I recoiled as they caved in a bit. Had he said it so flippantly?

"Sorry. Clearly, you're struggling with the possibility."

"You think?" I asked, checking his face for a reaction.

"I know. I'm sorry. This must be tough for you to process." He nodded thoughtfully. "It's gotta be a lot." He reached for the carafe and refilled our glasses as if the alcohol it contained was an elixir and would solve my issue. I was happy to indulge and see if it did.

I gazed across my rim at our server carrying a white oblong plate with golden brown pastry pillows nestled next to a ramekin with dark chocolate dipping sauce. Her cheeks were ablaze and her jaw set.

"Here they are, Kathryn," Mason said with a hand flourish. "These are reason alone to come to Charleston. Your taste buds will never be the same."

"Here's your *damn* beignets." Scyler plunked them onto the table.

I was relieved to see she was speaking to Mason.

"But you almost got me fired."

His lips parted as if to speak but thought better of it.

"I can't afford to lose this job, Mason. It may just be a crap waitress job, but it pays the bills for now. I don't have the luxury of a cushy job working in my parents' firm like you do."

"I'm sorry," was all he could manage.

"Your entrees will be out soon," our server announced in a flat, disinterested tone.

"You're the best, Scyler. The best," Mason cooed.

She glanced back and then left his synthetic compliment unanswered as she strode away. I sensed they shared some sort of a backstory but not necessarily a positive one. And it seemed their stories were of different genres. Mason's sniffed of historical fiction, and Scyler's reeked of true crime.

Turning back to me, he crumpled his brows and asked, "So you could *see* what transpired in the kitchen?"

Averting my eyes from his, I said, "Something like that."

He seemed to be searching for his next question.

Hoping to diffuse his interest, I offered, "It comes and goes. Not very predictable."

"That's crazy. How long have you been able to do that?" Clearly the diffusion tactic was ineffective.

"I don't know. Since I was little."

"What? I'd love to be able to do that. Can you teach me?"

Repressing a groan, I said, "It's not that simple. I don't even know how I do it. It's really not that big of a deal."

"*You* say..."

"Well, it isn't, and I'm done talking about it. Can we get to these infamous beignets before they get cold?" After all they'd come at a price, one we hadn't had to pay.

"Of course. Sorry. Yeah, they're not as tasty when they're cold. Here, dig in." He nudged the small platter toward me.

I had to admit I'd never tasted anything so scrumptious in the sweet category and doubted much had gotten past me over the years. It seemed a tad odd to be having them before our savory entrees, but I saw no reason to question it. No respectable guest would.

Mason held up a beignet dripping with chocolate before he popped it in his mouth. "Amazing, right?" He wiped his chin with the back of his hand. "Dessert first," he mused.

"Incredible. So glad you ordered them." Hopefully Scyler wouldn't have to deal with any lasting backlash from her clash with the chef.

"I knew you'd love them," said Mason.

"Can't imagine why they took them off the menu."

"Yeah. Don't know. Maybe the chef got tired of making them. But they really are the best in Charleston," Mason said. He chuckled. "Or maybe it's a secret menu item that you have to know about. Only insiders get to have them."

I doubted the latter scenario but let it go. After the unfortunate beignet distraction, I needed to bring him back to my original concerns.

"Mason… this whole thing with my uncle is more than I can fathom right now. He was the sweetest guy. Had the biggest heart. The police are looking into the possibility of his death not being an accident… that someone wanted him dead."

His face fell. "They said that?"

"Yeah. The left rear of his car had collision damage."

"Couldn't it have been when he… the car hit the bottom of the harbor?"

"That's what they initially thought, but then they found silver paint that had been transferred from another vehicle."

He sat back, hard against his seat as if someone had shoved him.

"Wow, this changes everything."

"Yeah."

He lost interest in the beignets. His face suddenly lost color. "Damn it, that's not right."

"Right or wrong, it's what happened."

"Could the body damage have already been there?"

"Are you kidding? The way my uncle took care of his prized cars? They would have been in mint condition. If one needed work, he could have taken the other. He wouldn't have been caught dead—" Unfortunate choice of words. "—in public driving a car in less than pristine condition." That much I knew about Gray. At least I thought I did.

Clamping his mouth shut, Mason seemed reluctant to share his thoughts.

"What's the *why* here, Mason? Who would want to see him dead?"

His nostrils flared, and he seemed to be focusing on his breathing. I desperately wanted to smack him to get him to speak his mind. Finally he unlocked his jaw and shared his thoughts.

"This is not a professional opinion."

I couldn't imagine why it wouldn't be. He was an attorney, and he was offering his opinion. But if that was what he needed to say to feel comfortable, so be it.

"I'm just trying to rationalize what's happening. But I think anyone in the area with an inkling of what's going on would say what happened to your uncle had everything to do with—" He shook his head. "I shouldn't even say this out loud."

"Spit it out, Mason." I jammed the words through clenched teeth.

He pressed his eyes closed and ran his outstretched fingers across his forehead. He took a minute before he opened his eyes.

"It has to do with him publishing articles about a certain attorney. Accusing him of bilking his clients, among other things."

"That's it? There's nothing original about that. Just because he wrote a few articles about some local attorney who screwed his clients…"

"Yeah, well, it's *which* asshole attorney he wrote about that's the problem."

"Who did he write about?"

He took another sip from his glass and deposited it back on the table, knocking his oversized frame against the back of the chair again. "Gilbert Hayes."

"So? Who's he?"

"A very well-connected attorney. Not just well connected, he's notorious. Can make anything happen. A regular Teflon Joe. No matter what questionable activity he's involved in, nothing sticks to him. He's gone years with rumors of wrongdoing circling around him but never gets charged, much less end up in court. He and his previous firm have represented some shady clients, and few have ever seen any jail time."

Mason took a moment with an extended yet remarkably quiet exhale. I waited for him to continue but soon Scyler reappeared with our plates of duck hash and shrimp with grits, dumping them off with a couple of thuds on the weathered wood table.

"Thank you, Scyler," I offered, hoping to sound sincere, and received a backhanded wave in response as she walked away. I chose to believe it was a positive gesture.

"So you were saying… about Hayes."

"Hayes is a powerful guy. Not someone you want to tangle with. He's too well connected. I think your uncle may have gotten in over his head doing an investigative series on him."

A palm frond nodded in the breeze on the edge of the patio behind Mason, making my vision blur for a moment. "So you think Hayes went after Gray?"

He scoffed. "It wasn't Hayes. It had to have been someone he hired." He grabbed a fork and the plate in front of him. "Here, lets split the two plates so you can try both."

"How does he get away with something like that?"

He let out a subtle snort, and I sensed I was being naïve.

"So you said, 'He and his previous firm.' Where is he now?" I asked, trying to steer the conversation back to the facts.

Mason put down his fork. "Levinson & Levinson."

"Oh geez."

"That's not the worst of it."

"What is?" I hated to ask.

"He's my stepfather."

"What?" I leaned across the table toward him. "What the—" It was a lot to process. "When were you going to mention that? Seems like a huge conflict of interest or something along those lines."

"Until there was evidence your uncle's death wasn't an accident, there was no reason to put the two together."

Dropping his fork on the table, Mason seemed to have lost interest in the food in front of him. It couldn't have been his first realization his stepfather might have been connected, but it appeared to be hitting him hard.

It was for me. "So where is he now?" I didn't know what I would do with the information but needed to know.

"Well, that's the thing. No one knows where he is."

"What?"

"Right after Gray's third article came out, he went missing."

In spite of his notorious past, Gilbert Hayes had been hired by Levinson & Levinson, the firm who was on retainer with my uncle. Were they keeping their enemies close?

And what came as even more of a surprise was that Gilbert Hayes was also Mason's stepfather, his mother's husband. Never having met Mason's mother, I had no idea what she saw in Hayes or what motivation she would have had to bring him into her law firm. But anytime you introduced love into the equation, business could get convoluted. Could the situation get any more incestuous?

Now Hayes' whereabouts were unknown. Was he responsible for Gray's disappearance? The damning articles would certainly have given him motive. Or was that too obvious?

Unaware of what awaits her
She's walked into the throes of danger.
And who will protect her?
Surely not an uncaring stranger.

I watch her like a common stalker
From my seat behind the curtain.
She goes about her day unaware.
Of this, I must make certain.

Who am I to her but a crippled man
Hands aching and getting worse,
Body aging, a shameful mess,
To wither further with the curse.

# CHAPTER TWENTY

"You're an odd one, Kathryn. But I like you," Mason mused.

I grinned at how childish he sounded. He seemed to hear it too, but he reached over with his can of spiked seltzer and clinked mine with a dull thud.

Over bourbons one afternoon on the carriage house patio I'd burst into tears. Fueled by the 80-proof brown liquid, I'd felt hopelessly helpless to resolve my uncle's disappearance. It had clearly caught him by surprise. He awkwardly attempted to comfort me. A one-armed hug. A couple pats on the back. Desperate to calm me, he asked what I needed from him.

Between sobs, it spilled out I wouldn't rest until I'd searched the harbor for Gray. The officer from SLED had done his best to convince me he wouldn't have survived the car plunging into the water, even with his seatbelt engaged. Perhaps I'd partially accepted that as a possibility, that his body was still out there somewhere.

It took only a beat before Mason announced he'd get me out on the harbor. And plans were made.

We'd found a prime location on the top deck of the Carolina Belle for the ninety-minute tour of Charleston Harbor, joining a throng of tourists with overly exuberant offspring in tow. *Wait until they get to the history talk and the part about Fort Sumter, kids. It will be riveting!*

Leaning on the railing and gazing over the side, Mason probably wasn't on the lookout for anything in particular, but in all of my morbid thoughts, I searched for anything resembling Gray's body. He had to be out there somewhere. And while I hoped it wasn't in the harbor, I had to at least acknowledge the possibility. I could check it off the list. Plus, it gave me more time with Mason. Was I subconsciously playing the part of the damsel in distress? I hoped it didn't appear that way to him.

For the outing, he'd worn colored jeans in a dressy charcoal and replaced his usual linen jacket and button-down oxford with a sherbet-colored polo, the collar popped, of course, his biceps testing the elastic on the short sleeves.

As we chugged along at an excruciatingly slow pace—we could cover more ground at a faster speed, I reasoned—the captain narrated, recounting historical events and sharing anecdotes visitors from out-of-town would find interesting. The engine droned with a monotonous, sleep-inducing steady tone.

"Seeing how calm the harbor is it's almost hard to believe there's a tropical storm coming," said Mason.

"What?" I'd been so fixated on my uncle's whereabouts I'd thought of little else. "Really?"

He examined my face. "You didn't know? Well, you should be aware, especially since you're downtown… and south of Broad. That area is notorious for flooding—on a good day."

"Yeah, you mentioned that."

"So be forewarned. The forecasters aren't very good at getting it right. They don't know what the storm will do. I heard talk it might strengthen to a hurricane by the time it reaches Charleston."

"A hurricane?" I'd never experienced anything like that in New England.

"Yeah, but probably just a Cat 1. I've seen worse. And you're in a sturdy old girl who has endured much worse. You'll probably be fine."

Unsure how I should feel about his revelation, I refocused on scanning the water as we moved through it. I enjoyed the silence we shared until there wasn't.

"So how do you... know and see things others can't?"

I pressed my eyes shut. Tight. It was too much to share with others. *Why did we have to revisit it?*

A near drowning accident when I was barely eight left me terrified of water. Years later, claustrophobia joined the party and turned me into a neurotic mess at the right trigger. All it would take was traffic grinding to a halt on the highway, getting stuck in a line of cars at a red light, or the doors closing on a crowded elevator and getting wedged against the back wall. Forget about enduring an MRI. It wasn't going to happen. I'd rather take my chances with a misdiagnosed medical condition.

Stepping onto a plane would send panic rippling through my body. It took everything I had to walk down the jetway, step through the cabin door, shuffle down the aisle feeling trapped between fellow passengers taking their time stowing their carry-ons in the overheads, and flop into a seat, sweaty palms clutching my tote. The flight attendant's distant voice gently reminded me to place it under the seat in front of me and fasten my seatbelt. My body always stiffened at the sound of the forward cabin door slamming shut. The meds usually took the edge off so I could pass as a marginally nervous flyer but at times didn't kick in in time or just weren't enough. Overdosing posed a risk, particularly when traveling alone, so I tried to err on the side of caution, which often resulted in inadequate dosing.

During the flight attendant's safety spiel with the bright yellow toilet-seat shaped life preserver around her neck, I'd fight off images of the plane crashing into the ocean, water filling the cabin around me, and the jammed seat belt trapping me in the seat. Reflexively I usually reached under to locate the life jacket and ran my fingers back and forth across the tab to assure myself it was there. But it would be useless if I couldn't get out of my seatbelt. So much to think about. So much to stress over.

The unpredictability of the attacks and my adversity to constantly being on meds led to a roller coaster of anxiety levels and chasing the symptoms.

The drowning incident also seemed to unlock my ability to have visions—the rare ability to see places and happenings at a distance called remote viewing. They scared me so I did my best to block them. The meds I took for anxiety did nothing to quell the visions. If anything they enabled them.

At first I didn't understand what was going on and rationalized the images were daydreams or the result of an overactive imagination. After all, creative people's minds never really shut off, did they? Mine never seemed to.

But when the images I was seeing—like a fatal, multicar pileup on Boston's Zakim Bridge one icy winter day—showed up above the fold of the Boston Globe the next morning, it frightened me. I kept it to myself, afraid to tell anyone—especially my mother. *What did it mean? Could I see the future?* With that would come the unbearable responsibility of warning those in danger. In desperation, I Googled how to stop the visions from occurring but have been no more able to accomplish that than to keep Dorchester Bay from coming onto L Street Beach in South Boston at high tide.

"I don't mean to pry." Mason was still on topic. The protracted time it was taking me to answer his question did nothing to steer him off course. "I think it's an amazing talent."

"You wouldn't if you had it. It's more like a curse." My eyes were trained on the dark water below as we chugged through the harbor.

"Curse? Are you kidding? I'd love to be able to see what other people are doing without them knowing it. I could have used that to figure out my last girlfriend was cheating on me long before I caught them in our bed together."

That was an image I didn't need filling up my head. But it also meant he wasn't gay. I was surprised how relieved I was. It was as though I'd let out a breath I hadn't realized I was holding. Could his last girlfriend have been Scyler from Blind Tiger?

"I'm sorry that happened to you, but it's not that simple. You can't just turn it on and off. At least I can't. I know there are people who have trained themselves to be able to do that, but I never have. No desire for that. I'd love to be able to shut it off and have it go away for good."

"Wow. I think you're missing out on an opportunity here."

"Of course you do. You can only see the upside of it. It's exhausting viewing remotely. It takes everything out of me. And since I'm not trained, I don't always know what I'm looking at. So then I get stressed that there's someone I should be warning away from danger, but I have no idea how."

"Wouldn't that be an incentive to work at being able to have more control over it?"

"If you look at it from the other side, you have to think about whether you should meddle with fate."

"Fate?"

"Fate… or destiny… or the master plan if there's some master planner watching over us. If I step in to keep someone from encountering something he or she was supposed to encounter, I've screwed up the way things were supposed to work."

Mason listened intently. Our eyes met.

"Do you really believe all that crap you just spewed?"

And that was where I stopped trying to get him to see my side of it. He'd never understand.

"I don't know what I believe anymore."

"Do you at least keep track of them?"

I chuckled at the irony of keeping a log of something I'd rather forget. "Yes, I do. I have a notebook." I patted my pocket but was surprised it wasn't there. "I jot them down as soon as I have one so I can remember the details. They're like dreams. As time goes on, the details are more difficult to remember and are lost forever."

It was then I wondered for the first time if the act of committing the visions to paper cemented them in time, and if they hadn't occurred yet, they would. Did I have a hand in forming the future?

# CHAPTER TWENTY-ONE

"What's that?" I grabbed Mason's arm to divert his attention and pointed toward the water. "Look. There!"

"What… uh… looks like a stick to me."

"A stick? Are you sure?" But the more I stared at it, my brain settled into interpreting what I was seeing as part of a simple tree branch. "Okay. Yeah, I see it. Sorry."

"No worries." He settled back into his comfortable slouch over the railing. Anyone else with his hulking frame would have looked awkward in that position. Instead, he projected an air of suavity. And he made it look effortless. Was it his Southern upbringing? His mother had done a stellar job. I hoped to meet her one day soon.

While the captain narrated, spouting riveting facts about the fort and surrounding harbor, I kept my eyes focused on the water. At times I glanced to Mason looking bored, nose to his cell, his thumbs tapping in rapid fire. I supposed it could have been work related. I hated that he seemed so disinterested in where we were and what we were doing. I'd never want to be the reason for someone yawning.

As we slowed near the fort, I caught sight of something in the water. Long and sizable. Moving. Bobbing?

"Oh! That's it. Look there!" This time I yanked on his arm. "It's him." I was so sure of it I dashed to the stairs and descended them two at a time, nearly tripping over my feet at the bottom. Was Mason right behind me? I couldn't tell. Didn't matter. I headed to the same place we'd been standing along the railing, one deck below.

My uncle was still there. He seemed to go under and then resurface. "He needs help. Someone needs to help him," I said with urgency to anyone who would listen.

But no one along the railing seemed to be seeing what I was seeing. It had to be because they didn't know what they were looking at. They weren't expecting to see a person in the water. I was and I'd found him. The police just hadn't looked hard enough.

Tossing off my sweater, I grabbed the rail with both hands and swung my legs over. It took a couple seconds before I hit the water, long enough to hear that side of the boat erupt in shrieks and gasps. The cold was a shock to my body, but I fought it off. I needed to get to Gray.

My body was like a projectile going straight down. I kept going. How deep? I thrashed with my arms and legs to slow my descent. Was it working? I felt myself tumbling. Finally it all slowed enough for me to realize my dire situation. *What have you done, Kathryn?*

In the murky depths, I grew terrified. I was suddenly reliving my childhood scare. Underwater. Unable to breathe. Panic erupted. Which way was up? *Think Kathryn.* There's no one to pull you out this time. You're down deep. This is not a swimming pool. Which way is it? If you start swimming the wrong direction you'll make your situation worse. Then who will rescue Gray? And his heart will be broken if you die trying to save him. Think!

Fearing my body was on the verge of paralysis, desperate to take a breath, I looked around and realized the water below my feet looked lighter than in the direction I was heading. Sunlight was making it lighter. *Kathryn, swim toward the light.*

Struggling to turn my body around in the water, I became acutely aware of the fire in my lungs begging for air. Then something brushed against my leg. I screamed a scream only I could hear, losing what little oxygen was left in my lungs, and swam toward what I thought was the surface. It took forever. Thrusting both arms upward, cupping my hands, and pulling them down with everything I had. Gradually the light above me got brighter. My lungs burned deeper.

I resurfaced, gasping for air. Between fitful coughs I heard shouts of, "Man overboard! Man overboard!"

The breeze off the water hit me in the face and sent a chill through me. I shook off a shiver and started swimming toward where I'd seen Gray, which was away from the Carolina Belle.

The water seemed rougher than it had looked from up above. I wasn't making any progress. I kept reaching out as far as my arms would reach and pulled with deliberate strokes amid shouts from the boat.

Something hit the side of my head with a clunk. Asterisks exploded. I faltered and went under, sucking water into my nose and mouth. *What had happened? Was the boat running me over?* I resurfaced, coughing and sputtering. Within an arm's length was a white ring. It struck me that it was plastic. The black block letters on it spelled out Carolina Belle. A life preserver tethered to the boat with a white cord.

As my head started to clear, I could make out shouts to grab on. I treaded water and searched the horizon for what I'd seen from the top deck. It was impossible to see much from my vantage point at the water's surface. And after plunging into the chilly water and getting whacked on the head with the preserver, I couldn't be sure which direction I was looking. Had the boat turned around to reach me?

"Kathryn, grab the life preserver." It was Mason's voice. Shouting. "For God's sake, Kathryn. Grab it."

My body jolted. He sounded entirely too much like my mother when she was losing her patience with me. Was she somehow on the boat too? Had she gotten there in time to ridicule me again? God, I couldn't escape her.

I had to concede I wasn't getting anywhere—likely swimming in the wrong direction—and reached out for the preserver. Someone was going to have to help me. Surely Mason had seen what I'd seen. He would help. I needed to get to Uncle Gray.

Just as I got the preserver wedged snugly into the crook of my elbow, I got a glimpse of the throng of gawkers on both decks—adults and children. The closer they pulled me, the more their faces came into focus. Some were laughing. Others had a look of concern, compassion. But I couldn't escape the sea of cell phones capturing the moment to share with the rest of the world. Everyone could get a chuckle even if they were nowhere near Charleston, South Carolina. Nothing was private anymore. Everything was instantaneous and potential humor fodder for the multitudes of social media platforms at the expense of the innocent person at the center of it all. No wonder psychological issues were rampant. No mercy.

# CHAPTER TWENTY-TWO

THERE WERE PLENTY OF STRONG HANDS to pull me out of the water and back onto the boat. Plenty of spectators as well. I would have thought the captain should have been concerned the boat would list to that side.

I felt a heavy blanket drape around me. As if it was only then I realized how cold I was, my body began to shake uncontrollably. Mason wrapped an arm around my shoulders and guided me to a bench.

"Kathryn, what were you thinking?" he asked. "Can you even swim? You were underwater for so long.... You scared me. I was afraid—" He didn't finish. And it wasn't until later when I replayed the events on the boat that his comment resonated with me. I might have realized then if I hadn't been so focused on my uncle.

I turned to look into his eyes. "You saw what I saw, didn't you? Tell me you did." I pleaded with him.

"What did you see?" he asked. I detected a subtle but very real shake to his head.

"Uncle Gray. I don't know if he was swimming or his—" I hated to use the word "—his body was bobbing. Surely you saw it too."

He fell silent. "Sorry. No, I didn't. What you saw was—"

The captain was in my face but asking Mason if I was okay. After multiple assurances from both of us, he disappeared and the boat started moving again.

The rest of the passengers seemed much less boisterous than they'd been at the start of the trip. There was an unnatural stillness, a pause with anticipation of what was to come. Was it because of me? Or just that we'd completed the narrated part of the trip and were heading back to the dock? I embraced the latter.

As Mason tightened his one-armed grasp around my shoulders, I heard a low whirring sound. As I listened it got louder. Over my shoulder a red helicopter approached.

"The Coast Guard!" I announced.

Springing to my feet, I stepped on a corner of the blanket and lost my balance, careening with arms flailing. I could sense Mason grabbing for me, but he only managed to yank the blanket from my shoulders. Not very helpful. I fell in a heap with a hard thud. I was a bit stunned but refocused on the helicopter.

Mason grabbed hold of one elbow and pulled me to my feet.

"They saw Gray too. They're coming to pull him out."

He laughed but I sensed he wasn't amused. "Probably looking for you. I think they have to respond to all man overboard emergencies."

The helicopter hovered not too far from the boat, stirring up the water in a wide circle beneath it. *Woop, woop, woop.* I dashed to the railing, leaning over, arms waving, frantic for them to hear me and yelled, "That way. Go farther toward the fort."

"Jesus, Kathryn. They can't hear you." Again, he sounded too much like my mother. He stood behind me with the blanket draped over one arm, like a parent with a beach towel trying to get a belligerent child out of the pool.

One of the crew in his hunter green polo stood up from his position along the railing and approached us.

I spoke before he could. "Are they searching for the person I saw in the water?"

"What?" He looked to Mason and back to me again. "What person?"

"Kathryn, there was no one in the water besides you," Mason said to me, then turned to the crewman. "They're looking for her, aren't they? They're responding to her jumping overboard."

"No and no," he said, looking at each of us in turn as he answered our questions. "You out-of-towners do get funny ideas in your heads. The Coast Guard regularly holds drills in the harbor. I think it's as much for practice as it is for the tourists. They wouldn't have had time to launch the helicopter and get over here this quickly for you." Our eyes met.

"Drills? No, they need to go check out… I saw someone in the water back there," I insisted.

"They're here to drill," he repeated. "And if you two wanted to veer from the tour, you should have booked the private sunset cruise." He turned and headed off, presumably to return to his maritime duties.

I felt a tug on my arm. Mason led me back to a seat in the center of the boat, away from the railing, and wrapped the blanket around me again. My shivering grew uncontrollable. He adjusted it so it covered my head and wrapped both arms around me this time.

"I think this is your sweater." The young boy with sunburned cheeks was holding it out before I realized he was talking to me. As I took it from him, he said, "You scared away the dolphins. Why did you have to do that? I wanted to see them. That wasn't very nice, ma'am."

He walked away but not before creating a lump in my throat. *How selfish, Kathryn.*

Dolphins. Was that really what I saw? Perhaps everyone else was convinced of that. I wasn't sure I was.

Mason stayed quiet. Probably figured the boy had said everything that needed to be said.

# CHAPTER TWENTY-THREE

As the crew of the Carolina Belle tied up at the dock, we were asked to remain seated until the rest of the passengers had disembarked. I knew that wasn't a good sign.

My shivering had evolved to near convulsions. All I could think of was a hot bath, a pile of warm blankets, and a strong cup of Earl Grey. I supposed if Mason hung around for a while after bringing me back to the Pink Lady, I'd forgo the tea and head for the makeshift bar in the armoire. Time would tell if he was even speaking to me after my diving-off-the-boat-in-mid-tour spectacle.

From within the abrasive maritime blanket scratching my cheeks, I looked out to see two men in crisp white Coast Guard uniforms approaching. The one in front looked more like an accountant eager to embark on an end-of-year inventory with his diminutive frame and clipboard in hand, but his partner, towering behind him with dark features and thick torso, more than made up for the lead ensign's lack of stature. I felt Mason's arm loosen ever so slightly from around my shoulders. Even he was knocked slightly off his firm base at the sight of them.

Taking the lead, Mason stood with a hand raised to stop them before I realized the warmth of his arm had dissipated. The captain pulled up the rear and stopped short, eyes darting between the guardsmen, Mason, and the pathetic drowned rat on the bench.

I couldn't make out much after Mason said, "Gentlemen, I'm happy to help resolve this unfortunate situation." Nodding to me, he said, "This is my client."

The four men continued, their conversation muffled by the hum of the engine. At one point, Mason pulled out his wallet and produced his license. The man with the clipboard took it and made some notations. Mason must have explained my ID was locked in the trunk of his car. I had nothing on me.

As Mason presented my case, probably embellishing where necessary, he glanced back from time to time, as did the other men. I felt as though I was in a cage on display in an aviary—an odd bird, out of her element, just passing through but managed to get her wing tangled in unfamiliar brush.

As it turned out, Mason was successful in pleading my case, a clever attorney after all. And I never had to utter a word in my defense. Mason signed something on a clipboard held out to him, and the three men departed with one final pitying glance at me.

Mason had saved my butt. I owed him one. A big one, but I still needed to get back to finding Gray.

# CHAPTER TWENTY-FOUR

I don't really remember much from the ride back to the Pink Lady. I'd had to give up the blanket that belonged to the ferry, but Mason pulled a reasonable facsimile—actually a softer one—from his trunk along with my purse. I dry-swallowed a couple of my meds—maybe it was three or four. More than double the usual dose, but I figured I could use it. I hadn't meant to relive my childhood near-drowning scare, but that was exactly how it had turned out.

My head was fuzzy as I opened my eyes. I was on my side with my face half off the pillow. The room was dark. It didn't come to me right away where I was. There was a slight pressure and warmth against my back. As I shifted to roll over, I realized there was what felt like an arm across my abdomen that slipped off as I moved.

"Kathryn, you're awake." His voice was quiet but it still made me jump.

"Mason." It came out more like a shriek than I had intended. The sound served to clear my head, and I recognized we were in my bedroom in the carriage house. He scrambled off the bed. I was under the covers, my clothes still drenched and stuck to my skin. Exceedingly uncomfortable. A briny odor wafted from under the covers.

I sat up with the bedspread scrunched in my fists. He started talking fast.

"I didn't know what else to do. You'd fallen asleep in the car. I carried you in. It was all I could do to get you up the stairs and—oh, that didn't sound right. That wasn't what I meant." Even in the dim light he looked flustered. Not characteristic of him.

"Couldn't get you to wake up and change your clothes—and I certainly wasn't going to try to take them off—so I got you under the covers, but you were still shivering. I had to do something so I… I got on the bed with you—on top of the covers—and tried to keep you warm. You finally stopped shivering and then I guess I fell asleep."

How sweet. I tried to keep from grinning at the thought but wasn't even remotely successful. It made me even more fond of him. I felt safe with him.

"But nothing happened. I swear."

"So that's how a Southern gentleman handles this sort of situation?"

"Yes, ma'am." He took a step back from the bed and clasped his hands behind him as if they were in cuffs and could do no wrong. "Not that a gentleman finds himself in this situation very often, but yes."

"Please don't start with the yes ma'ams again."

He nodded. "Sorry. I didn't know what else to do," he repeated.

"Thank you. I appreciate what you did… and didn't do."

Looking awkward in his rumpled clothes that looked damp from his chivalrous deed, he said, "Why don't you grab a shower and some dry clothes. I'll go pick up some food."

Sounded like a fabulous plan to me. After he left, I peeled off my smelly, harbor soaked top and capris. It was only then I realized my shoes were missing. That was the least of my worries. I cranked up the shower and stood underneath it, soaking up the heat and breathing in the steam. Scrapes on my calves stung. My chest felt sore. Guess that was what happened when you deprived your lungs of oxygen for an inordinate amount of time. *"God, it's a miracle I didn't drown,"* I said to no one.

Then I had an intriguing thought. If Gray had passed—and I wasn't willing to acquiesce on that notion just yet—but *if* he had, perhaps he was there today… in the harbor… guiding me to safety. It was oddly comforting, given my aversion to believing he was gone. But I was sure he would have if that were the scenario.

I put a couple extra layers on to keep the chill away, changed the sheets and blanket on the bed, leaving the wet ones in a pile for another day, and headed downstairs to the tantalizing aroma of barbecue. Mason had arrived and was setting out a feast on the coffee table. It didn't hit me until then how famished I was.

"This is incredible, Mason. Thanks for picking it up."

"It's one of my favorite barbecue places. I love having a reason to go there."

"Glad I could be your reason." I surveyed the spread. "Looks delicious. I think I recognize most of it: ribs, coleslaw, potato salad, mac and cheese… oh, and cornbread. Is that pulled pork?"

"Yeah," he said and scooted to get closer from the sofa, pointing out the rest. "And brisket, collard greens, pickled onions…" He poked his head in the bag everything had come in. "And don't forget dessert." He pulled out two small plastic containers with spoons and held them up. "Banana pudding." He grinned. Clearly one of his favorites.

"This is quite a spread. More than enough for the two of us."

"I wanted you to be able to have a taste of it all. Barbecue is one of those things that every chef has their own take on—like shrimp and grits—and you have to try a few before deciding your favorite."

Then I noticed the two glasses. Bourbon neat. Either I was out of ice or I'd graduated to serious Bourbon drinking. Either way, I got the impression he'd set those out first before the food.

"Let's dig in." He lifted the two glasses and handed one to me. "Here's to both of us safely back on dry land again."

"Cheers." We clinked rims. I didn't dare laugh. It was clear he hadn't meant for it to be humorous.

Once we'd devoured an embarrassing amount of barbecue and sides, we settled in for a second bourbon and what I knew would be a serious chat.

Turned out, after my unscheduled swim in Charleston Harbor, I was facing some sobering charges. Could have been arrested and escorted away as soon as we returned to port. Tens of thousands of dollars in fines. I tried to envision how uncomfortable the handcuffs would have felt on my wrists. Then I thought of my mother. Surely she would have found out. Her backlash would have been far worse than anything the Coast Guard could have doled out.

Mason described me to the guardsmen and captain as distraught over recently losing a family member. Wasn't thinking clearly. He would take complete responsibility for getting me home, finding the appropriate mental health assistance.

After hearing the sorry story Mason had spun on my behalf, which sadly contained little embellishment, the captain wasn't interested in pursuing charges against me. He had to file a report though and had the option of describing what happened as an accident. An overzealous tourist anxious to get a closer look at the dolphins would work. There was probably less paperwork if it was handled that way.

"I'm sorry," I offered after he'd filled in the blanks for me. It pained me to have put him through the exercise with the authorities. But he'd done it, which said a lot.

"Kathryn, what were you thinking?" Before I could answer, he said, "Your uncle—his body—is not in the harbor. They would have found it by now. It would have washed up somewhere like the other body."

"Then where is it? The other man's body showed up."

He hesitated, then said, "At this point, it probably made its way to the open ocean. I hate to be so blunt. But you just don't seem to get it. It's not going to show up. It's gone. He's gone."

I didn't agree, but it served no purpose to argue with him. I'd already angered him, and I needed him on my side. But how was I supposed to accept my uncle's death if there was no body? Everyone else seemed to be able to very easily. Not I.

Besides, if I conceded Gray's body was out in the ocean, it would conjure up images of sharks tearing it to pieces, devouring his flesh, fighting each other over it. No, that was entirely too ghastly to picture. It didn't happen. And it wasn't going to.

"I'm sorry. I was certain I saw Gray. It seemed to be the right size as a man's body. Long too."

"You're not hearing me. It wasn't him. And you won't find him there. You need to drop it before you get yourself—and anyone else within range—into any more trouble."

"I'm sorry," I tried again. "I didn't mean to put you on the spot like that."

"Well, you did. I signed the report and now my ass is on the line. And I saved yours."

"And I appreciate it. I owe you."

"Be careful, Kathryn. Payback can be rough."

I had a feeling I was going to learn that soon and regret it.

# CHAPTER TWENTY-FIVE

Lifting my head from the arm of the couch, I took a moment to grasp my surroundings. The carriage house. Uncle Gray's monstrosity of a house—a manor—looming nearby. Bolting upright, I grabbed my cell vibrating next to my feet on the coffee table.

"Yeah." There was more than a hint of scratchiness to my voice.

"Whoa. Rough night, sis?"

My feet hit the floor with a dull thud. "Delaney." It was more of a verbal smack in the face for my own benefit—get alert fast—than a greeting.

My little sister always put me on edge. Delaney had an annoying way of making me feel grossly inadequate. It wasn't anything in particular she said. All she had to do was be Delaney. Pretty. Thin. Confident. Successful. Delaney.

"Yeah, that's what the caller ID said, I bet. What's going on Kat?"

I clenched my jaw. My sister had picked up on the ridiculous nickname our mother had invented for me.

"What's going on? Not much. Just taking care of things down here."

"So what's it like?"

"Gray's house? Charleston?" I thought it odd that children brought up in a family with means had never traveled to the South. Europe?

Yes. Charming Charleston and the stunning Lowcountry of South Carolina? No.

"Both."

"Well, the house is pretty cool. A lot larger than I expected. The views are amazing out to the harbor. Even the carriage house is charming. I could live there quite comfort—"

"Carriage house. How big is the property?"

I dug my teeth into my lower lip. Delaney was a conduit to our mother. Everything she heard got passed along at breakneck speed.

"You know, it's an old house. That was just the way they built them back then." I hoped my hedge would be enough to repress further questions about the property. "Charleston is amazing though. You should see it." *Should she? Careful Kathryn. She might take you up on it and show up on your doorstep looking for a personal tour.* "The cobblestone streets. Horse drawn carriages. Flickering gas lanterns. Intricately forged wrought iron gates."

"Sounds so romantic."

"I guess it is." I had begun to think of it that way, and it seemed to fit. Or was it Mason who was making it feel romantic?

"And the food. Shrimp and grits."

"Yuck," Delaney protested.

"No, really. You should try it." *Careful, there you go again.* "The fried chicken and biscuits. Seems like everything is chicken fried. And the beignets. Those are to die for."

"Oooh, careful Kat. You don't want to have to ask for a seatbelt extension on your flight back."

"Nice, Delaney. You sound like Mom when you say things like that."

"We're hoping you'll listen to one of us."

Jesus. Who needed enemies when you had a mother and sister to gang up on you. It wasn't like I was obese. Not even close. Just a few extra pounds that I didn't care enough to do anything about. I didn't do spin class every other day like them and suffer through intermittent fasting like they did so I could don a pair of leggings to run errands.

"Just kidding, kiddo. But seriously, speaking of Mom, she's getting worked up about you being down there so long. What's up with that?"

"What does she expect? It's not so straightforward."

"Okay, well, I thought I'd give you a heads up."

"Thanks for that. Let me ask you something."

"Shoot."

"Don't you think it's a little odd that Uncle Gray left his"—I stopped short of calling it a mansion—"house to me?"

The harrumph that came from the other end of the line sounded more like a gruff scoff. "Are you kidding? Odd doesn't begin to describe it. Dad isn't saying much but—"

"Dad's still shaken over his brother's death."

"Nah, I don't know about that. Maybe. He's never been one to share his emotions. But Mom is pissed."

"Pissed. About what?" I asked, but it seemed to get drowned out by another voice on Delany's end.

"Yeah…" She shared a laugh with someone else. "Peyton says Mom is so pissed she's on the verge of chewing her fingernails."

"You and I both know that's not going to happen." Our brother rarely contributed anything of importance to a conversation.

"I know. But you get the idea."

"So what is she so pissed about?" I tried again.

"Why you?"

"Why did I get Gray's house… and not her?" I asked.

"No… just… why not bequeath it to Dad or the family as a whole."

I'd asked myself the same question and hadn't arrived at a reasonable answer.

"I mean, I know you were close. Probably closer than anyone else in the family."

"Without a doubt," I spoke up. I loved Gray and had a connection with him that was tighter than anyone else's.

"There's still the matter of blood relations," Delaney continued.

"Blood relations? What the hell does that mean? We're all related by blood."

"Well, technically Mom isn't."

"Exactly, and I am," I said. "So why is she getting so bent out of shape about it?"

There was a pause. I'd backed my sister into a familiar corner with her usual faulty logic. Delaney often got so caught up with our mother's ridiculous rants she didn't stop to think through if they made sense. It probably wouldn't matter. She'd still take Posh's emotionally charged side. None of it made sense to me. My entire crazy family didn't make sense.

"You know Mom," Delaney finally came back with. "She can go off. It gets scary sometimes."

"Scary. What are you talking about?" Was I so detached from my mother there was more to her than met the eye?

"She doesn't let you see that side of her. But this thing with Uncle Gray has pushed her to the edge."

"Do you think it's just her twisted way of coping with the loss?"

"I don't think she's all that broken up about him dying."

"How crass," I murmured.

"Mom never was close to him. Not that I remember anyway."

"That doesn't mean she's not sad. She may show it in a different way." My words sounded silly, but I needed Delaney to think I wasn't throwing our mother under the bus, even if I'd been considering it.

"Like when she heard his death was ruled suspicious... saying someone had beat her to it?"

"Oh, Delaney. There's no way. That's just crazy talk. She didn't mean it." I had to cast doubt on its meaning while talking with Delaney, but it added fuel to the fire—the viability of Posh following through on her threats—already smoldering in my mind.

"You know how she is when things don't go her way."

Maybe I didn't. Could our mother have meant it? Where was her anger toward Gray coming from? What had happened in their past?

# CHAPTER TWENTY-SIX

It started out as a lightheadedness, but I knew it would become more than that. I rubbed my eyes with one hand while locating the nearest place to safely plunk down my backside. The flickering along the edges crept in like a stealth jet crossing enemy borders—streaking across, delivering searing pain before you realized it was already past you.

I was in a car. The passenger seat. Mason's Jag. His hands clutched the steering wheel. He was sitting forward as if anxious to get where he was going. The details were remarkably vivid, unlike what I usually saw.

The ride from downtown took us across the iconic Ravenel Bridge and through Mt. Pleasant with retail and restaurants on both sides. He never turned off. We were passing through. Where was he heading?

As he changed lanes to enter an entrance ramp my vision started to fade. I was losing my connection. Was this happening live? No! *Stay with it. Focus.* I'd never tried to reconnect before, but I felt this was what I needed to do.

I struggled for a while. *Breathe. Focus.* Imagined myself back in his car. Gradually I noticed blurry movement, and it grew clear again. I realized I was watching from outside the car as he pulled up to a sprawling house with a meticulously landscaped yard and a wraparound piazza that went on forever.

Mason left his Jag in the circular drive behind another car and rapped hard on the front door. I caught up to him again and was standing to his side. When there was no answer, he tried the door and slipped in, not noticing me staying close to him. White begonias with deep green leaves in a generous vase filled the entryway. I noticed I couldn't smell their sticky sweet aroma.

He headed into the kitchen but no one was there—only a light pink flowered teacup and matching saucer with a teabag steeping in it sat on the granite counter. A demitasse spoon and a jar of honey waited next to it.

Passing through the kitchen, he entered a narrow hallway.

Mason grabbed onto the first door jamb and poked his head in. He appeared to say something, but I couldn't hear his words.

I could sense someone else deeper in the room, but Mason didn't take his eyes off a sizable mahogany desk in the middle.

A woman was slumped in the chair, her head tilted at an uncomfortable angle and resting on her shoulder. His mother? Mason stepped farther into the room. I moved with him. A man stood with his arms at his side, a pistol dangling from one hand.

Lunging toward the woman, Mason took her limp hands in his.

Behind him, the man spit words through clenched teeth.

Mason ignored him.

I couldn't take my focus off the woman. Her eyes shut. Not moving or looking like she might. A dark stain the size of a man's fist interrupted the swirly pattern on the front of her navy and burgundy print blouse. It was then I noticed the entry wound, nearly camouflaged by the large, stylized pattern.

Scooping her up from behind her shoulders with long, strong arms,

Mason pulled her to his chest. He rocked her limp body gently. He had to feel the man's eyes and remember he was holding a gun.

Laying his mother gently back in her chair, Mason whipped around to confront the man. He pulled his own pistol from the holster inside his jacket and aimed it at him. The man shrank away, putting his hands out in front of him.

They seemed to exchange words. Mason wagged the pistol as he grew more agitated. Who was the man?

Glancing back to his mother, reaching for her again, Mason picked up her limp hand from her lap and leaned against the side of the desk.

The two men exchanged more words. Both seemed to be shouting.

The room went black. Two silhouettes formed by the ambient light spilling in from the hall. Indiscernible movement. Three shots. They were the first sounds that penetrated the veil of the vision. It sounded as though someone went down. At least one of the shots had to have reached its target.

Gasping for air on reentry, I came out of it with a jolt.

Was my vision in real time? Who was shot? Please let Mason be all right. Did he shoot the other man?

My gut ached. It couldn't have ended well.

THE KNOCK MADE ME JUMP. I wasn't expecting anyone, and I was still shaken from my last vision with Mason. It had felt so real. I hoped it didn't materialize.

It was well after sunset and the carriage house was bathed in shadows from the grand oaks in the yard. No moonlight could penetrate the thick foliage and the flickering gas lanterns next to the front door gave out no discernible light—merely ambiance. A quaint ambiance I loved, but not very useful.

Peeking through the curtain on the side window, I recognized Mason's stocky frame and yanked open the door. I needed to play it cool. I had no idea if what I'd just witnessed had happened yet and prayed it never did.

Sucking in a quick breath and letting it out slowly to signal to my body to release the pent up tension, I pulled open the door. I decided to take a humorous approach.

"I thought Southern gentlemen were supposed to call before dropping by for—" Then I noticed his ashen face and swollen red eyes. I couldn't tell if it had been a physical fight he'd been in, but he'd taken a beating, for sure. I saw what looked like dried blood on his shirt. "Mason, what happened? Is this your blood?" *Don't let it be his mother's.*

He didn't speak at first, so I guided him to the sofa and slipped a bourbon on ice in his hand. Reflexively he drank but stared at the pattern in the rug. I grabbed one for myself, sat on the edge of the wingback chair as near to him as I dared without touching, and waited for him to come around. He'd been through some sort of trauma. Hopefully lubricated with a few sips of Woodford Reserve, he'd be able to converse.

Eventually he looked up.

"It's all a blur. I've been driving around. I don't know how long. Trying to make sense of it. At times, I wonder if it actually happened. Then I look at the blood on my shirt. My mother's blood."

"Oh my God. What happened to your mother?" I was afraid I already knew the truth.

Even with the whiskey lubrication, I couldn't get him to spill.

His voice was low. "No, Kathryn. I can't say. It's best that way. The less you know, the better." Then he added, as if talking to himself, "I threw the gun out the window once I got on the Ravenel so it's as if nothing happened."

Silly talk from an otherwise rational, logical, sharp attorney.

"What? You don't think they'll find it?"

He suddenly became quite lucid as he said, "If they can't find your uncle I don't think they're going to find my gun."

I remained silent. He'd made an excruciatingly painful point, but I wasn't going to engage in a discussion over it.

"Okay, point taken. So do you think there were any witnesses?"

He shook his head. "I don't know. I don't think so. I hope not. But I don't really know. I don't really remember leaving. I don't remember driving here."

"Leaving where?"

He shook his head. I wasn't going to catch him up that easily.

"Should you call the police?" Did I really want to know? Get involved? "How about an ambulance?"

"How can I? I'd be admitting—at a minimum—I left the scene of a crime. But I also could be implicated for—" He stopped short before revealing too much—although I could guess. Could he have shot the other man?

"I need to go back."

"Why don't you call the police?"

"And say what… No, I need to go back first… to see what the scene is. Then I can bring them in."

"When you left, what did it look like?"

Mason still wasn't going to get sucked in with my feeble attempt to get more info. But it seemed as though he hadn't heard my question.

"It wouldn't take even a rookie cop long to figure out who had the stronger motive."

"All right. Let's talk this through." I was no expert in crime scene investigations, but I was the only one he had to help him think clearly at the moment. "Stop by your office. Put your empty holster in your desk drawer. That way it looks like someone took the gun to frame you."

"Okay… wait. He had a gun."

"Right… well at least it will look like yours was stolen. Do you know if the gun he used was his?"

"I'd have no way of knowing."

I felt like my questions were taking him in a circle. It was how I wrote too. All over the place. There I was, in my uncle's carriage house, coaching a man on his next move based on my as yet unsuccessful novel writing and the research that went into it—a man who could very likely be arrested for manslaughter in the next few hours.

Guns. What a crazy place, the South. Everyone carried a gun. Like the Wild, Wild West.

"Chances are—if this was premeditated—Hayes got the gun from somewhere else so it couldn't be tied to him."

"So we are talking about Hayes."

His eyes met mine with the realization he'd slipped.

"But what if it wasn't premeditated? What if they got into an argument and he pulled the gun on her in a moment of extreme and violent passion?"

"Then he would have used his gun and the ballistics will match. He'll be nailed."

"And you shot him?"

Setting his glass on the arm of the sofa, he considered my question.

"I assume so. I thought he went down. I left to let him bleed out, die a slow death. Perfect."

I didn't like the way he was talking or the look in his eyes.

"The bullet you shot him with can't be traced to you because your gun is missing."

Staring at the rug again, he said, "He kept saying it wasn't what it looked like. I wouldn't let him talk. I was so sick and tired of hearing his voice over the years I just wanted him to shut up. I *hated* seeing him with my mother. *Hated it.*"

"It would be best if you kept that hatred to yourself. You don't need to provide them with a motive and make this a slam dunk case for the DA."

He nodded and returned to sipping his bourbon.

"Okay, I think I like your idea of heading back over to your mother's house just like you did earlier."

He knocked back the last of his bourbon.

"Where does she live?"

"Daniel Island."

"Call her a few times on the way like you're desperate to reach her. Make your first call now. Retrace your steps. Only this time when you get to the house call 911."

"I don't know that I can."

"Yes, you can. You didn't do anything wrong." *At least not here in South Carolina where everyone is carrying.* "You went to check on your mother, and Hayes pulled a gun on you. You defended yourself." I hoped what I was telling him to do was right because it sounded like I was talking him into it. He had to do something to make it look like he was innocent. He'd simply gotten caught up in the moment.

"I don't know... I don't know that I can see her like that again."

Deep down I knew I would regret my next four words, but he needed a friend right now. "I'll go with you."

His face lightened ever so slightly and he thanked me softly.

"But first we need to get you a new shirt."

"Why? It's my mother's blood."

"Yes, but it's dried. It will give you away when the cops come."

# CHAPTER TWENTY-EIGHT

At his apartment, he lent me a baseball cap he'd scrounged from under the seat, and I ran in, in case there were security cameras the cops could pull from to check the timing of his movements. Surprisingly he didn't hesitate to hand me the key to his place but then again he was probably still in shock. Certainly desperate.

The other surprise was how close he lived to the Pink Lady. His apartment was one of four above a gin bar and was well within walking distance. The outdoor tables of the bar were full. The Edison lights strung across the space in a random zig zag gave it a festive feel that seemed incongruous to the bloody mess Mason and I would be contending with that evening.

"Call your mother while I'm gone," I instructed as I exited his Jag.

I slipped into a compact elevator to head to the second floor but vowed to find the stairs for the return trip. The doors hadn't opened as promptly as I'd expected them to, and I found myself fighting off my anxiety, my breathing quickening. Tight spaces and I rarely got along.

When I slid the key into the lock and turned the knob, I felt a tingle slither throughout my body. There was something about slipping into

Mason's apartment unescorted. What would I find? How did he live? Would I be disgusted at his mess or seduced by the décor?

Expecting something along the lines of college dorm grunge, I was stunned to walk into a meticulously maintained space with modern furnishings and unique lighting. It even smelled good, as if he'd been burning two candles simultaneously: clean linen and woodsy knoll. The colorful and unusual artwork distracted me from my task at hand as I strolled through his open-concept living room—or was I procrastinating? It felt as though I was in a Beacon Hill art gallery with an impressively well curated collection of modern art pieces. Who wouldn't want to spend time absorbing it all? I was getting to know Mason in a sneaky sort of way and enjoying it thoroughly.

Offering to accompany him back to his mother's house blurred the line between friendship and being an accessory to a crime. Would I be able to claim he was my attorney, and I was merely listening to his direction? *For God's sake, Kathryn, that's ridiculously lame. You'll have to do better than that.*

Crossing the threshold into his bedroom made my stomach lurch. I seemed to be treading where I was forbidden, which was entirely enticing. I couldn't resist running a hand across the end of his comforter, a dark colored geometric print, and then sitting on the corner of the bed. My body tingled as I imagined being under the covers with him. We had gotten close once after the mishap on the ferry, but it wasn't under the right circumstances. In the shadows of the room lit by a single bedside lamp, I could feel my face flush.

Knowing he couldn't walk in on me and risk being seen on cameras in a blood stained shirt, I pulled down a corner of the comforter and got in to satisfy my curiosity. I took in his smell. It was so exhilarating I lay there for a moment, warming my side of the bed. Or was it his?

A voice in my head scolded that I took procrastinating to a whole new level. I'd trespassed long enough so I reluctantly slipped out, tucked the corner back where I'd found it, and grabbed a smart-looking button-down and khakis hanging in a neatly arranged closet. Scooping up a pair of loafers to complete his dressy casual ensemble, I headed for the door.

I'd had him wash his hands and arms thoroughly at the carriage house. Hopefully with a fresh set of clothes, there would be no gunshot residue for the police to find.

When I returned, he didn't ask what had taken me so long, but I could sense it was hovering on his lips.

"Nice place," I said after settling back into the car with my armload of clothes.

"Thanks. It suits me… for now." Clearly he had grander aspirations. Perhaps he needed a place more fitting to his ride.

"Here's your change of clothes. I brought you a complete outfit. Take off the ones you're wearing first. Here, I brought some wipes for you to use." I pulled the container out of my tote. "Then put on the clean clothes."

Averting my eyes as he changed in the car, I watched a group of twenty somethings strolling into the bar, seemingly carefree and out for a fun evening. How I longed to join them. I pictured Mason and me walking in behind them—anywhere but where we were heading.

Once Mason had changed, I shoved his Sperry's and pants into the bottom of my tote for safekeeping. After folding his soiled shirt in on itself to conceal the blood stain, I held the bundle for a moment, still warm from being on his body, before jamming it in the bag. *Kathryn, your actions are approaching twisted. Rein it in. You could be getting into bed with a gun-carrying man who may have just killed a man. You don't know the circumstances during which it all went down. So don't be fantasizing about actually getting into bed with him.*

Next stop was his office. He took care of dropping off his holster, out of sight of cameras under his jacket. He looked the same on the way out as he had on the way in, except for the file he'd grabbed for good measure.

On the ride to his mother's, while Mason made another call to her cell, I thought about my role in the bloody mess. Mason had involved me just by showing up on my doorstep. But then I took it upon myself to provide unsolicited guidance on how to handle it. *Did I think I was in the throes of writing my next murder mystery?* Now involved nearly as intimately as Bonnie Parker with her accomplice Clyde Barrow, I thought I could at least summon my best horror movie scream at the appropriate moment for the benefit of the neighbors.

We got stuck at more traffic lights than I knew existed on the straight shot through Mt. Pleasant so I got him talking to keep him calm. "Is this the house you grew up in?"

It took him a moment to realize I'd asked the question.

"Uh… no. We were over in West Ashley." He let out an abbreviated laugh. "Much more modest than this one." His gaze was a long way off. "Hayes insisted they build it before they got married. Six thousand square feet on two building lots. In-ground pool. Pool house. Tennis court. Unobstructed marsh view. Hardly cozy. More of a statement of their success with all the trappings to go with it."

"So you don't consider this home," I asked but knew what his response would be.

"No." His answer was terse, which he underscored by shaking his head. Certainly understandable if Hayes had insisted they build it. "But my mother seemed to enjoy it."

"Do you visit very often? Holidays?"

"Yeah, I do head out for holidays. Dinners, usually. The occasional party I get invited to. But no, it's not my home. And I don't walk in. I always knock. The damn doorbell is so ostentatious with its loud clanging that goes on forever, I refuse to use it." He paused as if listening to it in his head. "So obnoxious."

As soon as we took the Daniel Island exit off I526 the charm of the island became obvious. Grand oaks draped with scraggly Spanish moss framed the road in and a golf course ran alongside. Long-necked great blue herons and bright white egrets intent on fishing among the reeds along the edges of ponds couldn't be bothered to turn their heads to watch us pass.

Impeccably landscaped grand homes were meticulously maintained, giving the island a Disney-esque appearance. It was the kind of place that felt encapsulated inside a safe bubble—where kids could ride their bikes to school and dog parents could walk their furry babies after dark—but the bubble could be popped at any time, revealing the vulnerability that was there all along, the false sense of security obliterated. Earlier that day, Gilbert Hayes had delivered the pin to pop it.

At least that was what Mason wanted the world to think. Was he fooling me along with everyone else?

As we neared his mother's house we could see the lights. Blue flashing. Mason wouldn't have to see his mother like he was dreading, but he'd have to dig deep to come up with an Oscar worthy performance portraying he was shocked at the news.

Mason let out a soft groan. Someone had discovered the crime scene. A nosy neighbor?

We pulled into the drive as far as the yellow tape would allow. A shiver rippled through me. We weren't stepping onto the set of a popular television show. This was the real thing. And I'd gotten sucked into it.

Even under the circumstances I was struck by his mother's grand home. It was much like you would see on the peninsula, south of Broad. Flickering gas lanterns. A welcoming arms staircase up to the front piazza. It was much grander in person than my fuzzy vision.

Mason stepped out first to meet an officer already closing the distance between them. I got out in time to see them greet each other as if they'd crossed paths before, which made sense. The jobs of the police and attorneys often intersected. The encounters and the relationships weren't always positive, but this one seemed to be—at least in initial appearances.

"What's going on? Where's my mother?"

"Mason, I'm afraid I have some devastating news."

Keeping his voice even, Mason said, "What happened? Please don't tell me it's my mother. Is she all right?"

"I'm sorry, man." The officer paused, appearing to struggle sharing the news. I imagined it was one of the worst parts of his job. And it had to be even harder to tell someone he knew. "It's your mom. Ellen. There was a break-in and she was shot. She didn't make it. She was gone when the paramedics got here."

Mason's knees buckled as if he were hearing it for the first time. Clearly no acting was required for him to confront his mother's death so soon after his initial encounter. I ran around the car to attend to him. He was pulling himself up by the door handle.

"She's gone… a break-in… can I see her? I need to talk to her." He was doing a good job of rambling senselessly. It seemed genuine.

"No, I'm sorry. You can't go in. Forensics needs to process the scene."

Mason stood rigid, his hand braced against the hood of the Jag. He stared straight ahead.

The officer continued. "Your father was with her when—"

"My father?" Mason lurched at the mention of him.

"Uh… I'm sorry. Your stepfather," the officer corrected himself.

"Hayes? He's resurfaced? What was he doing here?"

I cringed that his tone was tinged with anger.

"He's married to your mother. Correct?"

At that point I thought it best to step in and layer in a brushstroke of naivety. Latching on to Mason's elbow, I said, "Officer, this is a horrible tragedy. Just horrible." I looked up into Mason's face. "He's got to be in shock right now. Give him some time."

"I'm afraid that's not possible. He needs to come in for questioning."

"Surely that can wait," I gently pleaded.

The officer clamped his lips together so tightly they almost disappeared. "In spite of his injury, Hayes was able to call 911 and told us it was you, Mason, who shot him." He had the cuffs off his hip and snapped around the young, shell-shocked attorney's wrists in no time.

So Hayes had gotten shot but it wasn't fatal. He'd lived to point the finger at Mason. Two different guns would have been used during their encounter, but one had little chance of being recovered. It would be one man's word against the other.

I watched as Mason folded himself into the backseat of the cruiser, no small feat for a man his size. Just as the officer slammed the door, I noticed the security cameras on the eaves, pointing toward the front door.

That changed everything. Mason's situation suddenly looked ominous. His comings and goings that evening surely would have been documented.

I needed to do my best to distance myself from him.

# CHAPTER TWENTY-NINE

The Uber ride back to the Pink Lady, with a tote full of evidence on the seat next to me, was a somber one. Fortunately the driver had no intention of making small talk. My head was buzzing.

Mason had been handcuffed, whisked away under suspicion of shooting Gilbert Hayes, and hauled into the Charleston Police Department, his fate unknown. Hayes lay in a hospital somewhere, his condition unknown but still alive, which complicated the situation. And I'd ridden up to the crime scene with the gun-wielding attorney who was their prime suspect in his shooting.

No one could accuse me of a mundane existence anymore. But I didn't think this was what my mother had had in mind when she'd said, "Kat, do something interesting in your life for once. Take a risk. Live a little. Make a little history for yourself. You know what they say, well-behaved women rarely make history." I'm sure she'd be proud.

Depending on Hayes' level of consciousness, he may have already spun a tightly woven account of Mason walking in on his mother and stepfather, becoming enraged, pulling his gun and shooting Hayes, and then using Hayes' gun to shoot his mother. Or some other twisted tale that would take himself out of the hot seat as a suspect.

It didn't look good for Mason. And it didn't look good for me. What reason would I have had to be with him? What would I tell the police when they asked? Surely they would.

I had to trust Mason knew enough to request an attorney. What choice did he have? Sounded like self-defense to me. But legal matters weren't my forte, and I was entirely too deep into the situation for my liking.

As we approached the bridge I thought of two intersecting, yet unconnected, events that had occurred there. My uncle's car hurtling over the edge and Mason disposing of the gun he'd shot Hayes with. Both could have happened in the exact same spot. Both Gray and Mason were heading the same direction on the bridge—southbound toward downtown. One individual made it back to the grand Pink Lady. The other did not.

I noticed the beat-up blue car across the street before the Uber pulled up. No one was in it. Instead, I found Stella sitting in a rocker on the piazza. She bolted out of it before we came to a stop in the driveway.

"I've been calling and calling you." She was in my face with jagged breathing before I was out of the car. "Texting and texting. . . where have you been? The shit has hit the fan at the office, and no one's talking. I gotta hunch you might be in the middle of it. You *and* your uncle."

Calling and texting? I glanced at my phone and an impressive list of texts and missed calls. A record for me. Must have had the sound down too low to hear. That and I'd been a bit preoccupied with aiding and abetting a criminal.

Stepping back to make room to shut the door and put distance between us, I nudged her with my elbow.

"Yo! Don't be shoving me, girl. You don't know who—"

"Stella, give it a rest." I raised my palm. "And give me some space."

The Uber pulled out, undoubtedly happy to put what appeared to be two squabbling females in his rearview.

Heading for the carriage house, I could feel Stella on my heels.

"Don't you walk away from me, girl. You better start talking."

*For God's sake, if I wanted to be berated and verbally abused, I could call my mother.*

Annalee was bent over, busy working in the garden again—this time by the light of a floodlight in the corner of the yard. Incredibly dedicated. She stood up and adjusted her wide-brimmed sunhat long enough for me to catch her eye and wave to her. It was impressive how very generous she was with her time. My guilt was mounting with each of her visits, but I would be of no help to her. I didn't know the first thing about it. Gardening was not something our family did. We always had landscape designers and gardeners.

My mother had been the president of her garden club for years, but I don't think a one of them had lifted a trowel or gotten peat moss under their fingernails. They were more along the lines of garden *admirers.* Their monthly meetings were field trips to the gardens of such destinations as the Isabella Stewart Gardner Museum, the Arnold Arboretum of Harvard, and the Newport mansions. On occasion they'd take turns hosting tea to show off their own gardeners' talents. In the winter months, they'd meet to discuss—argue might be a better word for it—the upcoming itinerary. As they say, first world problems.

Annalee was cut from an entirely different cloth. Down to earth. Not afraid to get her hands dirty. Appreciated the gardens of the Pink Lady. I'd have to remember to do something for Annalee in return. A flower arrangement? Homemade cookies? It certainly would just be a token of my appreciation. I could never repay her for all the time she was devoting. Sweet soul.

As I reached the door of the quaint B&B, I noticed something in my peripheral. Something that hadn't been on the bistro table out front before. A small flat light-blue box and a sizable spiral bound pad of paper. Taking a step closer I could see it was pastels and drawing paper. Both were still wrapped in plastic, never before used. Something inside stirred. I wanted to rip them open and get elbow deep in pastel dust.

Scanning the yard, I was perplexed as to who would have left them there. Had someone been inspired to draw the old Pink Lady or the carriage house but had had to step away for a moment before getting started?

Intrigued by their sudden arrival, I left them where they lay. If they were still there tomorrow, then they were meant for me, I decided.

There were more pressing matters to contend with. Getting Stella off my back.

Unlocking the door, I was painfully aware she wasn't going anywhere until I filled her in. I tossed the key on the sideboard and held the door for her.

"I need to know what's going on. I need this job. It may be shitty—they treat me shitty—but it's all I got. Is the firm going to dissolve because of all of this? Spill already."

"Well, you're going to hear about it on the news, so…" I motioned toward the sitting room where I filled her in on Mason's mother and her husband, Gilbert Hayes, getting shot as I'd heard about it from Mason. A sterile, reporting of events with the feel of a newspaper headline and first paragraph. I left out the part about Mason showing up twice, with me in tow the second time. We'd have to see what the media did with the story and how much digging they would do. With a firm as established in the Charleston community as Levinson & Levinson was, this would turn into the top story of the evening news, perhaps it would qualify as breaking news during Jeopardy! which would annoy a fair number of the game show's fans, I would imagine.

But Stella wasn't fooled. She squinted, then untucked her legs from beneath her and leaned forward in the wingback. "And they don't have any idea who shot them?"

"By *they*, you mean the police?" I asked, having trouble making eye contact with her. An errant thread on the seam of my pants suddenly needed my attention.

"Yeah, the police. And where's Mason now?"

"Mason? Last I knew he was heading to the police station to answer questions—voluntarily, of course." *Liar!* I tried to reframe it in my head as stretching the truth. "Poor guy. He must be absolutely devastated. To lose his mother like that. I think they were close."

"Bullshit."

"Excuse me?" I tried to keep my voice steady. Stella's street smarts were shining through. I wanted to walk her down to The Battery wall and push her over.

"I know a liar when I hear her. There's more than what you're lettin' on. Mason is somehow wrapped up in all this. And so are you." She ran her palms up and down her thighs as she considered the situation, rocking slightly as if to shake things into place in her head. When she looked up, she said, "Girl, you need me more than ever. You're knee deep in the pluff mud, aren't ya?"

Fine, I'll bite. "Pluff mud?"

"Pluff mud. It's that crap along the marshes in the Lowcountry that smells to high heavens at low tide. You get used to it, but you best hope you never step in it. It's like quicksand. It sucks you in, and the more you squirm, the deeper you go. Usually you just end up losing a shoe, but I've heard stories of worse."

"What makes it smell?" The question sounded odd. Discussing the qualities of marsh mud when there were much more pressing concerns. I was trying to steer her away from them.

"It's a bunch of decaying stuff. Marsh grasses. Fish. Oysters…crabs."

"Sounds lovely."

"Well, you're in it. But good. And it's starting to smell in here."

# CHAPTER THIRTY

I DIDN'T CARE FOR THE IDEA of collaborating with Stella, but at that point I needed an ally. Particularly one with an in at the attorney's office who also knew her way around a police station. And it was slim pickings.

Heading for the armoire that held the liquor, I asked on my way by, "What's your poison?"

Without turning, she said in such a low drone I had to lean in, "You got that right. That stuff is poison. I stay away from it." She wagged her head once with intention. "My mother called it poison, but she couldn't stay away from it. And it got her. Sucked her in and took the life out of her. Almost got me. That DUI was my wakeup call. It saved me." She turned as if to gauge my reaction. "But you go ahead. I'm not your mama," she added, "even if you might need one now."

Stella sure wasn't and my mama wouldn't have stopped me; she would have joined me. Since I was still getting accustomed to and didn't trust myself with bourbon quite yet, I grabbed a familiar poison: vodka, a heavy-handed pour with a splash of seltzer. It would have been nice to have a slice of lime but what had been left in the refrigerator had turned brown and unrecognizable as any sort of citrus fruit, so I'd tossed them.

The irony of drinking vodka or my newfound bourbon was that

my family's business—ridiculously successful and looking for a future CEO—was beer, which had never been my thing. I'd gotten my fill of the sticky sour smell the morning after keg parties very early on at college and never acquired a taste for anything with hops, much to my parents' chagrin.

One might be inclined to ask the question: How does someone with such a lack of basic qualifications run a beer manufacturing company? She doesn't. Thank you, but no thanks. But it wasn't that clear cut. My parents had other ideas, and there was no way to escape what they saw as my destiny. I no longer had Gray to back me up. And I also didn't have a book deal to legitimize my preferred alternative. Bottom line was they had no one else to take over the reins. I was it.

"What the hell is going on, Stella?" I flopped on the couch and pulled my legs to the side, drawing a long sip. "Do you think Mason's mother getting shot is connected to my uncle's disappearance?" I still wasn't going to concede Gray was gone. No body. No death. He could still be out there.

"Your uncle was publishing a series of articles about Hayes when he disappeared. For the *Post and Courier.* Right?"

"Right." I loved that she left open the possibility Gray was still alive. And I loved that she had shifted from accusatory to productive.

"Where do you think he would have gotten his information? Who could have been his source?"

With those two simple questions, it couldn't have been any more obvious.

"Of course, Mason's mother," I said. "But why would she rat on her own husband?"

"I don't know. Maybe that would make it easier to divorce him or kick him out of the partnership. And maybe it wasn't her. After all, that would have been quite risky. I guess it could have been anyone in the office who stumbled on to evidence of his indiscretions. But my money is on her."

"That would certainly give Hayes motive for killing her. Seems a bit extreme though." And Ellen was no longer able to defend herself.

"Desperate people do desperate things," Stella offered.

I considered the source.

As if reading my mind, she snickered and said, "Yeah, you could say I know what that's like."

Redirecting, I said, "Okay, let's say Hayes did shoot Ellen. How did he think he would get away with it?"

"How the hell do I know?" she snapped.

"Well, what I meant was how could he possibly think he would get away with it? Had he thought it through?"

"Maybe it wasn't planned. It was a crime of passion. He confronted his wife and accused her of leaking info to the press and things got out of control."

"Certainly feasible," I conceded. "And with everyone carrying guns around here, a weapon was readily accessible."

"Then if he knew Mason would be stopping by, he lay in wait to frame him."

"Or it happened so fast and Mason happened to show up before Hayes could get out of there. Otherwise why wouldn't he just slip out and let Mason find her? Why risk a confrontation? He had to know Mason and his mother were close… he'd defend her, go after him."

"Yeah, maybe he didn't know Mason was coming and he showed up… unannounced."

"Yeah… could be."

I felt my pocket vibrate. The number on my cell made me cringe.

To Stella, I said, "Hey, I need to grab this."

She nodded.

"Hey, Dad, what's up?"

He chuckled. "What's up? That's why I was calling…to see what's up with you."

"Oh, uh, not much. Just trying to—"

"Why are you still there?"

I hesitated, not knowing what the real reason for his call might be. That was one way he and my mother were similar—their motivation wasn't always what it seemed at first glance.

"I thought your mother already talked to you about this. Didn't she call?"

"Uh, yes, she did. But—"

"Then why are we having this conversation? Do as you are told," he said in his best teenage parent lecture voice.

Feeling the heat rush to my face, it took everything I had not to lash out at him. I was long past puberty, and this was how he spoke to me. Made me want to rush back to Boston and get right back to work for him.

The line fell silent, and I rushed to fill the air space with, "It's complicated."

He scoffed. "You're *making* it complicated."

"You don't understand."

"No, it's you that's missing the big picture here. Hire a Realtor to put the place on the market and get back to your job. I need you. There's been turnover in the short time you've been gone, and I'm spending my days putting out fires."

*So you want to delegate the firefighting to me. Great. Can't wait. Maybe I'll never come back. How about that? Charleston has turned out to be a pretty special place after all. I love it here.*

He wasn't finished. "I expect you home in two days."

"Two days." My voice was probably louder than it needed to be. "That isn't possible."

"Two days. Now get it done. Goodbye, Kathryn. I'll tell your mother you said hello."

"Wait!" I wedged in before he could pull the phone from his ear. "Don't hang up on me. It's *you* who doesn't understand." I had to talk fast. "It's not so simple. I got here with every intention of doing just as you said: put Uncle Gray's house on the market and come back." I was relieved he didn't jump in when I took a breath. "But something isn't right. It doesn't look like Gray's accident was an accident. He—"

"Of course it was an accident."

"Dad, no. It may not have been. I've been doing some digging—"

"Leave well enough alone, Kathryn. That's not why you're there. You have no business *digging*."

"Just listen. He'd been publishing some articles—a series of articles—an investigative series about an attorney here. The guy's been stealing from his clients and—"

"His death has no connection to that." His use of the word death was like a fist to my gut.

"How do you know?"

He fell silent on the other end. If I hadn't heard his desk phone ring, I would have thought he'd hung up on me.

"I've got to go." He was finished with our conversation.

"But Dad. How can you be so sure?"

"We were close. We were brothers. I was in contact with him. I have more information than you do about what went on the night he died."

"You do? What? Tell me."

"No, it's not for your ears. I've got to go. Now stop sticking your nose where it doesn't belong and come home. Bye Kathryn." Our conversation was over.

The click wasn't as loud as when Posh hung up on me, but it was annoyingly close.

What the hell? What could he possibly know about the night Gray disappeared? Had he been in touch with the police and gotten more information out of them than I could?" I flopped in the wing chair. "God I hate being treated like a child."

# CHAPTER THIRTY-ONE

ONE OF THE LAST PEOPLE I expected on my doorstep was Mason, and I was conflicted about opening the door. He was connected to his mother's murder and her murderer. He'd disposed of evidence that would have implicated himself, but I didn't know exactly what else he'd done. I doubted that he did. The lights had gone out before he started shooting—at least that was what I'd seen—and he'd pulled me into the whole sordid mess.

I abhorred the idea of carrying a concealed weapon, but if I was honest about it, it might have saved his life. Hayes could have shot him, and there would have been no one around to dispute his side of the story.

I let him in. Gun and all, I assumed. It was hard to tell. Did he own more than one? He looked a little worse for wear, what with being dragged off in cuffs the last time I'd seen him, but the added crease in his forehead somehow made him even more attractive. Was it a matter of his seemingly impenetrable fortress, a protector of those needing protecting, letting his vulnerability show? Yup, worked for me. I couldn't pour him a drink fast enough.

Over our dueling bourbons, which were becoming a habit when we were together, he filled me in. The police had let him go with the understanding they'd be back in touch. His gleaming past and reputation as a respectable attorney had to have played a role. They seemed to buy his story more than Hayes' version, at least for now. Understandable with the latter attorney's history. The police had tested Mason for gunshot residue, but the results were inconclusive. I shuddered to think of how quickly they'd yank him back into custody once they viewed the security footage.

And he'd have company; they'd taken Hayes into custody. His injuries weren't life threatening so as soon as the hospital had discharged him, he headed straight for lockup. They were charging him in connection with Ellen's murder. He claimed Mason had shot them both, but it didn't add up for the police. The gun left behind was unregistered and wiped clean of any prints, Mason's or anyone else's.

But then Mason addressed my unspoken question about the security cameras. When the police pulled the footage, it appeared as though a new sim card had been inserted after the shooting. It picked up fifteen minutes before the first responders arrived, and no one else was seen going in or coming out on it. There was so much blood on the floor of Ellen's office with shoe prints on top of each other, it was feasible Hayes accessed the security camera monitoring system set up in plain sight there. Would the absence of the footage be enough to keep a jury from convicting Hayes? Or would it contribute to his conviction? Had Hayes done Mason a favor in the process?

Sitting back against the couch, one ankle casually resting across a thigh, he took a swig and said, "Kathryn, he could be responsible for your uncle's death."

"Disappearance," I corrected.

"Okay, well, either way, he's a dangerous man. And he's becoming more dangerous as time goes on. As his indiscretions come to light, he's getting desperate. And desperate people do things a prudent person wouldn't even consider."

"So he thinks he can get rid of his problems by eliminating the two people who had the guts to expose him?"

"Exactly."

"Why would your mother take that chance?" A better question might be *what did she see in Hayes?* Did he seduce her with some sort of boyish charm? With the power he wielded in legal circles? It had to be something like that.

He fell silent. I'd hit a nerve. I waited.

With an almost indiscernible shake of his head, he said, "Hard to say. I wish she'd said something to me. Maybe I could have helped. But I don't know what their relationship was like behind closed doors. Perhaps it was the only way she could think of to get out of it; she was trying to save herself and her law firm." He fingered the rim of his glass. "Hard to say," he repeated. "Hayes is…"

"He's pretty twisted. First he steals from clients. Then he murders to cover it up? Sick pup…"

He blinked with such deliberateness, I thought he had something in his eyes.

"The police are now looking seriously at the allegations outlined in Gray's articles. Looks like the pieces are falling into place. Time will tell if the charges stick."

"Well, the son of a bitch is not going to get away with taking out my uncle like he was a dispensable peon. Given what he did to your mother, I certainly hope they don't lose sight of the fact he went after my uncle."

Mason's steely blue eyes met mine. "What are you thinking, Kathryn? You're going to take on this maniac?"

"I'm just concerned that the investigation into my uncle's disappearance could slip to a lesser priority. If my uncle was willing to put his life on the line to expose Hayes, I need to look him in the eye and confront him. I want to hear him say it. Get him to confess."

"Kathryn, you have no idea what you would be going up against."

"May be. But I'm going after him anyway. Where do I find him?"

"Hayes? Kathryn, he's an animal. You need to stay away from—"

"Just tell me."

"You're not going to get too close to him."

"Where," I pressed. "I'll bet they allow visitors."

"Kathryn."

"Tell me."

Mason's jaw tightened. "What are you going to do, go ask him if he killed your uncle?"

"We'll chat," I conceded. "Where is he?"

"I won't let you put yourself in that situation. That's foolish."

I let it go. Although his concern for me was very sweet, he wasn't the only person I could get the information from. I had Stella.

# CHAPTER THIRTY-TWO

After sending Mason home to get some rest I got Stella on the phone.

"Are you crazy, girl?"

I'd already been through that discussion with Mason. "Just tell me. Crazy or not, I'm going."

"Whooeee, you got more guts than I gave you credit for. Just give me a sec. I'm pretty sure they would take him to Cannon…" I heard the clatter of a keyboard. "Yeah, that's where he is. Al Cannon Detention Center."

"Okay, thanks. Where is it?"

"North Charleston." There was an eagerness in her voice; I guessed tickled to be involved.

"Thanks, Stella. You're the best."

Googling the name of the detention center, I pulled the Aston Martin out of the garage and followed GPS to North Charleston.

Two large cement buildings with oddly spaced and undersized windows loomed ahead before I spotted the sign for the Sheriff Al Cannon Detention Center and turned into the parking lot.

My breathing had quickened and the uncomfortable feeling I wasn't welcome there crept under my skin. I was totally out of my league. Relatively young, white girl, naiveté painfully obvious from my scared expression. Did I really have the guts to face the monster who'd arranged to have Gray killed? Did I expect him to admit it? I needed to hear him say it, but he probably wouldn't, knowing conversations would be recorded.

A heavyset woman with blonde streaked dark hair pulled into a tight bun, sitting low at the counter, looked up as I approached reception. Her expression read, "Honey, you don't belong in a place like this." Communication was through a round metal insert in what could have been bulletproof glass, much like the ticket booth at a movie theater, except for the bulletproof feature.

Once the officer established I didn't have an appointment, she asked for an ID and the name of the prisoner I wished to see. It took a moment and an enormous effort to utter his name, but I finally said, "Gilbert Hayes."

The officer's hand paused midair after retrieving my license from the slot under the window and then she scrutinized it for longer than seemed necessary. Massachusetts may have been a different state, but it wasn't a different country. She made a copy and slid it back through the slot.

The sound of a heavy metal door slamming shut nearby made me jump. I tried not to show how much it shook me. A couple of male officers in dark uniforms came in through the front doors mid-conversation, and she watched them disappear down the hall. My stomach was a mess. I didn't belong there. Another door slammed shut. I envisioned being thrown into a cell and the door locking behind me. Trapped. Alone. No one the wiser. The woman's voice yanked me from my self-inflicted daymare.

"When you hear the buzzer, push that door—" She gestured with a tilt of her head. "—and take the third seat. If he wants to speak to you, an officer will bring him out. Good luck, honey."

Good luck? Wouldn't there be security so he couldn't hurt me? A dividing wall? A buzzer? Wait! My extremities tingled. I wasn't ready.

Tucking my license in my pocket I asked myself if I could go through with it. The buzzer sounded before I could come up with an answer, so I squared my shoulders and leaned against the door. The moment of truth.

The visitation room was deserted except for a young, animated Latino girl speaking Spanish into a gooseneck microphone at the far end. As instructed I took the third hard plastic seat in a string of chairs set up in front of what looked like television screens. The visit wouldn't be face to face after all. The relief was palpable but did little to calm my nerves.

As the edges of my vision blurred, I grabbed onto the narrow counter. I saw a man sitting on his bunk, looking up to a corrections officer, no doubt asking who his visitor was. He grew miffed when the officer shrugged his shoulders. He probably told him it was a way to get out of his cell for few minutes.

The vision faded and the florescent lighting blasted back through, causing me to squint. A more muted door slam announced prisoner Hayes' arrival, escorted by a refrigerator-sized Black officer. I watched on the screen as he shuffled closer—his wrists and ankles in shackles—in his prison-issue black and white horizontal striped duds. Not a good look—for him or anyone, for that matter. I'd been expecting orange. Probably had seen too many movies. This looked more like a Halloween costume. It was hard to picture him as a suit in an attorneys' office, much less a court of law.

Hayes stopped halfway over and squinted at what must have been his monitor projecting my image. Faded, thinning red hair plastered the top of his head, framing his pasty white face. A protruding gut tested the strength of his shirt fabric and suggested he hadn't been in long enough to suffer the effects of inedible prison food. The officer tugged on his arm, guiding him toward me. Hayes closed in and flopped into the chair, his handcuffs landing on the counter with a soft clunk through the speaker.

"Who the *hell* are you?" He sized me up with bulging eyes. Clearly not who he'd been expecting. And not the charming seductive attorney I was expecting.

I stared him down, gathering unexpected strength from the memory of my uncle.

"Well? Either say something or I'm leaving because I've got better things to do."

The sound of my laugh surprised me. "Sure you do."

His eyes flared and then he turned to the guard standing nearby. "I'm outta here."

"All right. Hold on," I said, scooting forward on the plastic seat. It would be a shame to miss the opportunity after gathering the courage to come this far.

Hayes held up a hand to the guard who had his hand on the doorknob.

"Go on," he pressed.

The girl at the other end of the room grew more agitated, but I could only hear her side of the argument. It was hard to focus. The guard appeared to step in and give the couple a warning, and the commotion simmered down a bit.

"I wanted to hear it straight from your mouth."

"Lady, I don't even know who you are. Let's start with that."

"The guy you had killed. Gray Moore. He was my uncle."

"Who?" He scrunched up his forehead, doing his best look of confusion.

"Don't even pretend you don't know him."

"I think you got the wrong guy."

"No, I don't. Gray investigated you. Found out what you've been doing—defrauding your clients, stealing money from your law firm—and published articles in the *Post and Courier*."

"And you think I had him killed. Interesting theory. But what good would that do me? What would be my motive?"

"To shut him up. Scare others from publishing in his place. Get revenge. Any or all of the above."

He stood.

"Wait! Don't you leave. At least have the guts to admit it to my face."

Hayes smiled with a slow, contemplative nod. "Even if I did do it, I wouldn't give you the satisfaction. You come in here so presumptuous, like you know exactly what the circumstances are. Well, you don't."

Taking in much needed air, I sat back in the chair and watched him shuffle back across the room. The refrigerator took hold of his arm and led him out and the door slammed shut behind them.

I hadn't gotten very far, but at least I'd shown him I knew what he'd done, and I wasn't afraid to face him. I'd given him something to think about at night when he was lying alone in his cell, contemplating his future.

# CHAPTER THIRTY-THREE

On the ride back from North Charleston, I did my best to shake the visit with Hayes. Even though I hadn't gotten him to admit what he'd done, I would have always wondered if I hadn't tried.

My thoughts returned to my chat with Sergeant Jennings and the search for a vehicle that could have been involved in Gray's accident. Perhaps the reason they hadn't come up with anything yet was because they were looking for a car. It seemed to me it would take more than a car to send another vehicle over the side of the bridge.

Deciding to take another look at the Ravenel, I headed back by way of Mt. Pleasant, which took me through a gauntlet of outdoor malls partially obscured by landscaping on the way to the bridge. Trees covered in stunning light purple buds lined the median, not what you'd see on Storrow Drive in Boston. Before long, the towers loomed up ahead but still in the distance. I could understand why Mason said you could see it from everywhere.

As the last traffic light before the bridge turned red, I downshifted to a stop and trained my sights on the ramp ahead. This was where my uncle may have sat, unaware what was going to transpire a few seconds later. Did he have any idea the vehicle pulling up behind him would send him to the depths of the harbor? Perhaps the light was green and they sailed through it together.

Once he was hit, what was going through his mind? When did he realize this was how it would end? I wished I could have kept him from suffering such a tragic accident. A senseless, preventable death. *Had I accepted that was his fate?*

My heart sank. What a horrible way to go. The time between the impact with the killer and the impact with the water must have seemed like a lifetime. What were his thoughts? Did he think of me? *How selfish, Kathryn.* After he hit the water, was he still alive? Did he get trapped by the steering wheel and pulled to the bottom? Did he try to swim back to the top but ran out of air? Darkness closed in as I pictured the late-night scene.

The traffic light was red, and I was the first car in my lane, but I didn't have a line of sight on the other lanes around me. Up ahead the towers and cables of the deserted bridge were lit up from below. The light switched to green, and I watched as the speedometer needle jumped to twenty-five miles per hour. I could feel the car buck slightly as I shifted from first to second. At forty, the car bucked again and I was in third gear. Lights flashed in the rearview mirror as I shifted quickly to fourth and then felt weightlessness as the car left the pavement.

A honk yanked me back and I hit the gas, moving into the far-right lane to be closest to the edge, crawling along to examine the low side wall of the bridge. It was no more than the height of a Jersey barrier until the point where the suspension cables attached to the side. Seemed wholly inadequate for a bridge so high above the water. But would it take more than a passenger vehicle to send a car over the edge?

Screeching and a horn blaring from behind startled me. Before I could hit the gas and get back up to speed, my body lurched forward, and I heard a heart-sickening crunch on the bumper. I tapped the brake and pulled up on the emergency brake lever.

*What had I let happen?* "Uncle Gray, I'm so sorry. Your car!" Gripping the sides of the steering wheel with both fists, I rested my forehead on the top and squeezed.

Soon came a rapping. I rolled down the window and looked up into the panicked face of a pimply-faced teenager who seemed to know he should stop in the case of an accident but didn't know where to take it from there.

"Ma'am, it doesn't look too bad," he stammered. "Take a look… see what you think." I figured he was trying to convince himself as well as me it was a non-event.

Reluctantly I got out with the other cars whizzing by and walked to the back of the Aston Martin where his mud splattered Rav 4 bumper had dented mine.

"Why were you stopped on the bridge? I didn't expect someone to be stopped dead like that. Why did you do that?" He was starting to come out of his shock. "That's just dangerous." Anger crept into his quivering voice. Probably thinking about the consequences awaiting him at home.

I knew I'd been in the wrong. It was a busy bridge. I was lucky the collision hadn't been more serious than it was. My heart tugged at my conscience to let him off the hook.

Glancing at the two kissing bumpers, I said, "Why don't you pull your car back a bit so we can get a better look.… And put your flashers on so you don't get hit."

He obliged and returned in no time; no doubt anxious to get the trauma over with.

"See? Not bad at all," he tried again. "Oh, my mama is gonna whoop me," he said in a shaky murmur.

Being a newer bumper, his vehicle showed no damage from the

collision. My uncle's car wasn't as fortunate, but it wasn't worth putting the kid through getting grounded at home. It wasn't a life-or-death situation. That had already happened on the bridge. And it was really my fault.

"You're right. We got lucky this time, didn't we?" I assured him.

"So I don't need to show you my license and exchange info and stuff like that?" His face started to brighten. Then he added a barely audible, "Ma'am?" as if horrified he'd forgotten his manners.

"No, I think we're good. No real harm done." My heart was broken for allowing the car to get dinged under my care, but it would only take some minor body work to make it right again.

His exhale sounded like he'd been hanging on to it since he'd rammed into the back of me. He'd live to drive his girlfriend to the mall another day in his mother's SUV.

"Thank God. I'd hate to have ruined such a cool car. What is it?"

As I filled him in on the make, model, and year, something over his shoulder caught my eye—slashes on a jersey barrier just ahead looked like the surface of the cement had been scratched off.

The teen thanked me and scampered back to his car, pulling cautiously away, then flooring it up over the bridge—his souped-up engine an improvisation I was sure his mother hadn't opted for when she first got the car.

Leaning into the Aston, I switched on the flashers and then walked along the side of the bridge to get a better look.

This was it. It had to be it. Running my fingers across the surface, I noticed an unmistakable dark blue patch along the top of the barrier—This was where Gray had been hit and sent over the edge.

Making my way back to the Aston, as cars zipped by, it saddened me to think of the number of people who traveled past the exact spot and had no idea what had transpired there. Too busy to look and notice. Too busy to care.

Flashing lights pulled up behind my uncle's car just as I reached for the door handle. My stomach churned. I'd stayed a tad too long and someone called it in.

"Ma'am, what seems to be the matter?" he called, already outside of his cruiser, adjusting the belt carrying his holster.

"Nothing of any significance, officer," I called back. "Just a fender bender and uh… we checked things out and decided there was no real damage." The cars passing us had suddenly slowed to a crawl, gawking as if I'd committed a heinous felony.

"So the other party stayed?" He approached with his arms hanging loosely at his side as if he were ready for anything I might try. *Yeah, because I have that look of a renegade criminal on the run. Nothing to lose. So look out.*

"Yeah, he just left."

"Okay, why don't you go ahead and get back into your car." He flicked a couple fingers in my direction.

*Excuse me? I'm not a threat to you, Officer. You don't have to treat me like that.*

As I climbed in, he closed the gap and leaned in on the open window. Mt. Pleasant Police Department was emblazoned on his shoulder patch.

"License and registration, please."

Not understanding why the exercise was necessary, I complied and dug through the glove compartment, producing the appropriate documentation.

"So what's the story? Mass license. Car registered to a William Gray Moore."

"That's my uncle."

"And he's letting you take this beauty for a joy ride while you're visiting?"

"Not exactly." I turned away, fingering the stitching along the leather steering wheel cover. "He passed away recently. He left his car to me." I wasn't going to get into everything else on the long list. Even I struggled to comprehend it all.

"Wait here," he commanded.

I watched in the mirror as he strode back to his car, my credentials in his possession, and climbed in, the lights still strobing above. I averted my eyes. The last thing I needed was a migraine on top of everything else. The only positive I could come up with about the situation was that it wasn't at night—making it much more of a spectacle than it already was.

Reappearing at the window, he handed back my documents. "All right. You're all set. Maybe next time you can pull off on the first exit after the bridge so you don't tie up this lane. You've got quite a backup behind you."

"I do?" I certainly hadn't intended to ruin anyone else's day, but the ripple effect of one's actions was fascinating, I had to admit. The rearview mirror showed a line of cars stopped in my lane, the closest with her signal on and trying to merge.

"And sorry about your uncle," he offered with a pat to the top of the window frame before turning to go. His words felt flat, but it was a kind gesture, nonetheless.

I pulled out and as I traveled the remainder of the two-and-a-half-mile span, a white tow truck with a push bar mounted on the front appeared in the mirror, then pulled to the left and passed. I made note of the company name on the side panel: T&O Towing.

I recalled a dream I'd had with a similar tow truck in it. How long ago had it been? It didn't make any sense at the time—without context, so many visions didn't—was I seeing what my uncle had been seeing that fateful night?

This kind of tow truck was a familiar sight in Massachusetts. The bar in the front was often seen on police cars and could be used to push other vehicles while minimizing the damage to the cruiser. It came in handy to remove disabled vehicles from state highways during New England snowstorms. Perhaps they had a different use for them in the South. Like pushing Austin Healy's over bridges.

I would start the hunt for a tow truck—larger, like the one that had just passed—with a push bar on front imprinted with flakes of navy-blue paint. And I would start with following this one. It may have been white, but perhaps white paint looked silver on navy blue.

Never having followed another car with the objective of staying out of sight, I wasn't exactly sure how close to follow without being obvious. I found myself hitting the brakes, switching lanes, then switching back again, all in a matter of seconds to keep up but not always in his rearview. Or had I made myself more obvious? Had he noticed? Was he playing?

At one point an eighteen-wheeler changed lanes and slipped between us. I gunned it and went around the truck on the left only to watch the tow truck heading down an exit ramp just beyond the end of the bridge as I passed by.

"Damn it, there he goes." But the annoying voice in my head dismissed my distress. After all, what had I hoped to accomplish had I caught up to him? Could have put myself in a precarious, even dangerous situation. I'd been doing that too much lately.

Before I could scold myself any further, my phone vibrated in my pocket. Slipping it out, my heart skipped a beat when I read the caller ID. Was this the call I'd been dreading?

"Sergeant Jennings. What's up?" My voice sounded oddly casual, even to me. Had I fully prepared myself for when the call came to tell me they'd found Gray's body? Could I withstand the blow to my psyche that it was all so final, even though I'd expended an untold amount of energy convincing myself otherwise and coming up with alternate scenarios?

I switched the call to speaker and dropped my cell in my lap.

"Miss Moore, I wanted to give you an update."

I waited, unable to urge him on.

"We received a report of a truck located at the airport that may have been abandoned. Appeared to have been there for a while. It had sustained damage to the front and right side."

"It was silver," I said, anticipating the essence of his call.

"Yes, ma'am. It's on its way to the state lab right now."

"Okay, great. Thanks for letting me know."

"I'll get back to you as soon as I have anything."

The news only further underscored the argument someone had wanted my uncle dead. I felt a pinch in my stomach. Why? He was an incredible man. It was becoming more obvious how it had all ended for him. It killed me to admit it.

"Sergeant?" Had I caught him before he hung up?

"Yes?"

"Did the truck have a push bar on the front of it?"

"A push bar? Yes, ma'am."

"Okay. One more thing." I needed to follow up on a previous call, one I was sure he hadn't followed through on. "Whatever happened with having someone check out the area hospitals… you know, to check for anyone who might be in a coma or possibly conscious but unable provide their name?" I wasn't going to let it go.

Silence on the other end spoke volumes. He'd never followed through. He didn't think my theory held water—not a drop. *Damn it, Jennings, do your job! Is that too much to ask?*

"Ma'am, I'm sorry that I—"

"That you didn't bother?" I was livid.

"No ma'am, I'm sorry that I," he started again, "didn't share the results we obtained from our calls. We were unable to find an individual at any of the hospitals that were without an identity."

Regretting my overreaction, I said, "I'm sorry. Thank you for taking my request seriously."

"I know you're disappointed, and understandably so."

"Yeah, I know it was a longshot, but I figured it was worth a try."

"Absolutely. It was my pleasure to take your suggestion and run with it."

Not what I'd been expecting. But it didn't cost him anything to say it.

# CHAPTER THIRTY-FOUR

THIS TIME MY HEAD FELT HEAVIER than usual, as if it would flop off my shoulders if it weren't connected. Yet the spots took longer to flood my line of sight. Once they drifted in and rendered me blind, my hands were already firmly clutching the back of a chair, holding on tight to ride the incoming tide.

I recognized the back of Mason's head. His sun-kissed dark blond wavy mop just overlapped the collar of his blue and white striped oxford shirt peeking above a tan linen jacket, his signature preppy look.

He was in a dark room lit only by candles. White tapers with wax dripping down the sides. No discernable candlesticks. That detail didn't present itself, probably because it wasn't a necessary detail.

Mason crept up behind a man with a stocky build, dark hair. The farther he got away from me, the less of the other man I could see. Something in Mason's hand caught my eye—the glint of flickering flames on the shaft of a knife blade. His fist tightened around the handle.

I watched in horror as he raised it above his head and drove the blade into the neck of the man in front of him. As his victim's knees buckled, his body twisted as he dropped to the floor. I was suddenly looking down on the contorted face of my Uncle Gray.

Bolting upright, I shrieked, startling myself out of the vision. It was so unsettling. I had to believe it was more like a bad dream where my subconscious pulled pieces of thoughts and stresses and twisted them into a nightmare that made no sense, yet left me anxious, wondering if there was any truth to it. I had a long list of such visions I'd racked up. I needed to come up with a different name for them. They usually didn't come true—thank God—but I never knew how long to give them before moving them into that category. I vowed not to enter this vision in my notebook.

# CHAPTER THIRTY-FIVE

It had been a few days since I'd checked the typewriter in the main house, and I had a sense there might be a message. There was.

TRY THE PASTELS

PAINTING SUITS YOU

*YOUR MOTHER'S RIGHT.*

The last thing I needed was *someone* telling me my mother was right about anything—because she thought she was right about *everything*. I hit the carriage return lever a few times to see if there was more. There was.

*YOU'RE NOT A WRITER*

"Yes I am, damn it!" I smacked the side of the Underwood and headed back out.

As I grabbed the knob of the door to the side piazza, I heard the unmistakable sound of the carriage return lever on the typewriter. I froze. Once the house had quieted again, I crept back to the sitting room and approached the tiny desk by the window. The paper stuck up farther than I'd left it. There was one more line.

*YOU'RE AN ARTIST*

"Gray, you don't know what you're talking about." He'd always been my support system. The *only* person who supported my dream of becoming a writer. Why was he changing his tune? Then it hit me that it might not be Gray leaving the messages. I didn't want to think who it could be.

Approaching the carriage house, I had the creepy feeling someone was watching me. I glanced around the property but couldn't discern where their spying eyes might be hiding.

Once inside the door, I secured both latches and cast a wary eye out the window in the door. I couldn't shake the feeling.

Then it hit me. I hadn't had to unlock the door to the carriage house before I'd entered. Had I forgotten to lock up? Highly unlikely.

Then I saw him. His head was protruding above the wingback chair. I'd recognize him anywhere, even from that angle. But why was my father there? His stern orders on the phone hadn't been adequate? He'd felt the need to pay me a visit.

Before I could speak, he rose and turned toward me. I froze when I saw it wasn't my father but a stranger dressed all in black. I grabbed the door frame but couldn't get my feet to run in the opposite direction.

"Please, come in, Miss Moore." He sounded convivial, but I sensed his visit was nothing of the sort. He gestured to the matching wing chair on the other side of the coffee table, dark leather gloves stretched tightly over his sizable hands.

Upon closer inspection I could see the man looked nothing like my father, his severe facial features not masked by his sunglasses. Broad shoulders and a thick chest made up for what he lacked in height. *Had he been sitting with his legs tucked under him so he appeared taller when I walked in?*

How could I have mistaken him for my father from the back? Even the hair color was from a younger version of him. Had I been thinking of him and hoping he'd come to my rescue? Take over and help find his brother? Or, perhaps more accurately, his body?

Reluctantly I entered the sitting room and took a seat across from the man, catching a whiff of cheap cologne and wrinkling my nose. Why hadn't I run? Then I noticed a second man had taken my place in the doorway, lanky but no less threatening with his height. My instincts had been spot on. I wouldn't have gotten very far.

"Thank you for taking the time to see me, Miss Moore."

As if I'd had a choice.

"I'll keep this short and sweet, but you need to listen to what I have to say." He ran a hand through slicked back hair.

I nodded.

He leaned in. "You need to get your nose out of where it doesn't belong."

"And where would that be?" In all likelihood my tone was more brazen than it should have been in the prickly situation.

He glared and said, "Don't get fresh with me. You know full well what you're doing and a certain someone doesn't like it. So back off." He patted the side pocket in his jacket.

"I would imagine he's got enough on his plate what with all the clients he's screwed."

I assumed Hayes had sent the goons. That was quick, and from jail, no less. "I'm supposed to believe he's got time to deal with a Yankee he didn't realize he'd pissed off?"

The man considered me while grinding a fist into his palm. "You have no idea who you're dealing with and, believe me, you don't really want to find out. I think he can overlook your little visit, but that's where it needs to end." He stood, stared me down, and then walked out, his silent partner trailing behind.

I followed them at a safe distance to the door and double locked it after them. They strolled down the driveway with no particular urgency in their steps. With no car in sight, they turned at the end and disappeared.

How had they found me so quickly? Was Hayes that well connected he could reach out from behind bars and send a couple of thugs to pay me a visit? I hated that they had barged in, violating what little sense of security I'd gathered so far during my short stay. And I'd sat there and let them push me around. *What were the options, Kathryn? With what was hidden inside the spokesperson's jacket, you were outnumbered three to one. Oh Kathryn, what have you done?*

# CHAPTER THIRTY-SIX

WATCHING THE OPENING TO THE DRIVEWAY, I wanted to assure myself they were gone, but movement in the garden caught my eye.

Unlatching the locks, I stepped out and crept toward branches on a bush that seemed to be keeping time to a song only the plants could hear. As I got close, a figure popped up, nearly bowling me over.

"Geez, Annalee, it's you." I latched on to the front of my shirt, willing my lungs to keep functioning.

"Hello, Kathryn. I didn't mean frighten you. Just wanted to keep going with the weeding. With a garden this size, you never seem to be done."

"That's very nice of you to do. I probably should hire someone to take care of that. It hasn't been a priority since I got here."

"Whatever you'd like to do, dear. It's yours to handle the way you see fit." She tossed a weed into a pile and rubbed dirt from her palms. "But I'm happy to help. Gardening has always been my happy place."

"Annalee, did you see the two guys that just left? Were you here when they showed up?"

She glanced down the drive as if she could catch sight of my uninvited visitors. "Two guys? No, I didn't. Guess my back was to them. Seems odd they wouldn't have spoken to me." She wrenched her lower jaw to the side. "Must not have been brought up around here. No manners."

"You didn't see them when they walked up initially?"

"I'm sorry, I didn't. Too busy with my nose in the weeds, I'm afraid. Why, what's troubling you, sweet pea?"

Hesitant to admit I was shaken by their visit, I said, "I'm not sure there's anything to be concerned about. Not yet anyway."

Leaving Annalee in her happy place, I returned to the carriage house. Eyeing the pastels and paper, I decided it was time to see if I could find my own happy place. And my mother wasn't anywhere around to pop in unannounced with nostrils flared and that annoying click in her throat. She didn't have to utter a word. I knew she didn't approve of anything resembling creativity. If it didn't have anything to do with moving the business forward, she wasn't interested.

Plopping my backside into one of the bistro chairs on the patio, I began sketching the Pink Lady, dappled with the afternoon sunlight filtering through the magnolia trees. The delicate, lace-like Spanish moss gave me a challenge at first but I stuck with it, scrunching up several sheets of drawing paper along the way, and finally got the hang of it. As I sketched, blending colors with the tip of my finger in just the right spots, the squared off edges of the pastels was a familiar feel in my hand.

Flipping another page, I scooted the chair around to take in the gardens and Annalee bent at the waist, tending to them. I added a flower to her wide-brimmed sun hat as my hand skipped around the page, bringing the gardens to life. Both hands became covered in the chalky residue from the pastel sticks. Colorful dust covered my lap, which I ignored. It had been a while since I'd drawn or painted in the required courses for my art history major, but it was coming back easily.

One professor had tried his best to convince me to change my major to visual arts. Though flattered, I couldn't imagine trying to earn a living by painting or drawing. Then again, my art history major hadn't exactly opened the doors I'd hoped for either.

By the time dusk started to fall on the peninsula, clouds had moved in and the wind picked up. Annalee wrapped up her weeding, giving a wave as she headed back down the driveway.

I gathered up my art supplies and headed inside but continued to crank out drawing after drawing of interesting features of the carriage house, adding a touch or two using poetic license.

To a cozy reading corner with a wingback chair and footstool, I added fresh magnolia blossoms in a vase on the side table that existed only in my mind. To the fireplace with intricate carvings in the surround I stoked a crackling fire that invited the onlooker to pull up a chair. To the wooden handrail on the stairs leading to the second floor I draped a magnolia leaf garland, perfect for a Southern Christmas.

As I drew with pastels into the night, secure inside the carriage house, outside the wind grew fiercer and the rain splattered the windows. The hours slipped away without much notice until a crick in my neck finally got my attention. After washing up in the kitchen sink, I only got as far as the couch before gathering up a couple of toss pillows to my chest and flopping on it, vowing only to take a short power nap.

A frightful storm bears down on us.
You can feel the tension in the air.
Building strength as the clouds gather.
Growing height, as if ascending a tall stair.

Who can foretell the power it will bring
When it arrives at our feet?
Will we have prepared adequately?
If not, we hope it's death we cheat.

Is my fair maiden aware of the perils ahead?
Has she been warned to vacate the house?
Rescuing the fair damsel, I'm afraid
Is for a younger, stronger man, not a mouse.

# CHAPTER THIRTY-SEVEN

THE WINDS FROM THE STORM RATTLED the shutters on the carriage house for hours on end and made for a restless night, more tossing and turning than actual sleeping. I'd spent it on the couch in the sitting room for no logical reason other than that was where I'd flopped and fell asleep. But if I was honest with myself I'd admit I'd felt more comfortable there than in the second-floor bedroom. Visions of a large limb getting torn from one of the old trees on the property and penetrating the roof fueled my anxiety.

By dawn when the storm seemed to be settling down, I drifted off into a much-needed deep sleep, unaware of what might be brewing on the other side of the door.

What finally woke me was an odd sound, one I didn't recognize and had not heard since I'd taken up residency in the carriage house. Still groggy, I sat upright and listened but was unable to discern what I was hearing. Early morning light had started to filter in through the blinds, but the room was still awash in shadows.

Swinging my legs off the couch, I plunged my bare feet into cool swirling water that splashed up onto my legs.

My shriek would have roused the neighbors if I'd had any close by.

"What the hell?" Scrambling back onto the couch, I lunged for the lamp on the end table. It's compact circle of light illuminated enough of the room to see the water covering the floor.

"Where is this coming from?" Then the smell of the water hit me. Briny.

Bolting off the couch and splashing through ankle-deep water, I made my way to the door. The water had to be coming from the harbor. Mason had said the wall that ran the length of The Battery didn't always keep the water out. When high tide and ordinary thunderstorms coincided, you could count on downtown flooding.

This was more of an event than that. This was a tropical storm. How deep was it outside?

Flinging open the door to gauge the situation, a rain-soaked gust of wind smacked me in the face. Water gushed in over my feet. The yard sloped down to the street, which meant the water was even deeper there.

My thoughts went to my uncle's prized Aston Martin. I needed to keep the water from reaching it. Would I be able to get it out of the garage and get it to higher ground?

Tearing down the brick driveway, I stopped partway and watched wave after wave crash over the seawall and dump more water onto the street—a surreal sight that transformed East Battery into a raging river. The wind buffeted my body and soaked my clothes through to the skin. Rain stung my cheeks.

Wading to the bottom of the driveway and out into the street, I tried to gauge if I could get the car out without stalling it. If that happened, I might as well push it over the edge into the harbor. A flooded antique car was a totaled car.

The scene was eerie. The street was clear of the usual parked cars—others had heeded the forecasters' warnings and moved to higher ground. The view to the harbor and out to Fort Sumter had been obliterated. It was a wall of white with horizontal rain. My anxiety ratcheted up. Probably the only person in fifty miles that felt claustrophobic outside.

It hit me the residents of the peninsula, particularly those in the lower half where I was, had hightailed it out of there before the winds had gotten severe. They'd been through this sort of event before. I was the newcomer—some might say an outsider—who didn't have a clue I was putting myself in danger or the extent of it.

Stepping off the curb, I was struck by the pull of the water on my calves. It was quickly splashing up past my knees. There seemed to be a current below the surface. There was no way to get Gray's car through that. It was too late. We were both stranded.

Wind off the water flipped my soaked hair across my face and was stronger than anything I'd felt before. Debris whipped past. A palm frond zipped by perilously close.

I took another look around, but there was no sign of anyone in the area. No cars on the street. No one dared drive in it. I'd been left behind, and no one would be coming to my rescue. What I thought was the storm dying down must have been the eye.

A sudden gust felt like a shove from my older brother, nearly lifting me off my feet. Flailing for something to grab onto, there was nothing anywhere close to my reach. I eyed a palmetto growing up between the street and the sidewalk, leaning with the wind but it was too far away. Desperate to get back inside, if I were going to have a chance of surviving this storm, I would need to grab onto sturdy objects along the way.

With one last look out into the white of the harbor, I turned back to make my way to safety. Another gust, this one stronger than the last, pushed me off my feet sideways. I plunged headfirst followed by the rest of my body, completely submerged in the fast-moving street river. As my nose and mouth filled with filthy water, I felt myself getting pulled along with the current feet first. Grasping with both hands, desperate to find something to grab, my knees and hands were getting scraped and raw.

My lungs were burning. I needed to take a breath. If only I could grab something to get my head above water.

Suddenly my body rammed against the curb, and I had the sensation of suction against my side. Groping around, I felt the edge of an opening—one of those gaping storm drains. Could I get sucked down it with the force of the current? Was the opening large enough? *Lord, please help.*

With my lungs afire, I shoved my head up enough to suck in some air, searching for something to grab onto but saw nothing within reach. Grasping at the curb, only to scrape my fingers, I tried to crawl away from the drain but the pull was too strong. In all my flailing, I wedged my foot in what must have been the opening in the drain. I pushed my torso up for another gasp of air.

Going under again I silently pleaded with the universe to help. Panic set in. Getting my head above the water to breathe grew harder. The water was continuing to rise at an alarming rate. My arms grew weak with each attempt to fight the current. It was winning.

Was this how it would end? It was far too soon. I'd barely had a chance to live. And to die alone... how sad was that? Would my mother be sad at my passing? Would she miss me?

My lungs burned more intensely. I lifted my head as far as I could. My nose and mouth almost didn't clear the water level. Coughing and gagging, I finally grabbed a couple of desperate breaths, realizing they were probably my last.

When I couldn't hold my head up any longer, I let it drop. I was spent. Nothing left to fight with. This was it. I had nothing else in me. This was how it was going to end. Not what I'd planned. But who planned their death unless... at least I'd be able to see Uncle Gray on the other side.

The sound of a vehicle approaching sounded very real, but it had to be my imagination playing tricks. It was just the raging wind. No one was foolish enough to be out in the storm.

But what if the sound was real? If I could get their attention, they could help. Then I realized with the water obliterating the sides of the road they could easily run me over and not know what they'd hit. Probably figure it was debris from the storm.

Even from below the water surface, with my lungs about to explode, the sound of a motor grew louder. It was getting closer. I needed to get my head above water again. Or a hand, at least. I threw up an arm and waved, hoping against hope they would see it. I needed to take in another breath but knew if I did, it would just be water filling my lungs.

Through the murky water I could see two figures. Towering over me. Looked like men. One grabbed onto the hand I'd managed to get above the water. My body jolted when I saw the tattoo on his. I'd seen it before. More than once. In nightmares. They always involved water.

The two men had my head above water, and I coughed and sputtered until they tried to lift me to my feet.

"Stop!" I yelled. "My foot. It's stuck in the drain."

The man with the tattoo held on to me with an arm laced under my shoulders while the other dove underwater. I felt him tugging and twisting my foot. I tried not to dissuade him from his efforts by crying out. I whimpered softly when it got painful.

At one point the man let go of my leg and resurfaced. The other man suggested removing my shoe. Diving down again, he began working on my laces, and before long I felt my foot wriggle free, and they pulled me to my feet.

What an incredible rush of relief. I'd live to weather the storm a while longer at least. My legs were wobbly, but the tattooed man hung on to me and steadied me on my scraped and bleeding legs.

"Are you okay?" The wind had blown strands of his shoulder length, graying hair across the face of the man who'd freed my foot and saved me from certain death. As he brushed it away, I froze.

"Sorry about your shoe. There was no other way." He smiled a familiar smile I hadn't seen in a long time.

"Uncle Gray?" I struggled to process what I was seeing. "How can this be?" I uttered breathlessly.

"Yeah, it's me.... I guess we need to talk."

# CHAPTER THIRTY-EIGHT

My uncle and his friend helped me into the backseat of the Jeep Wrangler with its oversized tires—scooping me up by my armpits and under my folded legs. Gray scrambled into the back with me. I managed to buckle myself into the middle seat, away from the windows, and averted my eyes from the rearview mirror.

"Let's get out of here before the water gets too deep for this monster." Gray patted the back of the driver's seat. His friend gunned it, and we started out slowly away from the waterfront with a vee of spray behind us. Wind whipping the rain against the windshield made it challenging to see out.

Gray introduced his friend as Blake who directed me to blankets folded up behind my seat. I grabbed one, and Gray helped get it tight around my shoulders. The guys declined my offer to grab a couple for them. My body shook uncontrollably even under the wrap. Gray scooted closer and wrapped his strong arms around me. I'd nearly lost my life, and it was none other than my uncle who'd saved me. My mind reeled with unanswered questions.

His grip tightened. He gushed, "I came so close to losing you, Kathryn."

I sensed we'd talk once we got to safety, but I was dying to say *I thought I* had *lost you.*

As we drove, I stole a glance at the side of my uncle's face with more creases than I remembered. The graying of his hair, shimmering and dripping, was unsettling. How long had it been since I'd seen him in person? Too long.

I was struck by the stark differences between the two friends' appearances, yet I guessed they were close in age. Blake had strong features similar to Gray, but with light brown, shorter hair and no sign of gray. He sported attractive, neatly trimmed facial hair that accentuated his jawline, but my uncle was clean shaven.

I took in the barren streets and empty sidewalks through rain-spattered windows. Charleston was deserted, as it should be during a severe storm. Everyone else on the peninsula must have been smarter than the girl from Boston. As we turned the corner I recognized we were on King Street where Mason had taken me shopping.

Gray spoke up. "Blake, it's one way on this section of King."

His friend laughed. "I know. But no one's out driving except us, and King is the highest elevation on the peninsula—not by much, but we need every inch we can get."

My uncle turned back and asked, "Didn't you hear that the storm was expected to strengthen to a hurricane this morning?"

"Hurricane?" Why hadn't I checked the forecast? I'd been so focused on the pastels, I'd become lost on the right side of my brain. Out of touch with reality. That side of the brain that caused me to lose track of time and place. Not the first time that had happened, but clearly it could be dangerous. I'd almost lost my life this time. "Jesus."

"Yeah, and the peninsula is not the best place to be. Flooding has always been an issue. Some homeowners have gone through the expense, not to mention the hassle, of having their homes jacked up and their foundations built higher. But this storm is hitting during a full moon and a king tide."

"A king tide?"

"They happen like three or four times a year, and they're unusually high tides. So all of these factors make for a very dangerous situation."

"How'd you know to come looking for me?" I asked.

"I had a feeling a northerner like you wasn't used to riding out a tropical storm, much less a hurricane."

"Wait... how did you know I was here?"

"We'll cover all that." I thought I caught a grin before he turned to look out the side window.

A gust of wind buffeted the Jeep. Blake gripped the steering wheel more tightly and fought against it. He glanced in the rearview mirror. "We don't have too much farther to go."

"Uncle Gray, I'm shocked to see you. Everyone thinks you're—"

"Dead?"

"Yes!" I swatted at his shoulder. Switching my gaze to his friend, I said, "Well almost everyone."

My uncle's expression tightened. "I'm sorry to have put you through that. I needed everyone to think I was dead. My life depended on it," Gray endeavored to be heard above the winds.

Blake piped in, "The people who wanted him dead wouldn't have stopped if they thought he was still alive."

"So I dropped out of sight, stayed with my buddy here." He playfully ruffled the hair on the back of Blake's head. "Fortunately he lives in the carriage house behind my place, so I could keep an eye on who came and went—including you."

"I had an annoying feeling someone was watching me. Thought it might even be some sort of creepy spirit, given the age of the property and the local history."

"Yeah, yeah, it was me. At first I didn't recognize you. It's been a while."

A stab of guilt returned to my abdomen.

"But fortunately you didn't recognize me either."

I flashed back to the tourist Mason and I saw leaving the property in a hurry. "That was you."

"Yeah, I got concerned when I saw a car in the driveway I didn't recognize. I was foolish to try to get a closer look. I brought some things to drop off for you but that didn't work out."

"You look so different. Your hair. You've never had it this long."

Gray laughed. "I haven't gotten it cut since the accident. Had to stay out of sight."

"But the gray…" I wished I hadn't said it as soon as the words escaped my lips.

He nodded and fell silent. Just the sound of the wind and the wipers working furiously to keep the rain off the windshield filled the car. I looked down at my cold feet, one with a soggy Keds sneaker that used to be white, the other pale, bare, scraped, and missing a couple of toenails.

# CHAPTER THIRTY-NINE

Past Calhoun we turned down a side street and into a narrow drive next to a Charleston Single near the College of Charleston. Even in the midst of the storm I could tell it needed some tender loving care.

Blake clued me in. "My son lives here with a couple of roommates. They won't mind if we ride out the storm here. They know we're coming."

There was something very familiar about the house. I told myself it was just similar to so many other Charleston Singles I'd seen on the carriage tour.

We scrambled out of the Jeep, pressed through the storm, and up to the house. I tiptoed with my bare foot to minimize contact with debris on the steps. A narrow piazza ran along the side of the house. The long wooden shutters on the front had been closed, I presumed to protect the windows from projectiles generated by the winds. We had no sooner landed on the piazza when the door flew open and we were ushered in. The stench of greasy pizza made my stomach lurch.

"Get in here, you fools. What the hell are you doing out in this?" A light haired, hazel eyed teen who was the spitting image of Blake slammed the door shut behind us. He glanced at my feet but thankfully refrained from commenting.

"Hey, watch your mouth, young man." Blake wagged a finger at him. "You're not too old for me to whoop your backside."

The room burst into laughter at the idea.

"Kathryn, this fresh mouthed kid is my son, Garrett, and these are his buddies, Eric and Jason." He gestured with an open palm to a freckle faced redhead and a dark haired, scraggly-bearded guy who was in dire need of a visit to a barber. His head seemed to be permanently tilted to the side to keep hair out of his eyes. I watched him repeatedly push a clump of wavy locks off his forehead until I finally had to turn away. My neck was starting to hurt.

All I could offer was a quiet, "Hey." I was spent; starving, soaked, chilled to the bone, bleeding in too many places to count, aching all over, and not in the mood to make new friends. I just wanted time alone with Gray.

Garrett returned from the kitchen with three beers he handed out to the new arrivals. I practically yanked it from him and glugged down half the bottle. A beer had never tasted so good, which was a lot coming from me. I watched as Blake took two bottles, unscrewed the top on both, and handed one to Gray. The gesture seemed oddly intimate. Had I misread my uncle? Was that why he'd never married? Was that why my mother distanced herself from him and kept me away as well? Was she homophobic? As they clicked the longnecks in a toast, Blake's familiar tattoo came into full view—some sort of dramatic bird.

The small front room was decorated in early dormitory shabby chic, complete with Brooks & Dunn and Toby Keith concert posters, a futon, two beanbag chairs, and a couple of end tables fashioned from plastic milk crates. The coffee table with pizza boxes scattered across it and a half-empty bowl of pork rinds was a rectangular piece of glass balanced on top of a wooden vegetable crate with some sort of faded printing on the slats. Nothing that would get them into the next issue of *Charleston Home + Design* but functional, nonetheless.

A flat screen TV on the wall across from the futon was set to The Weather Channel and droned on about the storm happening all around us. I looked away from the images of waves crashing over the storm wall and a foolhardy reporter clinging to the railing that ran along the sidewalk. I had nearly lost my life there just minutes earlier. I had my uncle and his friend to thank for not becoming a casualty. And the tattoo.

Blake sent his son to fetch a change of clothes for the three of us. He returned with an armload of sweatshirts and sweatpants—apparently there was no shortage in a college student's wardrobe. I hoped they were clean. They appeared to be, but I wasn't in a position to complain if they weren't.

Allowing me to go first, we took turns changing in the tiny powder room off the hallway to the kitchen. Blake then gathered all our wet clothes and tossed them into the wash. Fortunately the power was still on, in spite of the intense wind.

"You guys hungry?" Garrett asked. "We ordered a bunch of pizza before it got bad and there are a few slices left so help yourself." He motioned to the boxes on the glass tabletop.

"Thanks, Garrett," said Gray. "Actually, would you mind if we have a few minutes to ourselves." He pointed between the two of us. "We haven't seen each other for … a hell of a long time, and we've got some catching up to do."

"Sure. No problem." He looked to his buddies and said, "Yo, let's go play some pool."

"I'll take you guys on," Blake challenged, and the foursome headed toward the back of the house. Poking his head back in, Blake said, "I'll throw the leftovers in the oven to warm them up a bit." He scooped up the boxes and disappeared into the kitchen.

Except for the enthusiastic anchor at the weather desk, the room grew quiet. Gray grabbed the remote and muted the TV, tossing it onto an end table. I watched with concern as the bottle in his hand quivered on its way down to the coffee table. I placed my nearly empty bottle next to his.

He pulled me into his arms and hugged me tightly. My knees buckled as I hugged him back. I didn't ever want to let go. I'd thought I'd lost him and now that I had him back, I wasn't going to let him out of my sight.

"God, it's so good to see you." Gray pulled back enough to look into my eyes. "Are you okay? Do you need me to get you anything?" He stepped back farther, assessing the scrapes on my arms and legs. "Antiseptic cream? Band-Aids?"

I shook my head. I didn't have the energy to think about addressing wounds. If sepsis didn't set in I'd get around to taking care of them. But realistically, there wasn't a Band-Aid large enough to cover it all.

"Why don't you have a seat, Kathryn. I need to fill you in on what's been going on."

# CHAPTER FORTY

"I don't know how much you've heard or what you've figured out on your own, so stop me if I drone on and get redundant."

I didn't care if he repeated something I already knew, I was going to let him talk as long as he was willing. He was there when the whole mess started and was keenly aware of the details. Shaking off a shiver, I pulled my knees to my chest, wrapped my arms around my legs, and nodded to encourage him to get started.

Gray settled onto the futon next to me and exhaled what sounded like a couple years of pent-up angst. The rain had turned his silver peppered hair into ringlets. As if he could sense where my eyes had landed again, he tucked as much as would fit behind one ear.

Finally he took my hand and said, "I'm so sorry to have put you through the last several weeks… letting you think I'd died." He shook his head, dropping his head. "What a horrible tragedy."

"If it wasn't you in your car, who was it?"

"At first when I heard on the news my car had gone off the bridge, I thought it was somebody who'd stolen the car and taken it for a joy ride. The more I thought about it though, I was pretty sure it was Larry, one of the guys at the shelter where I volunteer. We'd become close over the years. He was so fascinated with my cars. I'd take him out for a drive every once in a while. He loved those rides. Absolutely loved them.

"Probably got his hands on some alcohol—that was always his downfall. Then he made bad decisions. He had to have known where I kept the key."

"In the console, in your gloves?" I teased. It felt good.

He looked up and smiled. "I guess you found the one for the Aston."

I grinned. "Yeah… what a rush it was to drive it."

"Glad you haven't forgotten."

"Are you kidding? How could I forget once you taught me?"

He playfully mussed the top of my hair. "Well I wish he hadn't taken it for a joy ride, but Larry probably saved my life. Gave up his for mine."

"Someone thought it was you driving that night."

"Yeah."

"Someone Gilbert Hayes hired?"

My uncle leaned back and feigned giving me a once over. "Well, look who's up to speed."

Releasing my hand, he patted my knee in an *I'm proud of you* gesture.

"It seems as though that's what happened. It would make sense. My investigative series for the paper turned his world upside down. It would be natural for him to want to go after someone. I was it."

"How did you find out your car went over the side of the Ravenel?"

"The morning after, Blake—" His eyes went to the ceiling as if he could see his friend upstairs "—called and told me to turn on the news. When I did, I watched a video of my car getting pulled from the harbor." His hand went to his heart. "I didn't know my car was gone." He shook his head again. "Hell of a way to go. Poor guy."

"You can't blame yourself, Gray."

"Oh, but I do. It has me written all over it." His gaze went to a large grease mark on the coffee table where the pizza boxes had been. "But I knew if they found out it wasn't me in the car, they'd keep coming after me until they'd finished the job. So I had to lay low. "Fortunately, Blake let me shack up with him. He takes care of the house behind me and stays in the carriage house. It was a bit tight, but he's a good friend."

I wondered if they were more than friends.

"So tell me about the investigative series you've been doing," I prodded.

He paused as though he wondered if he should continue; finally he did.

"It's all centered around Gilbert Hayes—extremely successful, very well connected—who's gotten himself into a mess he thinks he's going to get himself out of because of who he is and who he knows and the positions of power they're in. And I'm not talking about fixing parking tickets."

"What exactly has he done?" Although I'd heard a version of the story from Mason, I was interested in hearing it directly from the one with a bullseye on his back.

"A better question might be what hasn't he done. Some of it is the usual crooked attorney crap like pilfering funds from clients' accounts as well as his own law firm—a South Carolina institution started by his wife's grandfather. I hear he was angry when he was brought in that his wife wouldn't change the name of the firm to include his. But other incidents connected to him have been labeled as a tragic accident or a senseless crime at the hands of a barbaric intruder."

"Like what?" I itched for specifics.

"Well… he'd been married before. A few years ago his wife suffered a fall at their home—down some steps—and ended up passing from her injuries."

"How sad."

"It gets worse." He took a moment to reflect. "His current wife, as you may have heard, turned up shot to death. According to his account he returned home one evening and found her lifeless and bloody body. Blamed it on an intruder. There was no sign of a break-in and nothing seemed to be missing."

"What would possess a man to do things so heinous?"

"Exactly, such heinous acts. Not one, but two wives."

I wondered if Mason had tried to warn his mother, keep her from marrying Hayes.

"So you think he's responsible for both deaths and all the missing funds."

"As they say, follow the money, so I did some digging and uncovered not only some shady business dealings but also his precarious financial situation. He had a drug habit to support that was wildly out of control. Power and money taints some people. He's got himself in deep. Owes money and doesn't have a way to pay it. People resort to desperate measures in that situation."

"But murdering two people?"

His eyes met mine. "He had life insurance policies out on both."

"That's disgusting." My stomach turned.

"I know, in my business I get to see the worst in people. This guy had a reputation for being ruthless in going after what he wanted. Someone who can murder his wives and write it off as an accident in one and a random intruder in the other, is someone who is one hundred percent evil, tainted by years of greed."

"So you put yourself in danger by publishing all this."

"Well, it's a series. I've only gotten part of it published. Looks like he was trying to prevent the rest of the story from coming out."

"It's so scary that he would want to kill you."

"This guy's vicious. He bulldozes over anyone in his way. Even though he's in custody, he's got a network of loyal associates who will do his bidding. Someone has to stop him."

A chill ripped through me. It was alarming to think how easily it could have been Gray who catapulted off the bridge and washed up on James Island. My heart went out for his homeless friend.

"After that I knew I had to stay out of sight. I had to do everything in my power to make him think he'd been successful. And I needed more time to get the complete story out to expose him."

"But you were declared dead. Your attorney executed your will." I recalled the moment I'd heard my mother's words: *your uncle has died.*

"I know. I got lucky with that—"

"Lucky!" How cruel could he be? "Gray, that was excruciating to think you were gone."

"I can imagine, and I'm sorry. It was necessary. As I said, I got lucky. After the police contacted your father to break the news to him, he followed up with my attorney and asked him to set into motion the process of having me declared dead."

"Even though they hadn't found your body yet?" I clenched my jaw, disappointed in my father. In spite of their long-standing differences, Gray was still his brother.

"Don't be pissed at your dad. All the evidence pointed in the right direction. It was my car. Suddenly I didn't show up at work and was no longer living at my house."

Gray took hold of my shoulder and gave me a firm, but affectionate jiggle.

"Kathryn, I'm sorry to have put you through all this, but you have no reason to hold anything against your father for what he did. Don't you see? I needed him to do exactly what he did."

"I just wish my parents would have pressed further for more answers from the police."

"Kathryn, they got answers, but not the ones they were hoping for."

They might have been the ones my mother was hoping for, but I kept that to myself.

"Why did you take the risk to write the articles? You had to have known what he was capable of."

Gray fell silent. "Perhaps… but he needed to be caught, and it needed to be a public spectacle. He'd been hurting so many people and getting away with it for so long. He went off the rails more often than most. And I couldn't have had a more reliable source."

I raised my brows to urge him on.

"His wife." He raised a cautionary finger. "Just between you and me."

"Brave woman." I studied the lines etched in his face. He was still very attractive, but he seemed to look older than I would have expected. Perhaps being on the run and fearing for your life did that to a person.

He reached for his beer and took a swig, his hand shaking as he returned it to the table.

I held in a gasp.

"She couldn't just divorce the son of a bitch. It wasn't that simple. He was a partner in the firm. If they had him arrested, he could work out a plea deal and the matter would get forgotten. He's so well connected in the local legal system. No, this needed to be a public humiliation, one that Charlestonians won't forget."

"And it was up to you to do it?"

With a tilt of his head, he said, "She reached out to me. Said she respected my reporting. Felt she could trust me. So I agreed to do it.… Who knows, maybe the people who hand out the Pulitzer Prize for journalism will take notice." He laughed.

"Please tell me you didn't do it for an award, or because she stroked your ego."

"Of course not, Kathryn."

I loved how he never called me by a nickname.

"It was the right thing to do. Period."

I loved his answer. I loved him. But his outward signs of aging were worrisome. Had it been that long since I last saw him that the change in his appearance would be that severe?

"You look…"

"Older? A lot older?"

I pressed my lips together, not trusting myself to find the right words. The last thing I wanted to do was hurt his feelings. All I could do was nod.

"Yeah, growing older sucks. And sometimes it happens quicker than you expect it to."

I waited for him to continue.

Swiping his palm across the stubble on his chin, he said, "Like with me. I knew something was wrong. My hands started to ache when I typed. I tried to ignore it. Just lived with the pain. Kept on doing my job. Lived on Ibuprofen for a while. It helped. But then it didn't. I thought it was carpal tunnel so I figured a quick surgery and I'd be back at it in no time. The doc showed me the X-rays and broke the news that it wasn't as simple as carpal tunnel. It's arthritis."

"You seem too young to have arthritis."

"I know. I thought the same thing. It's Rheumatoid Arthritis, which can strike adults anywhere from thirty to fifty years old. Lucky me."

"I'm so sorry."

"Yeah, same. It really sucks. It's getting very difficult to use my laptop to write. It seems to be moving into my ankles and feet, so walking isn't as much fun either. It's getting worse. It's painful to do just about anything with my hands."

That would explain why Blake had opened his beer for him. Was he just being a good friend?

"Is there anything the doctors can do to help you?"

"There are meds I hate taking, but they help. I've tried acupuncture and massage. Both seem to help. It's an ongoing journey to find relief as the disease progresses."

The irony of the tragic situation was not lost on me. Although I'd miraculously gotten my uncle back, his physical condition was beyond concerning and his prognosis alarming. How could he continue to pursue his writing career? His future seemed grim. My heart broke for him.

# CHAPTER FORTY-ONE

We fell silent and listened to the wind continue to batter the house, rattling the windows and shutters. The lights flickered and nearly went out but sprang back to life again.

Then I remembered the tattoo. "Uncle Gray, I need to ask you about the tattoo on the back of Blake's hand."

"What about it?" His expression turned serious.

"I just met him today, but I've seen that tattoo before. I don't know when, but I know I've seen it." I thought about the nightmares I had on a regular basis. They felt like flashbacks. "Something happened when I was younger."

Gray's face grew ashen. "The two of you met before."

I looked to him to continue.

"You were little… about eight or so."

"He saved me from drowning, didn't he?"

He closed his eyes and emptied his lungs. "God, I'd hoped you wouldn't carry that with you."

"What happened?"

Gray shook his head.

"Please tell me. I have a recurring vision of what happened, but I want to hear it from you."

"All right." He took my hand again and led me away from the couch, through the kitchen and the aroma of warming pizza, to the back windows in the dinette. Animated chatter from the raucous game of pool spilled down the back stairs. "Does this look familiar?" He pointed to an above ground swimming pool that nearly took up the entire tiny backyard. This isn't the original, but it looks just like it."

"It happened here?" As the vision came rushing back, a sudden dizziness sent me off balance. I grabbed the windowsill for support.

He nodded but averted his eyes from the backyard.

"Blake and I lived together then. We were both starting out as freelance writers for the *Post and Courier*. We rented this house. You and your mother were visiting."

"I didn't think I'd ever been to Charleston."

Ignoring my comment, he continued his confession of sorts. "It was a brutally hot, humid day in August. You begged to go for a swim. So we let you. And as adults sometimes do, we got distracted."

"And I went under."

"Yes." Gray choked getting the word out. "I'm so sorry. We almost lost you that day."

"It was Blake who grabbed me."

Gray nodded.

"He grabbed me with the hand his tattoo is on. Looks like a Phoenix. I've never forgotten that."

"I'm so sorry," he repeated, as if begging for forgiveness but not expecting to receive it. "I wish it had never happened. I wish I could go back and change it."

"Why would just my mother and I have been visiting?"

Looking pensive, he finally said, "I don't recall the details."

I knew there was more to the story but let it go for the time being.

# CHAPTER FORTY-TWO

By the grace of a higher power, the old Charleston Single never lost power, so we were able to track the path and the pace of the hurricane along with the anchors on The Weather Channel. From time to time, they'd cut to their cohorts out in the field, demonstrating the strength of the storm, getting buffeted by hurricane force winds. I never understood why someone would take that kind of risk when the rest of Charleston and the Lowcountry were under evacuation orders.

Apparently, in spite of those orders, locals didn't get too excited about a Category 1 hurricane—at least not those north of Broad Street. They hunkered down and rode it out, that was, after making sure they were well stocked with essentials. For college students, that included pizza and beer.

Hours later the winds died down and the sun poked through the clouds. The air was thick with humidity, but it was a relief to be able to walk outside.

Palm fronds and small branches from the towering magnolia tree and grand oaks in the neighbor's yard littered Blake's Jeep, but it seemed to be intact. Mother Nature's way of pruning what the humans hadn't gotten around to.

After clearing off the Jeep and piling the branches at the curb, Blake, Gray, and I thanked the boys for their hospitality and headed south of Broad to survey the damage there. What condition would the grand Pink Lady be in?

This time when we traveled down King Street we were moving in the right direction—with traffic. And downtown had started to come to life with pedestrians exploring the streets and a few cars inching down the usually bustling thoroughfare. The boarded-up windows gave the street the feel of a city suffering from urban decay, but the plywood was temporary and there to protect the windows of the much-loved buildings.

"What do you think south of Broad will look like?" I asked.

"Hard to say," Gray answered. "We might not even be able to get through if the police have put up barricades. We won't know until we get there."

We rode the rest of the way to the sound of the engine winding down to a stop and back up again, veering around downed tree limbs and garbage cans that had been left out and relocated by the storm. The traffic lights on Broad Street were all blinking.

"Well, that's not a good sign," Blake grumbled. Taking a left onto Broad, we went as far as Church Street where we turned right, zigzagging around debris until he pulled slowly into a driveway on the left. I understood it was where the guys were living.

"Not too bad. Not too bad." Blake scanned the property—a large two-story home and a carriage house. "The owners will want a full report, but it looks promising. All right, let's get you over to East Battery." He put the Jeep in reverse.

"You want to leave it here and walk over?" Gray suggested.

"Good idea. If anyone is watching the house, it's best if we don't go wheeling in there with this tank and draw attention."

"That and if the roads are blocked we may not be able to get through." They shared a laugh.

"There's a shortcut through the hedge," I added.

"Is that so?" Blake asked.

"Yeah, there's a neighborhood boy who uses it all the time, supposedly. He says he visits you, Gray."

He turned toward the back seat. "A neighborhood boy?"

"Yeah, he's probably about eight or ten. Cute kid. Dark brown hair. Kind of a page boy cut. Doesn't sound familiar?"

Deep crevasses formed in his forehead as he thought. I may have stared a bit too long at them. It was unsettling. Longing to break the tension I'd created, I laughed. "Well, maybe he spies on you, and you don't even know he's there."

"How 'bout that, Gray. Someone was spying on you while you were spying on Kathryn," Blake said with a playful jab to Gray's arm.

"Great. Just what I need. A midget spy. He reached for the door handle. "Okay, show us where this cut-through is."

We scrambled out and headed for the row of tall bushes separating the two properties. The rain-soaked ground sounded gushy and squished beneath our feet, mine in oversized flip-flops Blake's son had offered.

"I don't know exactly where it is, but it can't be too difficult to find." I pushed ahead and led the way. My strides got too long and one foot slipped out from underneath me. The other quickly followed and I slammed onto my back, my head thumping hard on the ground. I heard on odd crunch somewhere inside my scull and my eyesight blinked off for a moment. The flip-flops flew off to parts unknown.

"Jesus, Kathryn, are you okay?" Gray was at my side in a heartbeat, grabbing my closest hand.

Groaning, I rolled to my side and rubbed the throbbing from the back of my head.

"We need to get you some ice." Blake had my other hand, and they pulled me to my feet. "Here, let me grab those flip-flops."

"Don't bother. They weren't much good. Probably why I slipped. Damn it, that hurt." Pressing my palm against the back of my head, I teetered for a moment and then the throbbing started. Gray steadied me with an arm around my shoulders.

"Yeah, that couldn't have felt good. Let's get you that ice. You've got some in the carriage house, right?" Gray asked.

"Yeah." Not finding an obvious opening to cut through, we pushed our way through a thin section at the end of the towering hedge along the side of the carriage house, adding a few scratches to my already banged up and bruised body.

Quickly scanning the property, from what I could see it appeared the main house hadn't suffered any serious damage, although I couldn't see the front, which would have taken the brunt of the winds off the harbor. Small limbs were scattered around the yard, and the legs of the bistro table and chairs from the carriage house patio were sticking up through the partially flattened vegetation in the garden. Had I realized the severity of the storm I might have thought to secure them inside so they wouldn't have become projectiles. Thankfully the winds hadn't plowed them through any of the many windows on the two structures. The garden Annalee had been working so hard on looked a little flattened, but I hoped it was temporary and would spring back up with little encouragement.

My heart stopped though when I noticed an unfamiliar car parked at the end of the driveway, practically on the sidewalk.

"You expecting anyone?" Gray asked.

"No, I can't imagine…" Opening the door to the carriage house, again without needing a key, because I hadn't expected to be whisked away when I'd walked out earlier, I saw the visitor was seated in a wing chair in front of the fireplace. This time he looked like my father because he was my father.

"Dad. What… uh."

My uncle was behind me. "Joe… wow. What are you doing here?"

With a smug look on his face, my father said, "I figured you'd be surprised. But I'm even more surprised to see you."

"Well, yeah. But a hurricane is an odd time to pay someone a visit."

"Oh, hey Joe." Blake brought up the rear.

Gray remembered his manners. "Joe, you remember my buddy, Blake."

Joe nodded slowly. "Sure, I do. I can only imagine the trouble you two have stirred up lately."

Blake read the room and excused himself, mumbling something about checking out the condition of the house he'd been charged with taking care of. After he closed the door, the sitting room fell silent. I had no idea what had spurred my father's visit, but I didn't have a good feeling about it.

"Why don't you both have a seat," my father said. It wasn't a suggestion.

I headed for the couch, leaving the other wing chair for Gray, but froze when my uncle said, "Hold it." I looked from one brother to the other. "I have a feeling this is between you and me." He looked to me and said, "Go get that ice from Blake. Your father and I need to have a chat."

"Now, William"—My father had never called his brother by his preferred name—"I said I want her to sit with us."

"If I know what this is about, you're not going to have the satisfaction." He turned me by the shoulders and whispered, "Go along. I'll come find you when we're finished. Don't look back. Just go."

# CHAPTER FORTY-THREE

Feeling the rub that I was betraying my father, I heard him calling from behind—accusing me of being disloyal, turning my back on him, threatening if I didn't stay—but I kept walking. It stung, but my instincts told me it was the right thing to do. There might be hell to pay, but so be it. My gut had never steered me wrong before.

Picking up my pace in case my father tried to follow, I slipped through the newly forged cut through the hedge and strode, mindful of the slippery yard, to the stairs up to the carriage house situated over the garage. Ascending the steep stairs, I felt the hard, cold wood on my bare feet. Each footfall was deliberate so as not to slip. At the top I knocked. Blake appeared at the door and opened it slowly.

"What's going on?" he asked.

I managed a smile but doubted it was convincing. "I need some ice."

He considered my request and pulled the door in wider, but only halfway. "Okay, come on in."

After wiping my feet as best I could without a welcome mat at the door, I shuffled past him, taking in the modest kitchen on the way to a cane seat chair at the table. How two men were able to exist in the small space was baffling. The stovetop consisted of two burners. The cupboard space—one door was missing—was limited. The size of the sink barely allowed enough room to wash a small saucepan. And the apartment-sized refrigerator couldn't hold much more than a week's supply of beer and a dozen eggs.

Fumbling through the freezer, Blake pulled out an ice tray and cracked it against the edge of the counter, filling a Ziploc with a handful of cubes and handing it to me.

Wincing as I applied it to the back of my head, I pulled it away, took a breath, and reapplied.

"Beer?" Blake leaned on the open door, his fingers laced between two long necks.

"Uh… sure." Again, not my favorite, but I wasn't going to be rude. It was doubtful he had anything else to offer.

I noticed an upholstered chair set under a window next to the front door and wandered over. No wonder Blake couldn't open the door all the way. It had to be where my uncle had kept an eye on the comings and goings at his house.

Shutting the refrigerator with a flick of his foot, Blake popped the two tops and tossed them slam dunk style into the open garbage can at the end of the counter, both landing securely inside. He'd had some practice under his belt.

"Yup, that's where Gray hung out most of the day, watching over you as best he could. Sounds kind of creepy but he did it with the best of intentions. He was genuinely worried about you."

I scooped up a few loose sheets of paper with what looked like handwritten notes on them.

"Did a lot of writing there too, was always writing… until his hands hurt too much," Blake said.

He was a *real* writer. Was I *always* writing? No. *Imposter!*

Upon closer inspection, it became clear that what I was holding was a poem. He'd turned his observations and concerns into poetic rhyming prose.

The first two stanzas read:

> *She arrived today. I noticed her*
> *From the window in my hiding space.*
> *At first, I thought her a neighbor*
> *Then spied hesitation in her face.*
>
> *She's a fine young woman.*
> *Attractive in her own sort of way.*
> *Not to tread long in my world.*
> *She'd never want to stay.*

Beautiful. I was tickled he'd written them about me, in spite of the sideways, almost half-hearted compliment in the second stanza.

Out of respect for his artistry, I stopped reading and returned the pages to the windowsill, vowing to ask him about them another time.

I joined Blake at the kitchen table. He handed me one of the beers and clinked his to the top of mine.

"So what's going on?" He tilted his head in the general direction of Gray's location.

"They wanted to chat just the two of them."

"So what's the urgency to arrive the same time as a hurricane?" Blake took a swig and swallowed hard. "'Course he had to have arrived before the storm. The airport was shut down today. No flights in or out."

"Why don't you tell me?"

He recoiled at my question.

"I have a feeling you know a lot more about what could be going on than I do."

"Uh… I don't know about *that*."

"Well, I do. You've known my uncle a hell of a lot longer than I have. You were around all those years ago when I visited Gray with my mother." I took a sip to let that sink in. "I remember your tattoo." I pointed with the top of my bottle to the hand holding his beer. "You saved my life when I almost drowned in the pool—the backyard of the house we were at today."

Blake's face fell. He took a gulp of his beer and then returned it to the table with a thud, keeping his eyes from mine.

"We didn't think you'd remember. You were little. That was a horrible day. I'm so sorry."

"You saved me again today."

He smiled. "Yeah, I guess I did." Our eyes met. "Your uncle and I did."

"So why is my father here?"

He laughed, pushing back in his chair so it balanced on the back two legs. "Your guess is as good as mine. Looked like we were all surprised to see him."

I wasn't buying his ignorance. "When was the last time he came here?"

"Your father? I don't know that he ever has. But I'm not exactly with Gray every waking moment."

"But he would have mentioned it to you—a close friend—if it did happen, since it would have been an unusual event."

"Hard to say."

"Blake, you're full of shit."

He sipped his beer and shrugged. I wasn't going to get anything out of him. He was a good friend to Gray. Loyal to the end. Couldn't fault him for that.

We both turned at the sound of screeching tires.

Darting for the door, I heard my chair hit the floor as I grabbed the knob.

"Wait! Let me go with you," Blake called out as I dashed down the stairs.

I had just slipped through the opening in the hedge when I saw my uncle bent over at the edge of the carriage house patio, spitting and wiping his mouth with the back of his hand. As I approached, he straightened up and I could see his bloodied face.

"Uncle Gray. Are you okay?" I grabbed his elbow, but he pulled away. "What happened? What did my father do?"

He waved me off, turning to spit more blood.

"What the hell, Gray?" The driveway was empty where my father's rental had been parked. I felt a wave of relief, but clearly he'd left a trail of hurt in his wake.

"He sucker punched me."

"He what?" I wasn't familiar with the term.

"Also known as a coward punch." Blake appeared in the opening of the hedge but retreated when Gray held up a hand. "I never saw it coming."

"I'm so sorry." I'd never known my father to hit anyone, certainly not his flesh and blood.

"I've had it coming for a while." Shaking off the encounter, he swiped at his mouth and shook off his hand. "We need to talk… again."

# CHAPTER FORTY-FOUR

AFTER RETRIEVING THE OUTDOOR FURNITURE FROM the gardens and setting it upright on the patio where it belonged, I fetched a bag of ice for Gray. I still had mine. We settled into the bistro chairs, quite the pair, both addressing our wounds. Gray got to the point.

"There's no easy way to deliver this news.... Apparently your parents are getting a divorce."

"What?" I hadn't seen that coming. "Wait... my father came all the way down here to tell you that? No... he didn't know you were alive. That must have been a shock for him to see you. That's what he wanted to tell *me*."

Gray pressed his lips together as if he desperately didn't want to have to say what was next out of his mouth.

"That and he wanted to share the *why*."

No words came. I waited for him to fill in the enormous blank he'd just created.

"Your mother has lived her life as a frightened woman. Frightened of being found out."

"What are you talking about? Is she gay?"

He let my questions hang while he shifted in the chair.

At what couldn't have been a more inopportune moment, my cell starting clanging. Slipping it out of my pants' pocket far enough to see the caller ID, I said, "It's Mason. I'll call him back." No sooner had it stopped ringing than it started again.

"You might as well answer. He's going to keep calling until you do. He's worried about you."

Clicking on the phone, I answered abruptly, "Mason, what's up?"

"Thank God, Kathryn. Just wanted to make sure you're all right. Did you have flooding? Is there any damage at the—"

"Mason, I'm fine. Really. Look, I need to call you back. This isn't a good time."

"Okay, sure. No problem. Talk later."

I turned the sound off and shoved the phone back, deep in my pocket.

Gray's eyes narrowed as he watched me. "Did you have that with you earlier? When we pulled you from the drain?" He tilted his head toward the street.

I allowed myself a grin. "No. I got lucky. I'd left it on the counter in the kitchen so when I got your ice, I grabbed it. I doubt it would be functioning now if I hadn't. I also grabbed some shoes that actually fit." I slid my feet out from under the table to reveal the navy flip-flops with a bow on the strap I'd bought on my shopping excursion with Mason. Bows had never really been my style, but they were growing on me. Mason had thought I looked great in them, and I'd always been easily swayed to buy something someone else liked when it came to clothes. I had a closet full of clothes other people would like to wear. But I liked the ones I'd bought on King Street. I loved the attention Mason had showered on me.

Dropping his ice bag on the table, Gray ran ten fingers through his hair. I waited for him to continue.

"Kathryn... first of all, your mother is not gay. Far from it."

I watched his clenched jaw relax and a grin appear. "Oh, I love you so much." He was almost gushing. Never having heard him speak the words before, his sentiment seemed to come out of nowhere.

"I love you too, Uncle Gray." The creases on his forehead returned.

"Well, I love *you* like a daughter… because you are my daughter."

My throat tightened. Had I heard him correctly? I fought off the fuzziness creeping into my head. This was no time for a vision.

"Your mother and I had a short fling. She and Joseph were at a bad point in their marriage. Some might call it the seven-year itch. Whatever. I was pissed at your father for turning his back on me after I left the family business. Clearly he made it work. Saying it's been successful for him would be a gross understatement. I don't know why he couldn't let me forge my own path. Perhaps it was more difficult for him to make a go of it alone, but he did have your mother by his side. You would have thought I'd sabotaged him." He stared into my eyes. "I didn't.

"I'm sorry we were unfaithful to your father. It has killed me to keep the secret from him all these years, but we felt it was the best way to handle it. Rose and I—" Gray had never acquiesced to her contrived name, Posh—"did what we did, and we regret it, but I don't regret you."

I couldn't find my voice. I sat there. Waiting for something to come out that would make sense.

"I know this must be a shock. But you need to know. This is what fueled her fury toward me."

All I could come up with was, "So this is why I look so different from my brother and sister?"

His face brightened. "I'm sure that has something to do with it." He reached out and brushed an errant lock dangling across my eye.

"The only thing I regret is not being able to be there for you as a father."

I leaned across the table toward him. "That would have been

amazing." I imagined myself as a published author following my real father's lead. My raw, nagging feelings of not fitting into my nouveau riche Boston family were suddenly validated.

"It's hard to know what it would have been like. It's easier to have fun being a crazy uncle than a responsible father, so who knows how things would have turned out."

He grew quiet, as if considering the possibilities.

"Your sister probably wouldn't exist."

"What?" I tossed the ice bag onto the table.

"If we'd been up front with Joseph and told him the truth, surely they would have divorced then."

The thought hit me hard. Delaney and I had had our differences over the years, but that was part of being siblings. *Wasn't it?* I couldn't imagine life without her.

"This is why my mother's hated me all these years… treated me differently than Delaney and Peyton."

"I don't think she hates you," said Gray.

"Every time she sees me, I remind her of what she did. How she was unfaithful to her husband."

"She certainly has grown to hate *me*. Tried to keep me from you. Couldn't stand that you wanted to be like me."

It was starting to make sense, but not everything.

"So why did she and I visit you here when I was little? When I almost drowned."

He shifted in his seat again, taking a moment to gather his thoughts. I waited.

"She's a complicated woman. She and I have always had a love/hate relationship. Particularly after you were born. I think part of it was an act so Joe wouldn't catch on. But I think there was always something there between us. Maybe she was trying out the idea of being together as a family, the three of us. Maybe she thought you should get to know me. But the older you got it was hard to justify coming down here."

"So how did my father find out? Did she tell him?"

He wagged his head in slow, deliberate movements.

"Did you have any bloodwork done recently?" he asked.

"What? Uh, yeah. A few months ago. I had my annual physical. Why? What's that got to do with this?"

"Did your father put any pressure on you to get it done?"

"Yeah, I was overdue—it had been a few years, but I'm young with no health issues. So I really didn't think it was such a big deal. He told me to get it taken care of. Laid on the guilt trip that I needed to set a good example for the rest of the officers of the company—as if they would know I'd done it."

"After he knew you had an appointment, he made a call to your doctor and added a test to your lab work."

"He can do that?"

"Well, yeah, when you're friends with the guy."

"Great." Mason's comment about seeing a doctor who was a family friend being odd bubbled to the surface. "What kind of test?"

"Paternity."

"So he suspected."

"Apparently so."

# CHAPTER FORTY-FIVE

"Hey, there's that boy from the neighborhood." I pointed over Gray's shoulder toward the far end of the hedge where the child had popped out.

Shifting in this chair toward where I'd indicated, Gray turned back with a puzzled look. "Where? Do you still see him?"

"Well, yes. He's right there." I pointed again and then waved to the boy. He seemed reluctant to come any closer and didn't return my wave.

Gray looked again but shook his head ever so slightly. That was when I noticed the boy was wearing knickers and a cap that looked more like a costume than something a boy in the twenty-first century would have worn. I shook off a chill as I watched him disappear back into the bushes. Right through the hedge where there was no opening.

"Damn it, I don't want to be able to do that."

"Better you than me," my uncle said as he feigned shaking off a shiver.

"Great... terrifying visions *and* being able to see the dead." Then I grinned. "Yeah, but you took him for rides in your car and didn't know he was there."

"That's okay. He was a silent passenger."

He reached out and wrapped a warm hand around one of mine,

pulling it toward him, placing a tender kiss on the back of it. "You're a special lady, Miss Kathryn. Special indeed."

I could feel my cheeks burning. He had a way of doing that to me.

"We can pick up this conversation another time. Once you've had a chance to process everything and figure out what your next step will be."

"I don't need time. I know what I want to do."

"Take the time anyway. There's no need for any rash decisions. I don't mean to be selfish. I realize your life as you know it just came crashing down on you. But my life is still in danger. Probably shouldn't be sitting out here like this. I need to resume taking precautions until we can get it all resolved."

"Of course."

"And I'm concerned for your safety. Maybe you should head back to Boston until this all blows over."

"Hell, no. I'm not leaving. I just got you back."

"I bet your mother could use your support."

I let out a sigh. "She's got Delaney and Peyton. I'm probably the last person she wants to see right now."

He considered it and dropped it. "Let's go get rid of these ice bags."

I headed into the carriage house with Gray right behind me.

"Whoa. What's this?"

Looking back, I watched him lifting one of my pastel drawings off the sideboard in the entryway, which revealed another beneath it.

"Oh don't! Those are just—" I reached out to grab them from him, but he put up a side arm between us.

"And this!" Gray slowly pawed through the pile. "Did you do these? Of course you did." He didn't wait for an answer. "They're... wow. They're awesome." He looked up as if to make sure I understood the genuineness of his enthusiasm.

I couldn't keep from grinning. I was pleased he liked them. "Well,

I did take a few hands-on art classes while I was getting my degree in art history. They were required."

"If I'd seen your talent back then I would have talked you into a visual arts major."

What came out of me was an unladylike snort, which startled him. "One professor did try to twist my arm, but my mind was made up."

Gray harrumphed. "It's not too late." Then he added, "I'm glad you found the supplies I left you."

"That was you?"

"Who did you think it was?"

"Well, certainly not you!"

We shared a laugh.

"I knew you'd be good at this." He'd returned to examining the drawings. "But I didn't realize *how* good. Damn, I think you found your forte."

"What? No. I was just fooling around. Killing time. Keeping my mind off the storm." Inside my head I was screaming, *No! No! I'm a writer, not an artist. A writer like you.*

"Exactly. There was no pressure to produce. You did it for the love of drawing and taking in the beauty around you."

I considered his words of encouragement.

"There are more," I offered.

"Really? Show me." His face lit up like a child's on Christmas morning.

"Yeah." Leading him into the kitchen, I pointed to where I'd tossed a stack of several more drawings on the counter. It was only then I realized how many I had cranked out in a relatively short time. Several hours had gone by but seemed more like one.

Gray carefully lifted each drawing to examine the next until he'd reached the bare countertop. Returning the stack, he took a step back and stroked his forehead.

"I need to borrow a few of these. For a short time. Would you mind if I did that?"

I scrunched up my face, trying to think of a way to say no.

"There's someone I'd like to show them to. They're really very good."

"Who?" I didn't feel comfortable with just anyone seeing my work. My father was biased. Naturally he would think what I produced was fabulous. But I didn't think I could handle a stranger—heaven forbid an actual art critic with verifiable credentials—judging my work to be mediocre and rejecting them outright.

"A friend. Someone who has an eye for art."

*Someone like that.*

"I don't know, Gray. These were just for my enjoyment. I never thought anyone else would see them."

"Are you kidding? These stunning drawings were meant to be seen. It would be cruel of you not to share them."

The snort returned. I practically guffawed. "Now you're getting carried away."

"Kathryn, I'm perfectly serious. Please say I can share them with one other person. She's a good friend of mine. I really think she would enjoy getting the chance to see them."

Gray could be so persuasive. And encouraging. "All right," I conceded. "But I want you to bring them right back. Or toss them when she doesn't like them." Just what I needed—a rejection from a Charleston art gallery after a rejection from each of the big four publishing companies. More ammunition for my mother.

# CHAPTER FORTY-SIX

After the hurricane blew through Charleston, leaving ravages in its wake, Gray and I took rakes in hand and got to work cleaning up the debris in the yard. It was slow work because of Gray's arthritis, but it gave us time together and a chance for me to appreciate the property from the outside.

"Gray, this place is incredible. You've done very well for yourself." Clearly my mother had a contorted idea of his success.

Planting his rake and shifting stiffly to a position leaning against the grand oak, Gray took in the three piazzas on the main house. He chuckled. "I can't take credit for this. I owe it all to my dear friend, Annalee."

"Annalee?"

He nodded.

"Your neighbor? She's very sweet. Stopped by a couple of times. Introduced herself. Even got busy weeding the garden. It was driving her crazy." I laughed but then quieted.

Gray's face had scrunched while I'd been carrying on.

"What does she have to do with it?"

Stripping off his work gloves and tossing them on the pile of sticks, he motioned with a handful of gnarled fingers and said, "Come on. I've got something to show you."

Depositing our shoes outside the front door—a twinge of guilt crept into my gut for not doing so previously—I followed Gray into the Pink Lady. My conscience forced me to steer him into the drawing room to confess my clumsy mishap with the coffee table. To my relief, he barely reacted, waved off my apology, and then headed for the stairs to the library. He took the steps methodically, one at a time. When we got there, he went to the desk.

"She's quite a beauty, isn't she?" Gray ran a hand across the metal plaque that read *Wooton Desk Co.* and then pulled open the side-by-side doors to reveal the dizzying array of slots, drawers, and small doors. His arm movement stopped short when he lowered the desk flap and saw papers scattered in it. "I see the police didn't put things back where they found them." He clenched his jaw.

"I tried to clean up after they left. I'm sorry, I didn't think to open the desk."

He raised a hand. "No worries. Thank you for doing what you did. It wasn't your responsibility, and I appreciate what you did." He pulled the chair out and sat down, leaning into the desk. "It just means it will take me longer to find what I'm looking for," he said as he started to sort through the papers. Once they were in a neat pile, he pawed through the tiny drawers, sliding them out by the small knobs, rifling through the contents, then pushing them back in with a soft thud.

"It's got to be here someplace."

"What is?" I asked, but he didn't stray from his task.

When he'd opened every drawer, he returned to the stack of papers and rifled through them a second time. Partway through, he said, "Here it is. No wonder I didn't see it the first time. It was face down."

Reassembling the papers back into a neat pile, he handed me a small piece of paper. A newspaper article that had been cut out. Seemed recent. It hadn't yellowed yet. "Here."

I took it and started to read. "Wait… what? I don't understand." It was an obituary. Annalee's obituary. I read until I got to the part that Annalee had passed away a year and a half earlier. So I had befriended another person who was only on earth in spirit form. Great.

"Annalee was a dear friend of mine. We met at a fundraiser for one of the historical homes on the peninsula. We became fast friends. Very close. Who knows, maybe we would have married."

"I'm so sorry," I offered.

"So she stopped by to meet you?"

I nodded, stunned I'd had a conversation with her, on more than one occasion, and never suspected she was anything other than breathing.

"Sounds like something she would do. She was always friendly with everyone she met. Went out of her way to make them feel welcome. Guess that was her Southern upbringing. And she loved this house and everything in it. And the history it represented."

"I think she loved you too."

Gray's face brightened. "I'd like to think she did." His smile disappeared. "I miss her so."

"What happened?"

"Damn colon cancer. By the time they'd diagnosed her, it was too late. It was too far advanced. There was nothing they could do for her. She always took care of everyone else. Never herself." Wobbling, he stood and headed for the front window. Laying a hand on the telescope, he looked out to the harbor quite a distance away. "I was with her at the end though. Got to hold her hand. She went out gracefully, just the way she lived life."

"I'm so sorry," I repeated. "What a gift you gave her to be with her when she passed."

He held out his hand, and I returned the clipping to him.

"What a generous gal though." He refocused on the obituary. "She left me this place because she'd never married and was an only child. Her parents were already gone. She knew I'd take care of it and carry out her wishes for it."

"Pretty cool."

"A bit overwhelming, but yeah."

"I'll help you with it."

Gray grinned. "I knew I could count on you." He reached out with a warm squeeze on my shoulder.

"So where were you living before this?" I was curious. I wanted the full picture. There was so much I was missing it seemed.

He laughed. "Keep in mind this was a gargantuan step up." He gestured around the room with an open palm.

"Okay."

"You know the house where Blake's son and his friends are living?"

"Yeah."

"That was where I lived. I still own it, but now I rent it out to them."

More pieces falling into place. That was why my mother thought Gray lived in a dump. And she couldn't have been aware of Annalee's bequeathment.

"And then Annalee left this incredible place to you." I brought him back to the present.

"Yeah. She was an amazing woman. I have to admit it's a bit mind-blowing to think she entrusted it to me. I only partially moved into one of the rooms in the wing."

I laughed softly. "Then you know how I felt when I thought you'd left it all to me."

# CHAPTER FORTY-SEVEN

THE SOUND OF MY CELL INTERRUPTED my precious time with Gray.

"Miss Moore, it's Sergeant Jennings."

"Have you heard back from the lab?" I wasn't going to waste any time with pleasantries.

"The lab tested the dark blue paint they found on the side of the silver truck and was able to determine it was indeed the same Basilica Blue paint found on a 1968 Austin Healey."

"That's great. And you were able to track down the owner?"

"I'm afraid it's not that straightforward."

"God, now what?"

"The truck was a rental. Not one of the national chains. They had no record of who rented the truck because the person paid cash for it. The lab searched the vehicle for something that would tell us who the person was but came up empty."

"Damn it." I refused to let it go there. "What about cameras in the airport parking garage. That was where it was abandoned. Correct?"

"Yes and we checked those. They were all functioning properly. The driver was pretty well disguised. Had on a hat, sunglasses, even a scarf around his neck. But I got some guys working on it. Unfortunately they didn't have much to go on and came up empty."

"I've got to say that's pretty disappointing." Had I expected anything else?

"I didn't let it go at what the lab came up with."

I waited for him to go on. Why did it seem as though he always had to add a dramatic pause? Was it a Southern thing? Slower pace? "And?"

"I took a look at the truck myself. Ran through it very carefully. Pulled it all apart. And I came up with something."

"What?"

"I found a pen wedged down between the driver's seat and the console."

"A pen." I didn't try to hide my disappointment. *That was it?*

"Yeah, it's the cheap kind that businesses hand out to advertise."

I was still waiting for the reason for his call. Enough suspense building. Or was it just me who felt a sense of urgency?

"It had J.W. Moore Brewery printed on it."

And there it was. He might as well have kicked me in the gut. The "J" was for Joseph. The "W" for William. Joseph had named the company, insisting on including Gray's first initial. Gray had lost interest, which turned their relationship contentious and never healed.

"Just thought you should know we've arrested your father."

# CHAPTER FORTY-EIGHT

Once the police understood the recent change in Gray Moore's familial status and how it related to Joseph, they had a motive to go along with the charges. The news he'd been arrested for Larry's death should not have been as much of a shock to me, seeing as though he was not actually my father, but it was. It was all still new to me. And the ripple effects of a simple blood test just kept coming.

Gray and I took a break from cleaning the Pink Lady one afternoon, making plans for the property as we went, and gathered nibbles and a bottle of wine to enjoy out on the first-floor piazza.

I asked him about the Underwood in the study and the notes he'd left for me.

"Notes? Sorry to disappoint you, but that wasn't me. I didn't dare show my face over here. I almost got caught trying to drop off the drawing supplies to you on my first attempt. That was a close call. I had Blake drop them off for me after that."

So if it wasn't him, who was it? It seemed we were both considering the possibilities.

I decided it was Annalee.

"But I do have something of yours I need to deliver." He reached into his pants pocket and then splayed open his hand. Snaked across his palm was a silver rice bead bracelet. "If I'm not mistaken, I gave it to you once already."

"How could it be?"

"The police found it in the desk upstairs. Thought there might be a connection to one of the crimes Hayes allegedly committed. Apparently his first wife loved to wear these bracelets and at the time of her death at least one was missing."

I slipped it from his hand and secured it to my wrist along with the others. "Thank you. I thought I'd lost it for good."

"You're welcome. Thanks for trying to figure out what had happened to me."

A gentle breeze off the water helped to cool us as we waited for an expected visitor.

Stella had insisted on stopping by to see Gray in the flesh for herself. It wasn't sufficient to hear about it in the news or see photos posted on social media. She needed it to be face to face.

Her faded blue junker had grown louder since the afternoon she'd picked me up at the airport. Gray and I were enjoying our wine out on the main floor piazza and could hear her coming down the road. The view was clear out to Fort Sumter, and a breeze off the water made it a perfect temperature. Not a cloud in the cerulean blue sky. Absolutely idyllic and I couldn't have felt more content.

As Stella pulled onto the brick drive, there was an audible *clunk, clunk* as if something underneath was loose. I fully expected to see part of her undercarriage had landed on the ground, but apparently it was hanging on by more than a thread. It couldn't be long before the death trap threw in the towel and refused to go any farther.

Stella was out of the car and around the back in no time. "Well, I'll be *damned*." Her eyes bugged out, making her look rather unattractive.

*Please stop. Do yourself a favor.* "I wouldn't have believed it if I hadn't seen it for myself." She'd mounted the steps two at a time and went straight to Gray's rocker.

He struggled to stand up to greet her as a proper Southern gentleman. It was painful to watch. I desperately wanted to reach out and grab his arm to help but knew he'd prefer to do it himself.

You could see in her eyes Stella didn't expect his wobbling. It seemed to put her off a bit.

"Jesus, you don't look good." She could be so blunt.

Gray scoffed and extended his hand. "Yeah, you should see me on a bad day."

"Wow." Keeping her sights on him, Stella nodded. At what, I wasn't sure. "Good to meet you. You're a gutsy guy. Thanks for what you did. The scumbag needed to get his due."

"That he did. But it got a lot messier than we all thought it would."

"Yeah, it's too bad about Ellen Levinson. That shouldn't have happened."

Gray fell silent, eyes to the weathered floorboards. Finally he nodded. No words came.

"Would you care to join us? We're having some refreshments and enjoying the view," Gray offered.

"Nah. Thanks.... I just had to see for myself."

Not ready to share Gray yet, I was relieved she'd declined.

"All right, well, you guys enjoy your new life together." Heading toward the steps, she added with a flip of her hand, "See y'all 'round."

I got the feeling she'd felt left out of the unofficial investigative process she'd longed to be a part of. With the arrival of the hurricane, Gray's reappearance, and the police moving so quickly to follow through on leads, it had all come together quickly.

Time would tell how Levinson & Levinson would fare from the

fallout, particularly after the murder of a long-time pillar of the firm as well as the arrest of the partner responsible for her death. The remaining partners and Mason had a great deal to process and no doubt many decisions to make. Not a position I envied.

At the bottom of the steps Stella whirled around with a grin. "Just be careful and don't get yourselves deep in the pluff mud."

In my peripheral, I sensed Gray's body stiffen but didn't understand his reaction.

"What's that supposed to mean?" I asked after she'd reached her car.

He wagged his head a couple of times in a deliberate fashion. "Oh, I think it's a Southern thing. Kind of like New Englanders saying don't get stuck without snow tires on your car after Thanksgiving."

That didn't sound right, but I let it go.

As Stella reached for her door handle, she yelled, "Bet that was a surprise. Hah!" She pointed at us with a quick jab. "Never crossed your mind it was me, did it? Nobody thought it. Couldn't get credit for anything at that place."

Then it made sense. Gray couldn't divulge his source, who was still living, but she'd made it quite clear she was the one who'd leaked information to him. But they'd never met. Stella would have had to convince him she was Ellen Levinson. Once she had, pluff mud must have been their secret code.

Gray sat still. Quietly taking it all in. "What the hell," he mumbled.

As Stella coaxed her car to life, it hit me that she'd had a hand in Ellen's death. Her prints weren't on the gun, but she was the one who had gotten the whole disgusting ball rolling. If she hadn't listened to her Libran instincts that drove her to make things fair, Mason's mother would still be alive.

Life wasn't always going to be fair. And meddling with it when it wasn't, could have disastrous results. Results everyone else had to live with. But would it have been fair to let Hayes continue his rampage? Of course not. Ellen's murder seemed too high a price to pay though. I wondered how Stella could simply carry on after the cascade of events she'd set into motion. A ripple effect. Had she not made the connection? She was smarter than that. More likely she'd reasoned away her ties to the murder, allowing her a complete denial.

Lifting my wine glasses as we watched her back noisily out onto East Bay, I thought it was conceivable that could be the last time we'd see her. I was okay with that.

Stella poked her head through the open driver's window and yelled, "By the way, if you haven't figured it out yet, Kathryn, there is no basement."

I watched Gray's expression fold into a frown. "What's she talking about?"

"Don't worry about it. She likes to kid. It's a bit annoy—"

The sound of metal on metal was deafening. A massive dump truck had appeared behind her. Didn't sound as though the driver hit the brakes until right on top of her. The air turned eerily still.

My glass slipped through my fingers. I heard the dull shatter on the wood floor and sensed Gray struggling to get out of his rocker. I forced myself to look at her car. I couldn't make it out. *No, it's just your imagination again. She's fine. She's fine.*

But then I saw what was left of her car. The front bumper and part of the hood were sticking out from under the truck. It had run over her—like I had seen before. This time it was real, a vision fulfilled.

# EPILOGUE

WHILE THERE WAS NO CONCRETE EVIDENCE to tie Stella to leaking incriminating information to the press, Gray and I knew the truth. But of course, Gray in his capacity as a reporter kept his source confidential, contending that was the only way the press could maintain legitimate sources for reporting. One could argue both sides but without confidentiality, sources would quickly dry up. The downside was that the public was left to infer it was Ellen who had squealed on Hayes.

Gray had kept his notes on the zip drive I'd found in his desk. But they weren't in the folder labeled XXX as I'd suspected. They were in recipes. Both were password protected, but he figured if they fell into the wrong hands, no one would spend time trying to break into what looked like his hobby of gourmet cooking. Each article had a name like Chateaubriand, Coq au Vin, and Le Cordon Bleu.

Gilbert Hayes was arrested for shooting his wife Ellen for outing him to the press. He may have been relieved to hear of Gray's apparent passing, perhaps saving him the trouble. That left taking care of his wife, pinning it on a random intruder—until Mason showed up—and collecting the insurance money.

Initially Hayes' plan was to use an unregistered gun and let the police think it was a random intruder. Perhaps a home invasion. He grabbed the sim card from the security system and put it in his pocket, no doubt intending to dispose of it later but never got the chance. Mason showing up, foiled his plan. Hayes went straight to jail by way of the hospital.

Eager to blame it on Mason, he first told police Mason had shot them both. But it didn't add up. Once an autopsy was performed, the bullet that killed Ellen didn't match the bullets found in her office from Mason's gun that had missed their target. So Hayes backtracked and said it was a couple of intruders, one of which reminded him of Mason. With Mason's gun at the bottom of the harbor, there was no way to compare the unidentified bullets to it and connect him.

It was the sim card that did Hayes in. They found it among his personal effects when they booked him into Al Cannon. No one realized what it was at first. It sat in evidence for a few weeks until someone got curious about it. It showed him walking into the house but not Mason, because Mason arrived after Hayes had removed the card from the security system.

Gray thought it was Hayes who'd sent his car over the bridge, and rightfully so. The crimes became forever intertwined.

The ripples from Rose and Gray's infidelity, along with the subsequent blood test Joseph had finagled, and Hayes' long history of indiscretions, coupled with Stella's need to right the wrongs, had intersected with cataclysmic results.

As to the matter of Joseph Moore's involvement, he was charged with premeditated murder. Even though he got his target wrong, he'd carefully planned and carried it out.

After Charleston police contacted Joseph with the news of Gray's accident and presumed death, Joseph did some research and found Hayes reeked of knowing the right people in low places, so he reached out to him. Before Hayes went into hiding, he was able to line up another attorney and a judge to handle the death declaration case. A staggering amount of money passed through the right hands to make it happen.

Joseph and Posh divorced. The Beacon Hill estate was put on the market in order to settle her half of their joint holdings. At first, the address became a tourist attraction with a murderer as the owner. But when it came to selling it, few serious buyers stepped forward until they dropped the price significantly. Posh was indignant at having to let it go for less than they'd paid for it but had no choice.

Not ready to give up J.W. Moore Brewery, Posh hired a brand manager away from a much larger competitor and expanded the business with the addition of Moore Distillery, a move she'd been trying to get her husband to do for years to diversify.

I hadn't needed much time to process what was happening to my family. It was as if I could sense the reality all along. I'd never felt I fit into the Joseph Moore family; I couldn't have been any more different from Delaney and Peyton. From all the reading I'd done, I'd learned that middle children often felt as though they didn't belong and searched outside their immediate family to their friends to find meaningful relationships and acceptance. Turned out I felt like an outsider for a valid reason.

It wasn't that I hadn't tried to fit in, tried to connect with my parents and siblings, but my mother couldn't have worked harder to make me feel inadequate. And different. No matter what I accomplished, it was never good enough. I lived in the shadow of my overachieving and invincible brother and sister. Their company, Peyton Delaney Inc., was ridiculously successful *and* all my mother could talk about. My dreams of becoming a writer were not only not supported, they were ridiculed.

But I'd always felt connected to Gray. Now I understood why. Not just because we shared a love of writing and the arts or that he was my uncle. But because we were connected biologically as a father is connected to his daughter. A much more intimate relationship.

Even after the dust settled, my mother never reached out to me. After being elated with the news Gray was gone, she had to have been crushed to learn the truth. And at that point Posh no doubt officially disowned me—blaming me for the spectacular demise of her life. While it hurt, it wasn't entirely surprising. I'd never felt close to her, like a daughter was supposed to feel with her mother. But my brother, sister, and I vowed to stay in touch. I hoped we would. We three were the only innocent parties in the foray, having no control over our parents' actions—actions that had started decades earlier—and we chose to move on. The way I looked at it, I didn't lose a couple of siblings, they merely transitioned to half-siblings. I didn't expect our relationships to change much.

For his part, Gray seemed tentative about his role as a father. It wasn't like I was a baby, and he could start to get used to the idea and figure it out as he went. I was an independent adult who had adored him as an uncle. But what were our roles now that the truth had come out?

Saddled with health issues that seemed to bourgeon about the same time the Gilbert Hayes investigative series was first published, Gray must have been terrified of what the future would bring. He had to be agonizing over his limitations and how they would affect his career as a journalist and a novelist.

Due to his deteriorating mobility, he'd made the decision to back off on his commitment at the homeless shelter. What had happened to Larry may have had something to do with it, but he didn't mention it. Clearly Gray was devastated, no doubt feeling guilty Larry had lost his life senselessly, yet it was Gray who'd been the target. But I'm con-fident after some time has passed, I'll be able to convince Gray to do a fundraiser at the Pink Lady which will benefit the shelter. He has a big heart and will want to help.

Now that Gray had helped me realize my talent was in visual arts, in particular pastels, I refocused my energies on drawing. Gray's friend who owned a couple of art galleries was tickled to discover a new artist who used a medium that wasn't common in Charleston. She was eager to represent me, having her attorney put together a contract the same day Gray brought in the drawings.

In turn, and I would hope it went without saying, I was determined to help Gray. Since his arthritic hands were painful to use, we devised a system where Gray would dictate his articles for the newspaper or book manuscript, and I would type them. I was delighted to be working so closely with him. As I observed Gray in his element, it reinforced my understanding that writing wasn't my strength. I'd been trying so hard to force it to happen, I couldn't step back and see what others were trying to tell me: I wasn't that good at it. I'd been driven by the desire to be like Gray.

As to what I would call Gray, we decided it best to just drop the title uncle and leave it at that. Saying *Dad* would have been awkward at that point in my life. Although I didn't hesitate to introduce him as my father—of that I was infinitely proud.

Finalizing plans for the grand house, Gray decided he and I would take over the third floor. With over three thousand square feet, we each had plenty of room to spread out to have our own private living quarters, as well as a designated common workspace, and still be able to enjoy the view of the harbor from the front rooms. At some point in the future, we'd look into installing an elevator when stairs got to be too much for Gray.

While the carriage house would continue to be used as a bed and breakfast, the wing of the Pink Lady's first and second floors would be offered for short-term lodging as well. Gray reinstated the previous property manager who had done a fabulous job running the B&B and the funds collected would be used to maintain the property.

The remaining first and second floors of the main house would become a museum, open for tours and special events arranged by an educational trust Gray partnered with to make the historically significant home available to the public on a limited basis. Furnishings from Annalee's ancestors had been lovingly cared for over the years so visitors would get the feeling of stepping back in time as soon as they entered the front door. He thought Annalee would be pleased. She'd been so proud of the grand Pink Lady and her family's role in preserving history. Gray and I pledged to carry on that role.

I'd expected the visions to continue. I had no reason to believe otherwise. Without Posh in my life, however, I'd been able to reduce my anxiety meds. Guess I shouldn't have been surprised at how that played out. She may well have found herself on some of her own.

But back to the visions… Mason, who had been pleased to hear I would be staying in Charleston, which in turn tickled me, encouraged me to get rid of my notebook. Whether or not the act of writing down my thoughts and visions manifested the bad that befell innocent people, it was hard to say. But now that I'd moved on to pursuing visual arts, I didn't need the notebook so I tossed it. I figured we were all safer that way.

National award-winning author Penny Goetjen writes mysteries and suspense novels where the settings are so colorful they become characters in their own right. A self-proclaimed eccentric, she enjoys the serenity of writing with the allure of flickering candlelight often late into the evening, the chaos while perched at a hi-top table in a local coffee shop with half the caffeinated world walking by, and the romance of strolling in a long flowy skirt while observing the world and collecting characters. Seven published novels in and her husband still sleeps with one eye open.

Find out more about the author and her books:

www.pennygoetjen.com

Connect on social media:

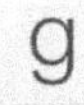

1. What did you like best about *Deadly Ripples*?

2. What did you least like about it?

3. How many ripple effects can you identify?

4. Do you think Kathryn's notations in her notebook caused her visions to come to fruition?

5. Was the notebook one of the ripples?

6. If you could have talked to Kathryn before she boarded the flight to Charleston, what would you have said to her?

7. Should she have pursued more of a relationship with her mother in the end?

8. If *Deadly Ripples* was made into a movie, who would you like to see playing the major characters?

9. Which character did you relate to the most?

10. If you could insert yourself into the story, which character would you like to become—an existing character or a new one of your own creation?

11. If you could read the story from a different character's perspective, who would it be?

12. If you could ask the author a question, what would it be?

13. Would you read another book by this author?

14. What do you think of the cover? Does it fit the story?

DISAPPEAR IN THE PAGES OF A MYSTERY
BEHIND OLD STONE WALLS

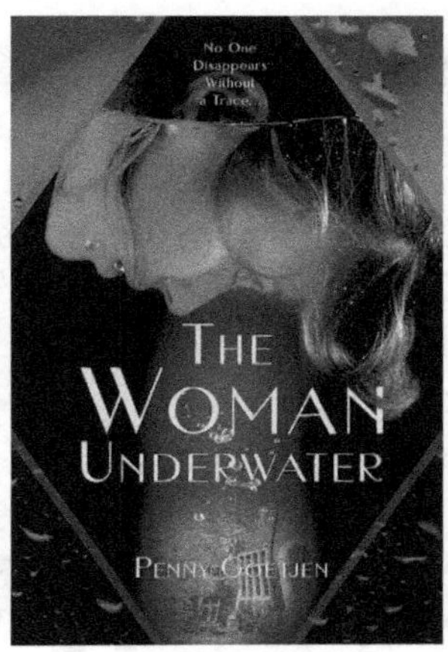

**No one disappears without a trace....**

Don't try to tell Victoria Sands that time heals all wounds. It doesn't work that way for a woman who's lost her husband the way she did. She was never able to say goodbye. Never able to arrange a memorial. Receive friends at the service. Write thank-you notes for the flowers and donations sent in his name. Because it didn't happen that way.

Victoria's husband never returned home at the end of a work day. And no one seems to know what happened to him.

In the seven years since his disappearance, no witnesses have stepped forward and no credible evidence has been collected—not even his car. The few tenuous leads the police had are now ice cold. He simply vanished on a field trip with the private boarding school where he taught behind stone walls—the same school their son now attends.

But someone has to know what happened. And that someone may be closer to Victoria than she realizes.

*"A vivid and poignant story of a woman haunted by an unsolved mystery from her past... I gulped it down in a single day."*
**—Megan Collins, author of *The Family Plot* and *Thicker Than Water***

**When Paradise Isn't a Sexy Character**

Young Olivia travels to St. Thomas to settle affairs after receiving word her mother, a highly-acclaimed photographer, has perished in a boating accident, but island police have no record of her death or even the accident. Could her mother still be alive? Olivia desperately needs the truth, if she has to find it herself.

Entangled in the same dark web of crime that may have ensnared her mother, Olivia is low on cash, high on mistrust, yet must rely on the ruggedly handsome stranger who seems to surface when she most needs saving. But is he her rescuer-turned-lover or her deadly foe?

*"Penny Goetjen uses the idyllic setting and island culture so effectively, the reader is tempted to savor ocean views from* The Empty Chair, *but don't pause too long—danger is never far away."*

—**Kathryn Orzech, Author of** *Asylum* **and** *Premonition of Terror*

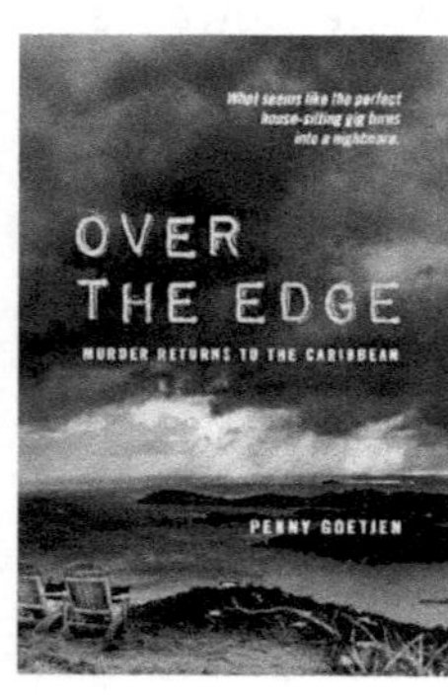

**The perfect house-sitting gig turns into a nightmare**

Returning to St. Thomas to rebuild her mother's bungalow after it was destroyed by fire, Olivia searches for Colton, her on again/off again love interest from her previous visit, but is left with more questions than answers, his whereabouts unknown. With nowhere to stay, she accepts the offer from an older, wealthy man to house-sit his spacious villa overlooking the Caribbean Sea while he sets off on an extended sailing trip. But what seems like a perfect arrangement turns into a nightmare. Before she can unpack her suitcase in the posh digs, Olivia stumbles upon the man murdered in his own home and becomes the prime suspect.

*". . . a well scripted murder mystery with deceptive characters and an unpredictable path."*

—*Suzy Approved Book Reviews*

## DISAPPEAR IN THE PAGES OF A MYSTERY
## ON THE COAST OF MAINE

**Caught on the rocks in the crosshairs of the storm**
*"Penny Goetjen has that rare ability to quickly capture the reader's attention and keep their interest from scene to glorious scene. There is elegance to her writings. She is a gifted storyteller and never disappoints."*
**—Martin Herman, Author of the Will James Mysteries**

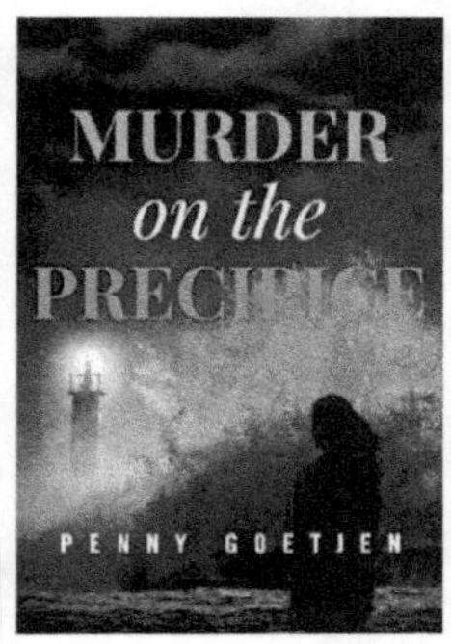

**Dearly beloved becomes dearly departed**
*"Goetjen is a competent writer who keep things moving along, throwing in hints of the preternatural that add to the overall ambiance....worth a read."*
**—Kirkus Reviews**

**When murder checks in, don't expect mints on your pillow**
*"Like the coastal waters of Maine, this story will lull you in with its seeming tranquility only to sweep you away in the undercurrent."*
**—John Valeri, Criminal Element**

www.ingramcontent.com/pod-product-compliance
Lightning Source LLC
Chambersburg PA
CBHW072205130726
47910CB00011B/1968